A NEXT GENERATION NOVEL

BEING Us

J.M. WALKER

IBSN: 978-1-989782-13-2

Being Us (Next Generation, #4)
Copyright 2020, J.M. Walker

FAMILY TREE

Angel and Genevieve "Jay" Rodriguez
(Grit, King's Harlots #1/Grim, King's Harlots #3)
Angelica "Gigi"
Ryder
Meadow

Asher and Meeka Donovan
(Stain, King's Harlots #2)
Aiden
Ashton

Coby and Brogan Porter
(Rude, King's Harlots #4/For You, King's Harlots #7)
Zachary "Zach"

Dale and Maxine "Max" Michaels
(Numb, King's Harlots #5)
Piper

Vincent "Stone" and Creena Stone
(Rust, King's Harlots #6)
Luna
Vincent Junior

Greyson and Eve Mercer
(Greyson, Hell's Harlem #1)
Jaron

Tray and Zillah Lister
(Tray, Hell's Harlem #2)
Beatrix "Bee"

John and Beatrix "Trixie" Butcher
(Hell's Harlem Series)
Cyrus
Samson "Sammy"

PROLOGUE

TANNER

WATCHING MEADOW RODRIGUEZ COME toward me as I sat at a nearby table, stirred every cell in my body. But not for what most would think. Truth was, she never did it for me. Hell, no one did. What woke the beast in me was the fact that she listened. It all had to do with control and control was what I intended to keep. No matter the cost.

But knowing what she thought of me, what everyone thought of me, didn't sit well. It was like a dead weight in the pit of my gut.

I let out a slow breath.

I tried with everything in me to let her know that I would never hurt her. I may have messed with her a little but that was only to maintain an image. I had worked hard over the years to get to where I was and I wasn't about to let it all go to waste over correcting some damn rumors. So, I let them slide into little ears. They were passed on from person to person. Maybe they were even used as bedtime stories to scare children into being good little boys and girls. I didn't know. I didn't care. Because it didn't matter. I used to try correcting the rumors but now, what was the point? People believed what they wanted to believe.

As Meadow neared the table I was sitting at, my gaze flicked to Sunny Harrison and Roy Allen, or Shade, as most knew him by. They stood by their SUV; their eyes locked on her. They watched, waiting for me to pounce no doubt.

It wouldn't happen. She had something I wanted and that was it. After she gave it to me, she would never have to see me again.

But the closer Meadow got, the more I saw the fear in her dark eyes. She had been a feisty little thing from the moment I met her weeks ago. I enjoyed toying with her, knowing it drove her guys crazy, but it would never amount to anything more than that. Although, they didn't appreciate my sense of humor.

"I won't hurt you," I said, as Meadow sat across from me.

"Isn't that what the villain usually says before they kill their victim?" she asked, her voice monotone.

I bit back a chuckle. Truth was, I liked her. She was fun. But rumors were rumors and she believed what was said about me. "Doesn't matter if you believe me or not. Doesn't matter if anyone believes me or not."

"Good because I don't." She looked around her.

I picked up the small mug and took a sip of coffee. I wished it were liquor, but alcohol was dangerous. Especially when I didn't know what was going on or if I would see tomorrow. There was a mole in my club, and I had no idea who it was. I didn't like that shit. I was used to being in control. For most of my life, I knew exactly what was happening day in and day out. My club, the way we made money, and more. They were all under my watchful eye, but this threw me off and I didn't like it. Not one fucking bit.

"Did you get what I asked for?"

Meadow reached into the front pocket of her jeans. "You never asked but yeah, I got it. I'm not sure if this is what you want though. My mom had no idea what you were talking about."

I leaned across the table and took the ring from Meadow. I did a quick scan of it, noticing the set of numbers engraved on the inside. I wasn't sure if this was what I had been searching for either, but it was a start. "I'm not sure actually," I confessed.

Meadow frowned. "What do you mean?"

"My dad was a twisted individual." I squinted as I read the inscription.

"Why didn't you ask my mom yourself?"

My gaze met hers. "Have you met your father? He's a scary fucker." Even *I* was man enough to admit that he was a person I did not want to mess with. "I've toyed with death before but I'm not stupid enough to cross your dad's path."

"Do you know my father?"

"Not personally, no. I've tried to stay away. Cause you know, I'm in Hell's Harlem territory and all." I winked, taking the words she had used weeks ago and throwing them back at her.

Meadow rolled her eyes. "This place is away from their clubhouse, so I think you're good."

"Listen, what happened before..." I hesitated, knowing I should apologize for the shit I had done. For touching her when she didn't belong to me. For making her think that I would have taken it further than what I had already done when she clearly told me no. I was an asshole, maybe even worse than that, but I knew when no meant no. Even though the rumors had said differently about me.

Meadow's eyebrows rose.

"I'm a bastard and I'd rather deal with animals than humans but...that...anyway, thanks." I stood from the table.

"Wait." She rose to her full height. "That's it?"

"What more do you want?" I demanded. "I suggest leaving before what happened earlier tonight is the least of your worries."

"I just..." She shook her head. "This doesn't make sense."

"Meadow."

I looked over her head, seeing Sunny coming toward us.

"Please, tell me why you would go through all of this trouble just for those numbers," Meadow said quickly.

"You ask too many questions." I stuffed the ring into my pocket. "Leave it alone, Meadow."

"He's right." Sunny grabbed her hand. "Let's go."

"No." She stepped around the table, blocking my path. "Why demand for me to get this from my mom? What's in it for you?"

I glanced over her head. "You need to put a muzzle on your pet."

"I want answers," she cried, shoving me.

Much to my surprise, she was a strong tiny thing.

A wicked grin spread on my face. "Listen here, little girl. I'd be careful who you demand answers from. My crew is not as nice as Hell's Harlem. Although, I seem to recall a time that they were actually much worse than my club." I chuckled for added effect. "Those were the days."

"Tanner." Meadow clenched her hands into fists at her sides. "How did you know that my mom had that ring or even that number you were looking for?"

"Because it was in my dad's will," I told her.

Her eyes widened. "What?"

BEING US

"If you must know, when my dad died, he had stipulations in his will that it be read at a certain time and on a certain date."

"I think he saw one too many action movies," she muttered.

I agreed. "That date has come and gone already. His lawyer called me right at the exact time my dad requested. I almost didn't believe it myself."

"I don't care what the numbers get you but why do I feel like there's a catch?" Meadow asked, staring up at me. "You can't just want those numbers and be on your merry way."

"And why not?" I turned back around. "You'll learn to leave well enough alone, Meadow. Don't make me change my mind." I started walking away, heading toward an alley that was past a few buildings. Once I reached my bike, I would head to the clubhouse and try and figure out what the hell these numbers were used for. There had to have been more in my dad's will, but I was too focused on getting Meadow to actually do what I wanted, that these numbers were my main focus.

As I was nearing the alley, I pulled my phone out of my pocket to let my vice-president know that it was done when something caught my eye. I stopped suddenly, looking around me. The hairs on the back of my neck tingled. Nothing was out of the ordinary. It was later in the evening, but people still milled about. It was the busiest area in town. With a few cafes, restaurants, a bar or two, the area was slowly building. But it was definitely busier than when I had visited as a kid.

Even though everything looked normal something was still off. But what happened next went far beyond just being off.

Pulling the pistol from the back of my pants, I lifted my arm, aiming at my target.

Gunshots sounded.

People screamed.

Sirens rang.

I heard it before I saw it.

I watched them fall, crumbling to the ground in a pile of limbs.

Meadow was screaming, trying to push the large body off of her.

My stomach dropped, my arm falling to my side.

Sinking back into the shadows, I watched the mayhem before me. They couldn't see me, but I could sure as hell see them.

People were running, trying to figure out what just happened.

I didn't know either. Maybe I would never know but I knew I would be blamed. Even though I never pulled the trigger, there were cameras. I tried shielding my head, but it was too late, knowing my face would be noticeable to anyone who looked at those security tapes.

One thing I did know was that I would do whatever I could to clear my name. Even if I died trying.

ONE

TANNER

WHEN YOUR CLUB BETRAYS you, that's when you knew life went to shit. Someone within Devil's Rejects wanted me out as President. It had been a feeling sitting in the pit of my gut for years. But I was never able to prove it. Not until it actually happened.

I was young. I did things to survive and make my way to the top. I had to earn my power and role as president. Even though I had done that, it didn't mean the other members liked it. Especially one.

Tommy West and I had gone way back. We were prospects together but even though we were close, I didn't trust him. I couldn't put my finger on it but there was something about him that was off. I always caught him looking at me with contempt. Like he should have been president instead of me. He could have been. He just never proved his worth.

I could still hear the gunfire and smell the powder from that night. But I was thankful that we had never met at the clubhouse. Sunny and Shade were smart that way.

Meadow on the other hand, wanted answers and she would have done anything to get them.

Lifting my hand, I watched the tremors rippling through it. It shook, pissing me off. The anxiety rushing through me had become worse over the past few months. Especially when I was trying to sleep. That was when the screams started. They shredded into me, tearing my heart in half. I didn't have a lot of morals. Especially when it came to humans but killing someone in cold blood was not my thing. Watching a fellow biker die, even if he was a member of a rival MC, while his girlfriend screamed beneath him, tugged at the last bit of decency I had left.

When that happened, I didn't stick around. I knew I would get blamed for pulling the trigger, but it had nothing to do with me. Whoever shot that gun and killed Sunny Harrison, started a war. And it was a war they couldn't win. Even *I* wasn't stupid enough to go toe-to-toe with Hell's Harlem.

I had spent weeks looking over my shoulder. It took longer than that for the screams to disappear. I wasn't a morally sound guy, but I didn't believe in shooting someone just for the hell of it. Although the rumors going around about me, said different. Bottom line, humans sucked.

Pulling the black hood higher up over my head, I picked up my speed while I walked the few blocks home. I was currently living in a shithole in the worst part of the city. It wasn't close to the Devil's Rejects clubhouse. I didn't know where Hell's Harlem did their business. Word had gotten around that they had a large house in the middle of nowhere while some of the members lived in a town nearby and in the same city that I did.

When my apartment building came into view, I breathed a sigh of relief. I had the money to afford better but was trying to lay low and out of sight. I needed to stay off the grid and was trying to get this target off my back as best as I knew how. Living in a big fancy house, would only make it worse. So, instead, after everything went down, I took my bike and drove to the city before anyone knew that I was gone. It was a pussy move on my part, but I knew that I would get blamed for shit I couldn't explain. Hell, I didn't even know how to talk myself out of this one. I needed to know why the mole in my club turned my brothers against me.

I would bet my life on it that it was Tommy, but I didn't know what he wanted.

Once I reached an alley, I looked behind me. Satisfied that no one was following me, I went down it and headed through the back way until I reached the doors of my building.

A homeless man sat by the doors. A blanket covered his body and was wrapped around his head like a hood, leaving his face hidden by the shadows. He had his arm resting on his knee with his hand held out.

"Hey, Kid." Even though I didn't know how old he actually was, it had been a nickname I had given him. I dropped a wad of bills in his open palm and made my way into the building. It had been the same routine ever since I moved in. Although I didn't like humans of any variety, I didn't take it out on the less fortunate. It wasn't their fault this was a fucked-up world with fucked-up people living in it. And it also wasn't their fault that vile human beings had taken it out on me as a boy.

I shook my head, forcing the unwanted memories out of my mind before they became too much and completely consumed me.

Taking the stairs two at a time, I stopped at the fourth floor and pushed through the dingy door. The security in this place was lacking. Not that anyone cared what happened here really. Graffiti marked the walls. Puke, piss, and other bodily fluids stained the carpet. The smell was overwhelming at first but after a couple of days, you got used to it. A gunshot rang out from somewhere off in the distance. Probably from one of the apartments nearby. Who knew anymore? It wasn't the safest place I had ever lived in, but it worked for the moment.

When I reached the end of the hall, I stopped at my door. Unlocking it, I pushed my way inside and quickly clicked all of the locks and deadbolts back into place. Call me paranoid, but when I watched a member of a rival club get shot and killed, it was bound to make a man leery of everything and everyone around him.

"Trigger," I called out, throwing my keys on the metal kitchen table.

A large German shepherd hobbled from the hall, coming my way.

"Hey, old man." I crouched as my dog closed the distance between us. He started licking my face, butting his head into the crook of my neck. I chuckled, running my hands through the fur at his throat and over his ears. "How was your day? Did you get some rest?"

He gave me a deep woof, leaning his whole body weight against me.

I kissed his head, reveling in the fact that this living, breathing thing, put all of his trust in me. I had found him in the alley when I moved in. He was old and beaten down. I could see his ribs after what was probably weeks of not eating properly. As much as I wanted to hunt down the fucker who hurt him, I took him in instead. But that didn't happen right away. It took over a week for me to earn Trigger's trust and we had been inseparable ever since.

"Alright, old man. Let's go get you some food."

He woofed again, heading into the kitchen.

I sighed, noticing the limp in his step. He clearly had arthritis. I tried making him as comfortable as possible, but I knew that it was only a matter of time before he passed away. Until then, I would do what I could for him and give him the best life before that happened.

I followed Trigger into the small kitchen. If you could even call it that. It had a sink, a fridge, a stove, and an oven that was stained. From what, I didn't want to know. I kept the fridge stocked and ate well constantly but living there, put a damper on things. The only good thing about it was that both Trigger and I were safe. For now. But I wasn't sure how long that would last.

After feeding him, I made myself something quick to eat and started moving around the apartment to make sure nothing was out of the ordinary.

Satisfied that everything was fine, I went to the spare room and began working out. It had been the same routine for the past several months. I spent the day trying to find answers as to who the mole was in my club and spent the nights working out and hanging out with my dog.

It was getting boring. And quickly. I needed answers. But no one I knew was able to give me anything.

After my workout, I was wired. I took a shower, cleaned myself up and decided to see if I could get some sort of answer. From someone. But I couldn't even call anyone in my club. Everyone had turned on me and I had no idea as to why. I wasn't easy to get along with. I got that. But no one seemed to care when I was paying them to keep their mouths shut.

Before I could leave the apartment, Trigger hobbled toward me. He gave me a deep woof, resting his body weight against my legs.

"I won't be gone long," I told him, scratching behind his ears.

He woofed again.

I crouched, earning me a lick.

I chuckled, the tension resting on my shoulders easing some at the mere affection he was giving me.

Kissing the top of his head, I ran my hand down his body. "You behave, alright? If you have a lady over, just put a sock on the door."

He woofed again.

I stood and headed to the door when Trigger barked. I paused in my steps, staring down at him. He didn't normally bark. Not loud anyway. It usually ended up being a deep sound, almost like a grunt because he didn't have the energy for more. But this time, for whatever reason, he did.

He looked up at me with those golden eyes of his.

"What's wrong?" I wished he could tell me. Something was off but I had no idea what he was trying to say.

Trigger slowly walked over to the door and sat, almost like he was telling me to stay home.

"I can't stay home. You know that, Trig. I have to get answers." I crouched back down, meeting him at eye level. "I need to get a better home for us."

He snuffed, shaking his head.

"Sorry, buddy. Dad has to go." I rose to my full height. He did the same and walked past me. Heading to the door, another bark sounded as soon as I placed my hand on the doorknob.

Looking over my shoulder, I found him with his leash in his mouth, wagging his tail. He hadn't wanted to go for a walk in over a week. Something was up with him tonight.

"Alright, I'll take you with me but if you cause trouble, I'm leaving you home next time." I grabbed his leash and clipped it onto his collar.

He gave me a deep woof, nudged his snout against my hand, and wagged his tail.

My heart warmed over the fact that I hadn't seen him this happy in a long time. He was hardly active anymore. He wasn't even active when he first came to live with me. But over the past few weeks, it had gotten worse. I wished I could have known him as a puppy and saved him from the hell he had lived in.

"Let's go, old man." I opened the door and led him out into the hall before locking up the apartment. Not that it mattered really. I had nothing of importance in it now that Trigger was with me at my side. The apartment wasn't my home but more of a cover-up instead. Just no one knew that unless I told them.

When we left the building, I gave the homeless man who was still sitting by the doorway, another wad of cash and started walking Trigger. Or more so, he was walking me.

"Hey." I tugged on the leash gently. "What's gotten into you?"

He tried dragging me, pulling me away from what, I couldn't be sure. But for a dog with arthritis and other ailments, he was strong as hell.

"Trigger," I said, my voice firm.

He stopped suddenly, sitting his butt on the ground beneath him, his tail no longer wagging. His ears stood up straight, his eyes locking on something. He was on high alert and I had no idea why.

This part of town was quiet for the most part. Surprisingly. Especially when other areas in the city that weren't as bad, kept the authorities busy. No, this area was only bad during the day. It was like the criminals wanted to challenge the cops by keeping them on their toes and showing their faces. It didn't make sense if you asked me.

Unsure as to what caught Trigger's attention, maybe it was a cat, I tugged on his leash again. "Come. We're going to visit a friend." Although, I wouldn't really call him a friend. He had been the only person I kept in contact with over the months I had disappeared. And the only person I trusted. Which was saying a lot. I didn't even trust myself half the time, but this fucker wormed his way into my heart until he became like the brother I should have had. Truth was, my own brother had died some time ago. He got caught up with the wrong people, ended up in jail and was killed because they had found out he was gay. I despised homophobic assholes. Ever since then, if I saw or heard someone giving a person a hard time just because of their sexual orientation, I kicked their ass.

As Trigger and I continued walking toward our destination, I couldn't help but listen to the noises around us. People milled about, going in and out of bars. It was still early in the evening. The sun had set about an hour before. A few cars drove up and down the street. A gunshot sounded off in the distance, followed by sirens. Trigger walked slowly, taking in everything around us as well.

"I don't know what you can hear, buddy, but I'm not a fan of this nervous energy coming off of you," I mumbled.

Trigger woofed.

I sighed.

A few blocks later and we were standing outside the entrance to Owan's Nook. It was a bookstore that held all kinds of books, reading paraphernalia, and more. It was a reader's wet dream if you asked me.

The shop always closed early on Saturday nights but tonight, it closed even earlier than expected. I gave the door two knocks anyway.

A lock clicked free, indicating for me to enter. Pushing open the door, I stepped inside with Trigger at my side.

"I'm surprised you brought him with you," came a deep voice.

BEING US

The room was dark, shadows danced over the stacks of books and other items displayed on shelves and tables but other than that, I didn't see anyone.

"He didn't want to be alone." And I didn't want him to be alone either with how weird he was acting.

"Fair enough." A large man finally stepped into the dim lighting of the moon, but I still couldn't see him properly. "Anyone follow you?"

"No." One of these days, I was sure I would say yes. I knew that. He knew that. It was only a matter of time. You couldn't stay gone forever. No matter how much you tried.

"Good. You know the drill." He headed to the back of the store, the sound of another door unlocking in the distance erupting through me.

Tightening my hold on Trigger's leash, I walked him to the back. When we passed through the open doorway, I was suddenly pulled against a hard body.

"It's good to see you, fucker."

I chuckled, wrapping an arm around Rowan Crane's shoulders. "Good to see you too."

Rowan leaned back, cupping the side of my neck and staring at me.

I shifted from foot to foot, unease twisting through my gut. "What?" I finally asked.

"My parents have asked about you. I told them you were fine, keeping well, ruining people's lives and all that shit. You know, the same old crap you do every day." He continued to stare at me, his words holding no hint of humor.

I huffed, pushing out of his hold and moved to the couch sitting by the far wall. I sat, unclipped Trigger's leash, and patted my knees.

He slowly jumped up onto the couch, laid down, and rested his head on my lap. "I haven't ruined anyone's life." Not in a while at least.

"Have you found out anything else?" Rowan asked, his gray eyes meeting mine.

"No." I ran my hand down the length of Trigger's body.

He sighed, his eyes fluttering closed.

You're safe with me, old man. I promise you that.

"Alright." Rowan shoved his fingers through his short light brown hair before scratching the scruff on his jaw. "And you haven't heard from anyone? Not your crew or Hell's Harlem or anyone else?"

"Nope." It was unnerving how everyone had been quiet. I cleaned up my tracks so I couldn't be followed. Rowan didn't even know where I lived. I didn't have a social security number. I didn't have a job. I didn't pay taxes. I didn't fucking exist in the government's eyes and that was how I wanted it. To them, I was dead.

"I don't like this," Rowan mumbled, cracking his knuckles. "I had my dad try and look up some information about your club and each member. Your supposed brothers."

I grunted. "They aren't shit to me anymore." And as strong as I tried to be, that shit stung.

"Good. You deserve better friends anyway." Rowan moved to the large chair behind the dark wooden desk at the other side of the room. "And you have me. So what more do you need?"

I rolled my eyes, but I couldn't help but chuckle. "Pussy would help." It wouldn't but I had a part to play. No one knew about my sexual preferences and how they were pretty much non-existent. "How's your sister?"

Rowan's gaze snapped to mine. "Married and fucking happy," he growled.

I chuckled.

Truth was, I hadn't had sex in months. Maybe even a year. Or longer. I couldn't be sure anymore. Not that I couldn't get it whenever I had wanted but the women I knew, knew my club and they would do anything to make an extra buck. They would let me fuck them, hell, do whatever I wanted to them, and then they would run back to Devil's Rejects and reveal all. I already had a target on my back, I didn't need any more of this shit added to it.

"Tell me again," Rowan demanded from his perch behind his desk.

I sighed, pinched the bridge of my nose, and leaned my head back against the couch. I didn't want to relive that night. That night that no doubt started a war. A war I could never win. Not on my own.

"I was meeting up with Meadow Rodriguez," I explained, telling him once again what happened that night. That night so many months ago that took a life and destroyed another's, including my own.

Gunshots. Yells. Screams. Blood. So much damn blood.

But what I remembered the most was the pain seeping from a rival club member. Shade lost the man he loved. He had his girlfriend, but I was sure it would never be the same. I didn't know who shot and killed Sunny, but I did know that both Shade and Meadow would think I had something to do with it.

"Tanner."

My eyes popped open at the barked use of my name. "Yeah."

Rowan turned his computer until it was facing me. "Who's this?"

I slid out from under Trigger and rose from the couch. Staring at the screen, I studied the image before me. A picture of a man dressed in a leather cut with my crew's name on it, sat on the left breast. It said President, with the Devil's Rejects logo on the right.

"That's Tommy West."

"Since when did he become president?" Rowan asked.

"Since I've been gone for months and everyone probably thinks I'm dead." He probably became president a few days into my disappearance. "I'm sure it was after they stopped looking for me."

"You think they were actually looking for you?" Rowan asked, raising an eyebrow.

"No. But the thought was nice." I began pacing. "Tommy wasn't my VP, so I have no idea how the hell he became president." None of this made sense.

"Well it looks like you were replaced rather quickly." Rowan turned the computer back around, clicking some more keys.

"Yeah, no shit." I nodded to the screen. "Where did you find that?"

"On Facebook. It seems like your club has its own page now." Rowan sat back, crossing his arms under his chest. "I'll see if I can get my dad or mom to find out where this page was created. I'll do some more digging and get back to you."

I muttered a thanks and let out a heavy sigh.

I never wanted to be on social media. I didn't care how good it made us look. Social media was dangerous, especially for our club, but clearly Tommy didn't care about that. He obviously wanted to be known. Maybe he wanted to be famous. But for what, I wasn't sure.

"I'm going to head out." I grabbed Trigger's leash and gave his head a scratch. "Time to go home, buddy."

He lifted his head, gave me a deep bark, and jumped off the couch.

"How much longer do you think he has?" Rowan asked gently, nodding toward my dog.

"I'm not sure but I'm going to give him the best last days a dog could ever have." And after he passed, even though I didn't want to think about it, I would rescue another dog and keep it going. Most people wanted puppies and while I loved them too, it's the old dogs I preferred. They helped slow me down. I had been going for so long, the next thing I knew, I would be an old man.

Trigger barked, pulling me from my thoughts.

I caught Rowan's gaze.

He raised an eyebrow. "Problem?"

Clearing my throat, I wrapped Trigger's leash around my hand. "Nope. No problem."

Rowan sat back in his chair, his eyes burning into me. "My dad gets that same look, you know."

"What look?" I shouldn't have asked, knowing it meant that I would have to give a little more of myself than I would like.

"It's that look that something happened but you're trying hard to forget about it." Rowan sat forward. "My dad has had years of practice on how to make it go away. He also has my mom to help him. But you..." He pointed at me. "You don't."

"I don't think your dad would like it too much if your mom helped me."

Rowan stared at me. "And you cover this shit up with humor."

"I have no idea what you're talking about. Besides, I have Trigger," I bit out through clenched teeth, hating that Rowan had me figured out. Even though I had known him for quite a while, it didn't mean that I liked him knowing my business. I had spent years keeping what happened, locked up tight. No one knew what I had been through or what I had done to survive and make it to where I was today.

"Right," Rowan said, drawing out the word.

"Either way. It doesn't matter." Sure, I didn't want to spend the rest of my life looking over my shoulder but when it came to the things I had done and the people who were after me, it would be this way for awhile. Maybe, forever. And there wasn't much I could do about it either. Even when I got the answers I was looking for.

"It does matter but you just don't see it yet." Rowan sat back in his chair, his light eyes burning into mine.

I grunted, gave myself a shake, and started making my way to the door. "Keep in touch."

"Always." He paused. "Take care of yourself, Tanner."

I nodded, leaving the room. "He's an odd one, Trigger."

Trigger snuffed.

"I'm glad you agree with me." When we left the bookstore, I stopped.

Trigger sat, his ears perking up.

Something was off tonight. He had felt it earlier. I knew he had because he wouldn't let me leave the apartment without him.

"Alright, old man. Let's go home."

TWO

TANNER

WE STARTED WALKING TOWARD our apartment. Nothing was out of the ordinary but something odd was definitely in the air this evening. It was still early. A few cars drove past us every now and again. No people were out though. Not like earlier.

Businesses in the area were starting to close. We didn't live in a busy part of the city. There were a few bars, but it was mostly locals in the area that frequented them. The only place that was open all night, was a local deli. They used to close at a decent time until they became so busy, they had to stay open to accommodate their customers.

Trigger headed in the direction of the deli, but I gently tugged him back.

"Not tonight, buddy. We have to head home." I went to cross the street when Trigger barked and tried walking in the direction of the deli again. "What's with you tonight? We have to go home. You need rest."

He looked back at me and gave a shake of his head as if he were saying, *Fuck off. I'm fine.*

As much as I could go for one of the deli's famous sandwiches, something was telling me not to. That familiar ache in the pit of my gut was warning me against it. I just wanted to go home, get some rest, and get back to figuring out what the hell was going on in the morning. But Trigger was having none of it.

"Trig, my man." I crouched in front of him, running my fingers through the fur beneath his ears. "What's wrong?"

He lowered his head.

I leaned my forehead against his. A sense of calm washed over me. It had always amazed me how animals could make me feel better. Even though they couldn't speak, I knew what he was thinking. He also had a different bark for when he was hungry, wanted to go out, or just wanted to chill and do fuck all. He spoke to me in his own way. I would forever be thankful to the person who didn't want him because he was mine. And I promised that I would give him the best life possible while he was still around.

"Alright, if you want a sandwich, I'll get you one." I could go for a meatball sub anyway.

Trigger did a little jump, his tail wagging back and forth.

I chuckled, grabbed hold of his leash, and headed across the street to Mama's Deli.

Once we reached the diner, I tied Trigger's leash to a nearby lamppost. Bending over, I scratched behind his ears. "Now don't go talking to any strangers, alright?"

He licked my face.

"I love you, boy," I murmured, kissing his forehead.

He gave my face another lick before lying down and waiting patiently for his sandwich.

Heading into the diner, the bell above the door dinged, indicating my arrival. I had been there before but as soon as I woke up that morning, I had been on edge. I could feel it deep in my bones. Even before leaving the apartment, Trigger felt it as well and tried stopping me from leaving. After giving in, he helped give me peace of mind that I wasn't overly losing it and that someone was after me. Or multiple someones. At first, I had thought it was all in my head. But after Sunny was shot, I knew I had to get out of there. And fast. I also knew that because Sunny had died, I was royally fucked.

Making my way into the small diner, I nodded to the waitress and sat at the stool at the counter.

"Same as usual?" the young woman asked.

"Two please." I usually got just one meatball sub and shared it with Trigger but this time, I ordered him his own.

She gave me a small smile, a flush of pink hitting her cheeks.

I smiled back but as pretty as she was, my body never hinted for more. It never hinted. Ever. There had been times where I thought a part of me was broken.

Glancing out the large window that took up the full length of the diner, I saw Trigger being petted by a dark figure. The hackles on the back of my neck rose. The person wore all black and I couldn't tell if it was a man or a woman.

"Here you go."

My head whipped around.

The waitress placed two wrapped subs on the counter in front of me. "Enjoy."

"Thank you." I grabbed the food and threw a couple of bills in its place.

When I went to head outside, I saw that the figure had disappeared. Once I neared the lamppost where Trigger had been tied up, I realized that he was gone as well.

Rushing to the leash that was no longer attached to the collar around my dog's neck, I looked around me.

Nothing was out of the ordinary but there were no cars on the street. Everything looked normal but a feeling of unease rushed through me. Who the hell took my damn dog?

A bark sounded, pulling me to an alley a block away. Dropping the subs, I quickly rushed toward it. When I rounded the corner, I wasn't expecting to see what was in front of me.

My stomach fell.

Two dark figures had backed Trigger into a corner. He was growling and snarling at them, drool dripping from the sides of his mouth.

Looking around me for a weapon, my heart leapt when I saw a pipe lying on the ground by a garbage bin. I picked it up, banging it against the wall.

The two figures turned toward me.

"'Bout time you show up," the one said.

I recognized the voice but couldn't place it. All I could focus on was the fact that my dog was cornered. He was old. Barely hanging on most days. He didn't need this added stress. The vet had told me that he only had months to live. If that. This would end him. If the bastards left him alone that is. But I had a bad feeling that tonight would be it for us as a duo.

"Trigger, I'm here, boy," I told him, keeping my voice as calm as I could. Calmer than it had been in months.

"Trigger," the one guy repeated, leaning against the wall. "I like it."

"What do you want?" I demanded, slapping the pipe against my open palm. "You want to play? Because I'm down for that. Although, I don't think you would like my dog ripping out your throats."

One of the men standing closest to Trigger stepped around him and in a quick move, had grabbed him by the throat.

Trigger struggled but even though he was big, he was weak thanks to his age.

"I don't suggest making threats," the bastard said, petting a hand over Trigger's head. "One move and I'll snap his fucking neck."

Bile rose to my throat. I was tempted to call this in and beg for help but then I remembered I had no one. I was all alone in this fucked up world thanks to a club brother forcing me out. Being the president meant shit when your whole club was against you.

"What do you want?" I demanded, keeping the pipe at my side.

"We have a message for you," the guy with his arm wrapped around Trigger's throat, sneered.

"From who?" I took a step toward them. "I have nothing you want." The closer I got to them, the more I recognized them. They weren't part of Devil's Rejects. Or if they were, they were new. Because they weren't part of it when I was president. But they were at the time, part of a puppet club. I had them do the shittiest jobs possible. Maybe that was the reason for this. "Listen, whatever I had you do, you know that most clubs make puppet clubs do their dirty work."

"Oh." The man leaning against the wall held his hand out in front of him. "You see, we don't actually give a shit about that anymore."

"Then what the hell do you want? And get your hands off of my fucking dog." I had enough of this shit. Trigger looked like he was out for blood, which I knew he was. But I didn't like the rough hold the fucker had on him.

"You think I'm stupid?" The man's arm tightened around Trigger. "This dog may be old, but I know that he could still rip out my throat."

"What do you want?" I was getting sick of this back and forth shit. Either they told me what they wanted or I was going to shove this pipe up their asses.

"Tommy sends his love."

Before I could question him, he lifted his hand and plunged a knife deep into Trigger's side.

He let out a loud whimper.

The sound forced me forward. I ignored the bile rising to my throat and rushed to them, not caring in the least that there was another fucker nearby. I had one goal in mind.

To save my damn dog.

THREE

Bee

LIVING WITH MEN HAD its hardships at times. Especially when I went out partying with friends and my ass got picked up by my two scowling cousins.

They were sitting in the front seat of their SUV, lecturing me and telling me how dangerous men were these days.

While they continued on with their tirade, all I could focus on was the alcohol gurgling in my belly. How much did I even drink?

My phone dinged from somewhere in the distance but even the sound was loud enough that it pounded into my skull.

"Bee."

I looked up, finding Sammy staring back at me. His dark eyes which mirrored his twin brother's, narrowed in the middle. Cyrus continued driving us to my place, glancing at me every so often in the rearview mirror.

"You need to stop doing this shit," Sammy said, pointing a finger at me.

"Yeah, because you've never done it yourself. Why is it okay for you guys to go out partying but I can't?" I could only assume I got the words out. But in my head, they sounded like a jumbled mess.

When Sammy's brows narrowed even more, I knew that I definitely got the words out.

"It's okay to party but when we show up and find you grinding against a fucker more than half your age older than you, that's when it's not okay." Sammy continued to stare at me, probably waiting for me to argue. But I was too tired. Since my fun was ruined, I just wanted my bed. And the guy wasn't that much older than me.

"My dad is older than my mom," I mumbled. "Why is it okay for them?"

"Because they are adults," Cyrus threw in. "*You* are acting like a damn child."

"I am not." I pouted. Okay, maybe I was but truth was, I was twenty-three and inexperienced. In every sense of the word. I had been watched my whole life and lived under my father's thumb. Hell, under every man's thumb who had taken on the role of being my impromptu uncle since I was born. Not that I wasn't grateful for the extra protection, seeing as my father was part of a motorcycle club, but they needed to let me live a little. Which had been what I was trying to do tonight until Cyrus and Sammy showed up.

"Don't pout." Sammy held back a smile.

I sighed.

"We hitting the club after we drop her off?" Sammy asked his brother.

Cyrus only grunted.

My head whipped around. "Take me with you."

Sammy chuckled. "No."

"Please." I leaned forward. "I'll behave. I just don't want to go home yet." My parents were out of town, spending the weekend away like they deserved. But I was an only child and our house was too damn lonely all by myself. I could call my best friends up and ask them to come over but knowing them, they were still dancing it up at the club Sammy and Cyrus had taken me from.

"Not happening, kiddo." Cyrus's voice was firm, leaving no room for argument but it didn't mean I wasn't willing to take a chance and try.

"You won't even know I'm there," I insisted. "Come on. Please. We never do anything together anymore."

Both of them scoffed.

"We always hang out," Sammy reminded me.

"Right." I snorted. "When you two are actually home and not fucking some stranger," I mumbled.

"Watch your mouth," Cyrus scolded.

I rolled my eyes. "Just speaking the truth. I've seen the women you pick up."

"Correction, you've seen the women Sammy picks up."

"Used to," Sammy muttered.

My ears perked up at that. "Oh, do tell! Is there someone in your life, Samson?" I waggled my eyebrows.

"Do not fucking call me that," he snapped.

I jumped, not expecting him to actually get mad at me over the use of his full name. I had learned throughout the years that he hated when people used his full name. It was always Sammy or Sam. Nothing else and he never said why. But I never expected that me calling him that would piss him off.

"Sorry," I whispered.

He huffed. "Don't worry about it."

"Listen, as much as we want to hang out with you, we are taking you home," Cyrus interjected.

I only nodded, looking out the window. I didn't mean to piss Sammy off, but I refused to apologize for stating the truth. How the hell could others get away with having a little fun and I couldn't? I was sure the women they picked up had filthy mouths on them too. Why couldn't I have one as well? Oh yeah. Because I was the youngest and it wasn't normal. I was a good girl. Blah. Blah. Blah.

While the guys continued talking about their plans for after they dropped me off, I stared out the window. I longed for the day that a man would come whisk me away. It was like my family thought I would fall into the arms of the first man who showed any interest in me. Maybe I would but that was none of their business. I just wanted a man who could stand up to the other men in my life and not back down.

"Hey, Bee."

I smiled as Alex came toward me. He was dressed in a light blue dress shirt that was tucked into black pants.

He smirked, causing that single dimple in his tanned cheek to pop. He ran a hand through his light brown shaggy hair when something caught his eye. His smile fell, the color draining from his face. "I…something's come up and I can't actually go on the date anymore."

"W-What?" I asked, my eyes widening. I followed his gaze.

My dad leaned against the wall, holding a shotgun in his hand. Uncle Greyson stood beside him, cracking his knuckles.

"See you at school, or not," Alex said quickly and ran toward his car.

Slamming the door shut, I spun on my father and uncle. "You have got to be fucking kidding me."

Ever since then, I hadn't been on a date. Word traveled around school rather quickly after that.

Did you know that Bee's father is a biker?

I heard he's in the mafia.

I heard her father just got out of jail after killing someone just by looking at him.

Just once I wanted to be able to live my life and not be under the watchful eyes of my father, his club brothers, and the guys I considered family. I knew I sounded like a whiny brat and I should appreciate having the protection and love that I did but it didn't make experiencing life any easier.

Once we pulled onto my street, a hard sigh left me. It was a Saturday night, not even ten yet, and I was going home to spend the rest of the evening doing nothing. All thanks to my cousins who were probably instructed by my father to watch over me. They were allowed to have fun but not me. Why? Because I was a female. It wasn't fair.

"Alright, Bee." Sammy turned to me. "Be a good girl and don't make us come get you again."

"How did you even know I was there?" I waited. When neither of them answered, I laughed. "You followed me. Didn't you?"

Cyrus scratched his jaw. "I guess you'll never know. Now will you?"

I swallowed a curse and left the SUV. I loved them. I really did. But Cyrus and Sammy needed to mind their own business and leave me alone. Let me live a little. Let me enjoy life. I needed to talk to my mom. I made a mental note to invite her out to lunch when she got home from her weekend away with Dad.

When I entered the house, my phone dinged, indicating an incoming text.

Sammy: We're just looking out for you.

Me: I'm a big girl, Sammy. I know how to take care of myself but thank you so much for your concern.

I shoved my phone in my back pocket, ignoring the next text that came through. I would get over this, I knew

I would, but that still didn't mean that I couldn't grumble about it for at least a little bit.

My phone suddenly started ringing, making me jump.

"Geeze, Bee. Get a hold of yourself." I pulled the phone from my pocket, when I saw one of my best friends calling me. "Hey, girl."

"Bitch, where did you go? I saw those hot as fuck cousins of yours storm in and the next thing we knew, you were gone," Heather Olle yelled into the phone.

I winced, pulling the phone from my ear. "Do you have to yell?"

"Sorry." She cleared her throat. "Where did you go?" she asked at a more reasonable volume.

"The twins took me out of there and now I'm stuck at home." I could have stayed at the club, but I wouldn't put it past one of them to throw me over their shoulder and carry me out of there kicking and screaming. I didn't need that sort of publicity, knowing it would only get back to my father.

"Oh, well in that case. Are they still there?" Whatever Heather was hinting at, only made me laugh and roll my eyes. She had a thing for the twins for as long as I could remember. It didn't help that they weren't interested. At all. But because of that, it only made her want them more. They brushed it off as a silly crush, but I knew her. It went far past just a crush.

"No, they aren't. My parents aren't here either." I sighed, kicking off my shoes and walking further into the house.

"So, you're on lockdown for the night?" she asked, knowing I hated when she used that term. Her and our other friend, Lori Alexander, would tease me whenever I wasn't allowed out of the house. They referred to it as *lockdown mode.*

BEING US

"Looks like it." I was sounding ungrateful for all the protection I had but growing up where it was constantly looming over my head, it got old and quickly.

"Well if you need Lori and I to stop by, let me know. And if the twins happen to be there, I wouldn't complain at all."

I could almost hear her waggling her eyebrows.

"You know that'll never happen." I laughed.

"Oh it will. Sammy likes easy women." She sighed. "I can be easy for him."

"You're such a slut." A bubble of laughter left me.

"Whatever. He's hot."

I made a face. "Sure. I guess. If you go for that grumpy brooding shit."

"He's not grumpy or brooding. That's Cyrus."

"Oh." I clutched my chest. "I'm sorry. I guess I don't know my cousins after all."

She laughed. "I wonder if they're into threesomes."

"Oh God." I gagged. "Stop."

Her laughter turned into a fit of giggles.

"Are you talking to Bee?" I heard Lori ask in the background.

"Yeah," Heather answered.

"Ask her if the twins are there."

"Seriously?" I smacked my forehead. "Her too?"

"Maybe they'd be into a foursome," Heather said.

"On that note, I'm hanging up." I shook my head, unable to stop the smile forming on my face.

"See you later, Buzzkill," Heather teased.

"Yeah, yeah," I grumbled, not liking the nickname they had given me whenever I had to cut my night short. "Love you."

"Love you too," both Lori and Heather said at the same time.

When I disconnected the call, I shoved my phone in my back pocket and stood there. Our house wasn't overly large. That had never been something my parents wanted. Especially when they only had me. There was a main level with no second floor. The basement was completely finished but I hardly ever went down there. Our backyard was my favorite spot. It held a swing set that we had ever since I was a little girl. It was one of those old ones made out of metal.

Trees surrounded the fence, closing in our yard. My mom would spend her afternoons in the summer planting her flowers and cleaning up the yard when she wasn't working at her shop. Now that I was trained in almost everything she knew about cars and motorcycles; she was able to take more time off to be with my dad. Even though she wasn't retirement age yet, she was slowly learning how to take care of herself more. Which was something Dad had insisted on.

My chest pained.

I longed for the day I had someone who looked at me like my father looked at her. Mom was much younger than him, but it had never stopped them.

Since they were out until the following day and I was home alone, a part of me considered going back out but then the rational part of me, thought better of it. I didn't need to ruin my parents' weekend by having it leaked back to them that their daughter couldn't follow the rules and take care of herself when they weren't home.

Swallowing a sigh, I grabbed a bottle of wine from the wine rack on the counter in the kitchen and decided to have a pity party for one. Not like I could do anything else with my cousins breathing down my neck.

A noise from the backyard caught my attention but I had seen enough horror movies to know not to check out the sound. When it didn't happen again, I let out a breath of relief. But my nerves were suddenly on edge. And I couldn't figure out why.

BEING US

(Tanner)

All thought control left me as I charged for the bastard who stabbed my dog, but I never got very far when I was jumped from behind. We fell to the ground but no matter how heavy the fucker was, it didn't stop me from kicking and punching. I knew how to fight but it was like as soon as I saw that knife slide into Trigger's side repeatedly, my body did its own thing while my mind was trying to catch up.

My fists landed against bone, my vision clouding.

The bastard released Trigger only for him to fall to the ground and roll to his side. A yell forced its way from my lips as I tried rushing for him.

"We'll tell Tommy you said hi."

A sharp slice of agony erupted through my shoulder, but the pain didn't stop me. I jumped the guy closest to me and forced him to the ground. Landing blow after blow, blood splattered my hoodie and face, the skin on my knuckles cracking the harder I hit.

Heavy arms pulled me off the guy.

"You should quit while you're ahead, Tanner." The man who stabbed Trigger towered over me, pressing a finger into the wound in my shoulder.

I winced, struggling beneath him.

He pushed off of me. The men laughed, their chuckles sliding over every inch of me and grating on my last nerve.

They grabbed their friend I had beaten and, much to my surprise, left the alley. I wasn't sure why they wouldn't finish the job, nor did I care. I would find out who they were and they would be the first I would kill.

I started crawling toward Trigger, sending up a silent prayer to whomever would listen that they would save him. But I wasn't a good man. I had never been a good man. Not even when I was a kid and stabbed a boy in the hand for hitting a girl. I had always done my best to protect those who couldn't protect themselves. But this time, I couldn't.

When I reached Trigger, a sob lodged its way in my throat.

It had always been him and I. Even though we had only known each other for a short time, he was the only thing I needed while I lived out the rest of my days in hiding. I didn't need a woman. I could pay for sex if I really wanted it. But I didn't care much about the physical contact of another person. Sure, it felt good, most of the time, but it wasn't something I had actively gone out of my way for.

But now, knowing that I would lose Trigger, it would force me to reveal myself. To come out of hiding. To start another damn war. One that I would be sure to win or, at least, die trying.

Even though I had visited Rowan every so often to see if he had any news on my club, a part of me just didn't care. I wasn't sure why. But I did know that the only thing that mattered at the moment was watching my dog struggle to stay alive.

"I'm so sorry, Trigger." I ran my fingers through the fur at his neck and down his side.

His breathing became labored, a soft whimper escaping him.

"I'm so fucking sorry." I leaned my forehead against his. "I'll find out who set this up. I'll avenge you. I promise."

He grunted.

"I'll be careful."

He grunted again in response.

BEING US

"Okay, not too careful."

He licked my face one last time before the life left his eyes. When he took his final breath, tears rolled down my cheeks. My nose burned, my throat working over the hard lump suddenly lodged in it.

I never wanted this to happen. I had tried so damn hard to give him a good life and then we got attacked.

I didn't know who all was involved but I knew that there was no way Tommy thought this up on his own.

Even though we had worked together and known each other for years, I still never trusted him. Not completely. I was all about keeping my friends close and my enemies even closer. He was the one who had been with Sunny's ex. I never pulled the trigger, but I was still there. I knew I had been set up. I just needed to figure out a way to prove it.

Pushing myself to my knees, I reached under Trigger's big body and lifted him into my arms. The weight of him enhanced the pain in my shoulder but I breathed through it. There was no way that I was leaving him in the alley.

Thankfully it was a little past ten at night and no one would notice me walking out of an alley with a dead dog in my arms. But I needed help and somewhere safe to keep him.

Taking as many of the back alleys as I could, I ended up at Rowan's again. Once I reached the back of the shop, I kicked the door. Knowing he was watching me through the security camera, I waited for him.

The inside door suddenly unlocked, followed by the second and third door. Most would call him paranoid, but I called him smart. You could never be too safe.

When he appeared in the doorway, his eyes dropped to my arms. "What do you need?"

"Burn him."

"What happened?" Rowan nodded, taking Trigger from me.

"They stabbed him and left me alive. I need to know why."

"I'm on it." Rowan took a step back. "Where am I delivering him?"

"Nowhere yet." I turned around and went to leave when his next words stopped me.

"You don't need to do this on your own."

I looked at him over my shoulder. "Yeah, I do. I also don't need your mom kicking my ass for putting her son in danger." His parents had already been through enough. I didn't know their story, I probably never would, but I did know by the little bits Rowan had revealed, that they didn't have an easy start. Especially his father.

"I put myself in danger." Rowan winked, pulling me from my thoughts.

"That's on you." I glanced at Trigger, who only looked like he was sleeping. Walking back up to them, I petted a hand down the length of his body. "Send me the bill for getting your clothes cleaned and for putting his ashes in whatever you can find."

"I'll find something special. Just for him."

I nodded, swallowing past the lump. "Thank you."

"You're bleeding." Rowan nodded toward me.

I looked down at my hand, noticing for the first time, the blood dripping off the tips of my fingers. "Oh, I guess I am." Before Rowan could say anymore, I made my way back down the alley.

I'll avenge you, Trigger. I'll avenge you and make those fuckers pay for what they did.

FOUR

TANNER

WHEN I ARRIVED AT my apartment, a laugh escaped me. It looked like a tornado had ripped right through it, leaving mass destruction in its path. The couch was torn to shreds, bits of stuffing spread out all over the living room.

Kicking the door closed, I headed to the kitchen and grabbed the first aid kit from under the sink. I didn't have time to stitch myself up, so I lifted my shirt and placed a bandage on my shoulder.

Satisfied that I wouldn't bleed out, I opened the top cupboard and pulled out a metal bin that once had cookies in it that Rowan's sister had baked for me. Even though I had never met her, I felt like I knew her. Rowan kept me from his family, understandably so, but he told me about them often. He also liked to remind me on more than one occasion how his sister was married and happy. Good for her.

Ripping the lid off the tin, I grabbed the wadded-up bills. Doing a quick count, I let out a sigh of relief that the amount hadn't changed. The fuckers who trashed my apartment at least didn't find this money. I could use it to hole up somewhere else.

A sharp pain suddenly erupted through me, reminding me that I had been stabbed. Fuck. I didn't even see it coming. Hell, I hardly felt it when the knife slid into my shoulder. I was too focused on Trigger.

My breath wavered. "Shit, Buddy. I'm so fucking sorry," I said to no one. I shook my head. As much as I knew I needed time to mourn, I couldn't. Not yet. I grabbed the money and quickly headed to my bed. The bachelor apartment didn't have an actual bedroom in it, but I was lucky enough to get this place when I did. I tried making it a home as much as I could for both Trigger and I but there were times that it did nothing.

Reaching beneath the mattress, I smiled when my fingers came into contact with my pistol. Looks like whoever raided my place, didn't actually look everywhere. I wasn't sure what they wanted. It wasn't like I had anything that could even be remotely considered important. The two most important things to me, were already taken away.

My club and my dog.

Suddenly, my phone started buzzing. Fishing it out of my pocket, I frowned when I saw *Mr. Awesome* flashing across the screen. Rowan was a funny one.

"Yeah," I said, answering the phone.

"You at your apartment?"

"I am." I shoved the pistol into the waist of my pants at the tail of my back. "Why?"

"You need to get the fuck out of there."

"I know that."

"No, Tanner. I don't think you do." Rowan paused which set my nerves on edge.

"What?"

"I couldn't sleep, so I did some more digging. Did you know there's a hit out on you? You're worth quite a lot of money dead."

"How much?" I asked, like we were talking about the weather and not the fact that my life was on the line.

"Five. Hundred."

"Aww." I pouted. "I was hoping for at least a mil."

"Tanner, you can't...fuck me. These people are willing to pay."

"Yeah, well, if they were willing to pay, they would have killed me in the alley. This shit doesn't make sense. Or someone's been watching *John Wick* too many times," I mumbled. "I'm not worth that kind of money, Rowan. It's not like I have any skills." I knew my way around a gun and was a dirty fighter. I wasn't sure those would be considered skills that you would kill someone for though.

"Right." Rowan said slowly. "Listen, I don't know why they didn't kill you. I know it doesn't make sense. They're probably just messing with you."

"That definitely doesn't make sense. Money is money, Rowan. You and I both know that."

"I'll keep searching."

"Good." I gathered my things and headed to the door. Stopping suddenly, I gave my apartment one last look before I stepped out into the hall. "I'm paying this month's rent and next and then I'm gone."

"Where are you going to go?" Rowan asked, concern evident in his voice.

"I'll find something." It wasn't like I had a lot of friends, if any at all. I did know some people, but most wanted me dead. Rowan was the only person I even considered more than just an acquaintance. Which wasn't saying much when half the time, I only contacted him because I needed something.

"Be safe, Tanner, but get the fuck out of there. Whatever you do."

"I'm on it." I disconnected the call.

Stopping in front of the super's door, I slipped some cash underneath it, along with my set of keys. The hundreds I left him should help him a bit.

Standing up straight, I couldn't help but feel...off. Trigger and I had traveled these halls so many times these past few months. I knew he would die. It was a given with his age and all but the way he went, was uncalled for. There was no reason for it. The guys could have come after me, but they didn't have to bring my damn dog into it.

Trigger was a part of me. He was the piece I had been missing from my life. A piece I never knew I needed. He kept me sane and calm, and prevented me from committing murder. Now that he was taken from me, I wasn't sure what I would do. I feared that I would fall back into myself or worse. That darkness would consume me. It had threatened to destroy me once before. I couldn't go back to that. But I had a feeling that I would meet that darkness long before I found the light I had been searching for, ever since I was a kid.

When I reached the bottom floor, the homeless man was still sitting by the door. I didn't know how old he was. Whether he was young or well into his elderly years. Either way, it didn't matter. I gave him a few hundred-dollar bills, hoping it would help him.

"Thank you," he murmured.

Those two words forced me to a stop. I glanced down at him. He had never thanked me before. Why now? But as much as I wanted to find out, I had to leave and find somewhere to lay low. I just wasn't sure where that would be.

Taking the back alleys once again, I eventually ended up in a suburban part of the city. I wasn't sure how I got there. The pain in my shoulder and the anxiety rushing through me, must have forced me to black out once or twice because the next thing I knew, I was standing at the backyard of a small bungalow. The yard was huge, with a swing set off to the side. It looked homey and inviting. Nothing I had ever experienced before, even as a kid.

The lights were on in the house but I couldn't see anyone moving around in it. Maybe they were in another part of the home. Or maybe they weren't actually there at all. But it didn't matter. It wasn't like I had a lot of options.

I looked behind me, tempted to run back into the forest I had just come from. Glancing down at myself, I noticed the tear in my shirt. The fabric must have torn on the fence I had jumped. I shook my head, trying to gather my thoughts, but was overwhelmed with everything that had happened tonight. The events of the night were all jumbled together.

The fact I needed to get the wound in my shoulder sewn up, pulled me forward when a woman came into view. Just the mere sight of her had me stopping in my tracks. My breath caught in my throat. Something foreign inside of me stirred. Something that had been dormant for so long, I thought it had disappeared for good, slid to the surface. I wasn't even sure it had ever been there in the first place. It wasn't like I was a stranger when it came to sex but I never went out of my way for it. But this woman made me want to drop to my knees just to have her smile.

The woman, whoever she was, brought a glass of red wine up to her lips. Her hips moved back and forth, like she was dancing to a tune that only she could hear. She placed the glass on a table before reaching up to her dark hair and pulling out the elastic. Her hair fell down her back in curls. It was so long; the ends almost reached her ass.

I licked my lips, letting my eyes linger down the length of her when I knew they shouldn't.

She bent over, showing me that full round ass of hers.

My dick throbbed.

I took another step forward when the wound in my shoulder reminded me what happened earlier tonight. Agony sliced through me, forcing my vision to fade in and out. The knife must have gone deeper than I thought.

"Fuck," I breathed, grabbing onto the nearest item to keep me from falling to the ground.

I wasn't sure how deep the knife had gone but I knew that I had lost a lot of blood. I wasn't a big guy, tall yes, but I had lost weight over the past few months.

I should have gone to the hospital, but they would ask questions. Questions I wasn't ready to answer. Not like I had the answers anyway. Just that Tommy fucking West took over my club, stole a rival club member's Old Lady and who the hell knew what else. I also couldn't risk getting the police involved. I would rather die on the street than get locked up.

But as much as I wanted to deal with this on my own, I knew when I needed help. I just hoped the woman wouldn't call the police before I died on her back step.

FIVE

Bee

CYRUS AND SAMMY CAME TO check on me. Again. I had a feeling they would just to make sure that I actually stayed home. I rolled my eyes at the thought. Yeah, I was home and bored. I put music on just to liven things up a bit because I was wired. While Slipknot played in the background, I drank my wine and stewed. I wanted to do something fun, exciting, but my cousins liked to be downers and ruin what little fun I was allowed to have. I sounded like an ungrateful brat but at the moment, I didn't care. I *did* notice how Sammy had been grumpier than normal when I saw him earlier in the evening. I went to ask why but Cyrus had shaken his head, silently warning me not to. I had no idea what that was about but was curious just the same.

Bringing the glass of red wine to my lips, I was about to sit at the dining room table when the hairs on the back of my neck tingled. My eyes lifted, a soft gasp lodging its way in my throat.

A large shadow stood in our backyard. I couldn't make out what he looked like, but I knew that it was a man. A very tall one at that. The fact that I was by myself and there was a stranger standing in our yard, made me wish Sammy and Cyrus had never left.

My eyes flicked to my bag on the coffee table. I could call them or the police, but I had watched enough movies to know that the man might not actually be alone. One wrong move and it could be the end of me.

The large shadow stumbled.

My heart jumped to my throat. Something was wrong with him.

When he reached the doors, he knocked on the glass. He mumbled something I couldn't quite hear. Should I call the cops? My dad? Cousins? The man wouldn't know that I was home alone. My parents' vehicle sat in the driveway while my dad had taken my mom on a little getaway with just his bike and the clothes on their back. It was their anniversary, so my father was spoiling my mother and gave me the house to myself for the weekend.

The man knocked again, muttered something else but I still couldn't understand what he was trying to tell me.

Taking a chance, I closed the distance between us and flicked on the light leading to the backyard.

He was pressing one hand against his opposite shoulder, his face pale.

I glanced up, finding him staring down at me. I swallowed hard. "Who are you?"

"I need..." A deep crimson liquid seeped between his fingers. "I need help. I've been stabbed."

My eyes widened. I went to unlock the door when a thought came to mind. "Are you armed?"

He hesitated, finally nodding after a couple of seconds had passed.

"Show me."

A mumbled curse left him, but he reached behind him and pulled out a small pistol.

"Throw it. Behind you," I instructed.

He looked over his shoulder, then back at me.

I raised an eyebrow. "You want my help? Do as I say."

He grunted but tossed the pistol behind him. It landed several feet away on the ground. I made a mental note to go grab it later. "Anything else?"

He shook his head and lifted his pant legs around both ankles.

Satisfied that he was no longer packing, I met his gaze.

"Please," came his muffled response.

I took a breath, unlocking the patio door. As soon as I opened it, his eyes rolled into the back of his head and he fell against me.

I grunted, struggling to hold him up. I had to do something but what, I wasn't sure. I wasn't medically trained. I knew my way around every single type of gun known to man, thanks to the men in my family, but that wouldn't save this guy's life.

"Alright, big guy." I dragged him to a chair in the dining room, gently sitting him on it as best I could without doing any more damage. "What happened to you?"

He blew out a slow breath, his eyes opening that time. They landed on me, something flashing behind them.

I wasn't sure what it was but the look he was giving me, made my heart flutter. I had never reacted this way toward a man before. Only because I didn't get out much, I was sure. And the guys I knew were either too old for me or they were taken already. They were also family even though we weren't blood related.

"You're beautiful," the dark mysterious stranger suddenly said.

I barked a laugh. "I think you've lost a lot of blood."

He adjusted himself on the chair, his face turning ashen. "Still the truth."

"Hey." I cupped his good shoulder, trying to stop him from moving too much. "Tell me your name," I said, attempting to distract him until I could figure out what to do.

"Tanner," he said between clenched teeth.

"Tanner what?" I moved his hand out of the way and saw blood soaking through a bandage.

"Horsch," he answered, his eyes dropping to the wound. "You need to stitch me up."

I was afraid he would say that. "You need to go to the hospital."

"Not happening," he bit out.

"The knife could have hit something vital," I argued.

"It didn't or I would be dead already. It just hurts like a bitch and the blood loss is not boding well for me."

"The hospital would be a better place for you," I insisted.

"I can't go to the hospital. I've been stabbed. They'll ask questions."

"I'm sure they won't." But I didn't know if that would be the case or not. I was trying to reassure him that he would be fine. They would operate or whatever else they needed to do, and he could leave.

"Sew me up. Please."

I laughed. "I am not sewing you up, Tanner." I was experienced in sewing up wounds, but it didn't mean that I actually liked doing it.

"Do it," his voice was firm, but he wasn't talking down to me or treating me as a kid like Sammy did half the time. "Please," Tanner's voice pulled me from my thoughts. "I don't want to bleed all over your floor." He pinched the bridge of his nose, taking shallow breaths.

"Alright, Tanner." I took a deep breath. There was clearly no sense in arguing with him. "I'm going to save your life." I jumped to my feet and ran to the bathroom. Grabbing the first aid kit from under the sink, I rushed back to where Tanner was sitting at the dining room table and dropped the bag on top of the table. "This is going to hurt."

"Don't care." He ran a hand through his hair, slowing his breathing. "Can't be any worse than this."

"How did you end up in this area?" I asked, trying to distract him from the pain.

"I walked. I ended up blacking out a few times I think, so I don't really remember much. Just…" His voice became thick. Oh God, did he lose someone? Was there someone else hurt?

"Are you alone?" I whispered.

He nodded.

"Did someone else get hurt?" I asked gently.

He nodded again, looking down at his hands on his lap.

Getting an idea, I went to the liquor cabinet that my parents kept stocked for whenever we had people over. I looked through it until I found the bottle of Mezcal my parents brought back from Mexico a couple of years ago.

Heading back to Tanner, I sat beside him and twisted off the cap before handing the bottle to him. "Take a swig of this."

Without asking me what it was, he did as he was told. "Fuck." He coughed, taking another swig and letting out a soft sigh. "That shit's good."

"Yeah, it's the strongest thing we have." I placed the bottle on the coffee table and started rooting through the first aid kit.

"Have you done this before?" Tanner asked, trying with one arm to take off his hoodie.

"Here, let me help." Together, we got his hoodie off without causing him more pain. When we got it off of him, I placed it on the table. I turned back to him, swallowing a gasp. Scars lined his torso. Small jagged lines sat on his abdomen, disappearing beneath his jeans.

"Hey," he barked.

My eyes snapped to his.

"I asked you a question," he said, his voice rough. The liquor brought some of the color back to his cheeks, but it was still a matter of time before the liquor no longer helped.

"To answer your question, Tanner. No. I have not done this before, but I have seen a bunch of movies." I shrugged. "This is no different, right?"

He stared at me. "You're kidding."

"Stop being a jerk and I'll tell you. You showed up here, asking for my help. So, either you be nice to me or you can leave and find someone else to sew up your booboo."

"I'm sorry," he mumbled.

"You should be. But yes, I *have* done this a few times before. The guys I know, play rough, so they needed someone to tend to their wounds because like you, constantly going to the hospital is bound to strike up questions they don't want to answer." I snapped my mouth shut, unsure as to why I revealed all of that. "What happened tonight?" I asked, cleaning up the wound.

"I was trying to save my dog," he answered, his voice becoming thick.

"What? You did?" I asked, while sterilizing a needle. "Ready?" I brought it to his shoulder, pausing while I waited for his answer.

"Yes." He inhaled sharply.

BEING US

When I dug the needle into the skin and began sewing up the wound, he didn't even flinch, which was impressive as hell. "What happened to your dog?"

"We had gone for a walk." Tanner pinched the bridge of his nose. "I needed to meet up with someone. After that, Trigger and I were on our way home, but we stopped at a deli, so I could get us some food. He..." His voice cracked. "He disappeared and I found him in an alley. Someone had him in a headlock and eventually...stabbed him."

I gasped. "I'm so sorry."

"He died because of me," Tanner said, more to himself than to me. His eyes took on a faraway look, like he was remembering the events from the night or something even before that.

"I'm sorry if this leaves a nasty scar," I told him, working away on his shoulder.

"Don't care," he mumbled. "Not like anyone's going to see it."

I paused. "What does that mean?"

"What do you think it means?" His gaze locked with mine.

I wasn't sure if it was his subtle way of telling me that he was single, but I knew, God did I ever know. With the way he stared at me and the intense air about him, he was dangerous. For me. For my health. For my damn sanity.

I cleared my throat. "I am really sorry about your dog," I whispered.

"It is what it is."

Which meant, he was going to get revenge. And I hoped he did. Poor puppy. I couldn't imagine losing an animal like that and having it done right in front of him, I was sure, only made it worse. Especially when there was nothing he could have done. He probably thought that his dog blamed him.

"Okay, I'm done." I put the needle and thread away, closed the kit and placed a bandage on the wound. Running my thumb along the edge, I hoped it didn't hurt as much anymore.

A shiver trembled through him.

"Sorry." I pulled my hand back, my cheeks heating. "I'm sorry."

Much to my surprise, Tanner grabbed my hand, placing it back on his shoulder. "Don't be sorry. I like it."

"I'm sure you do." I laughed lightly. "Don't most guys like it when a woman touches them?"

He smirked, his dark eyes dropping to my mouth. "I'm not like most guys, little one."

My breath caught.

A heavy knock sounded on the front door, interrupting our moment.

"Expecting someone?" Tanner asked, his brows narrowing.

I pulled away from him and jumped to my feet when the knock sounded again.

"Coming!" I called out. Knowing that it was probably Cyrus and Sammy checking up on me for the millionth time, I quickly disposed of the first aid kit. Maybe they were coming over to apologize for being jerks. Unlikely, but a girl could hope.

After putting everything away, I stopped at the hallway that led to the front door. I looked between it and Tanner.

He raised an eyebrow.

I didn't know him. Hell, I had no idea why his dog was killed in front of him either or why Tanner had been stabbed. He obviously knew people that wanted to harm him, or he was just in the wrong place at the wrong time. But I had a feeling that he knew more than he let on. He didn't give me a lot to go on, just that they had been attacked.

BEING US

Before I got lost in Tanner's stare, I rushed to the door. Checking the peephole, my stomach somersaulted. Cyrus and Sammy stood on the other side of it. They were going to rip me a new one for inviting a stranger into my home.

I unlocked the door and stepped outside before the twins could barge into the house.

"What's wrong?" they asked at the same time.

"Nothing." I gave them a smile for reassurance. "Why are you guys here a third time? Did you miss me that much?"

"What the hell is this?" Cyrus grabbed my hands, ignored my question, and turned them, palms up. They were covered in Tanner's blood.

Shit.

"What happened?"

"I was doing the dishes and a glass broke," I explained, surprised at myself at how easily the lie slid from my lips, and pulled my hand back.

"You're lying." Cyrus grabbed my hand again. "There's no cut. Who the fuck's blood is this?"

I pulled away. "Listen, thank you guys as always for stopping by and checking up on me but I'm perfectly fine. You can go now." I went to head back inside when a heavy hand slapped the door closed.

"Who the fuck is here?" Cyrus growled, his large body looming over mine.

"You know, my daddy won't be too happy if he finds out how much of an asshole you're being right now," I threatened.

Sammy chuckled, puffing on the smoke between his lips. "You can't always use the daddy card, Bumble Bee."

I rolled my eyes, but I couldn't stop my heart from warming at the nickname our Uncle Catch had given me when I was a baby. It stuck and everyone started calling me it.

"Johnny."

Except for Cyrus, who insisted on calling me by my middle name just to piss me off. But I could never complain, seeing as I was named after their parents who died before I was born.

"You can't tell my parents," I said, entering the house with the twins hot on my heels.

Tanner slid the hoodie up and over his head, covering his scarred torso. He was now sitting on the couch in the living room. He stiffened when he saw us coming toward him.

"What the ever loving fuck?" Sammy laughed. "This shit is unreal. Even for you."

"Johnny," Cyrus barked. "What the hell is going on? Why is *he* here?"

"Your name's Johnny?" Tanner sat back on the couch like he didn't have two men trying to drill holes into the sides of his head.

"It's Bee." I glared at the twins. "Short for Beatrix." I crossed my arms under my chest. "Tanner showed up and needed help. I was going to call 911 but he told me not to."

"That's because of who he is, who he knows, and the shit he's done," Cyrus said through clenched teeth.

"I don't know what any of that means." I lifted my hand when he went to speak again. "Listen, it doesn't matter. He needs help. He was stabbed and I sewed him up as best I could, but he needs to go to a hospital."

"I'm fine," Tanner mumbled.

"Sure you are," I threw at him.

"How the fuck did you get here and why would..." Sammy pointed his smoke at me. "You're really in for it. You know that, right?"

"Yeah, sure." I rolled my eyes. "My dad will yell a bit and then get over it. Cause remember, I am his baby girl and all." I batted my eyelashes.

But the twins were having none of it.

Before I could stop him, Cyrus grabbed Tanner by the collar of his hoodie and lifted him from the couch.

My eyes widened. "Cyrus." I rushed to him, trying to get him to let go of Tanner who was clearly in no condition to be manhandled.

"What the fuck do you want, Tanner? Got more of our members to kill? Want to ruin more lives?" Cyrus released him roughly.

Tanner stumbled back, landing on his ass with an oomph. "Fucking hell. I showed up here because I saw the lights on. I didn't know who lived here."

I went to Tanner, helping him to his feet.

"Thank you, Busy" he said gently.

My heart stuttered at the unexpected nickname he had given me.

"I know the Hell's Harlem clubhouse is a couple hours from here," Tanner added. "I would have gone there directly but I think I would have died on the way."

"Too bad," Sammy muttered, shoving his hands in his pockets.

"Sammy." I glared at him.

He only shrugged.

Tanner lifted his arm, wincing when he couldn't lift it far. "I didn't know she was your property."

"I am no one's property," I snapped.

Something flashed behind his eyes. I wasn't sure what it was, but it sent a shiver racing down my spine. Something happened to him. Long ago. Maybe recently. Besides losing his dog, he was struggling. I knew because I had seen it in the men I had grown up with. Either way, I had a feeling that there was more to Tanner's story than just his dog dying.

"You have no idea who lives here. Do you?" Cyrus asked, taking a step toward Tanner.

"How the fuck could I know?" Tanner held on to the back of the couch for support. "I've been keeping to myself for months. I don't know shit."

"Right." Sammy's brows narrowed in the middle. "Like you don't have any contacts that you keep in touch with. I'm sure you could get any information you're looking for."

"No." Tanner shook his head. "I've laid low. Kept to myself and took care of Trigger. That's it."

"Who's Trigger?" Cyrus asked, leaning against the wall.

"He was my dog," Tanner's voice cracked.

The pain etched on his face tore at my heart.

"Was?" Cyrus stuck an unlit smoke between his lips.

"He...uh...he was killed in front of me." Tanner rubbed the back of his neck.

It took everything in me not to go to him and comfort him as best I could. No matter what the twins said, no one should have to watch their pet die like that in front of them. Even though Cyrus and Sammy stood nearby, I moved to the couch beside Tanner.

He looked down at me.

"You gave him a good life and I'm sure he knew that," I said gently.

"Bee," Sammy barked.

Tanner continued to stare at me.

I gave him a small smile, lifting my shoulders in a shrug.

"Johnny." Cyrus's rough voice pulled me from Tanner's intense scrutiny. "We need to get this shit sorted. He can't stay here."

"I'll leave," Tanner said, taking a step away from me.

"No." I thought a moment. "We need to take him to the hospital and then we can take him to Uncle Greyson's."

The twins laughed.

"Right," Sammy said slowly. "Because that'll go well."

"I'm saying that we can take him to Uncle Greyson and then we can find out what's going on." I wasn't sure how well it would go over with him, but it was worth a shot. Tanner had shown up for a reason. One that I couldn't explain at the moment but a reason nonetheless. And he was also stabbed for a reason as well. Whoever hurt him, didn't just kill his dog because they felt like it. They were clearly making a point.

"Who killed your dog?" Cyrus asked, moving beside his brother.

"I don't know," Tanner confessed. "I had never seen them before."

"I'm making a call." Sammy pressed his phone to his ear and walked away, heading down the long hall that led to the bedrooms.

"Cyrus, please." I went up to my cousin. "You know helping him is the humane thing to do. You don't want his life on your hands, do you?"

Cyrus searched my face but before he could answer, Sammy came back out into the living room.

He looked between all of us. "We're going for a ride."

(Tanner)

I had no idea where we were going. It wasn't like I had much choice in the matter. The fact that neither Sammy nor Cyrus had killed me yet, earned them both a pat on the back. And maybe a raise. No, definitely a raise.

Sammy was the smaller of the two.

While Cyrus's eyes were cold, Sammy's were lacking something. Heart, warmth, life. Who the fuck knew? I didn't know their story. But even though my club had been a rival of Hell's Harlem for as long as I could remember, word traveled fast that their parents had been murdered.

I had never experienced that kind of pain. Losing Trigger was hard enough. He had been the only thing I had ever loved. I never even loved my club. I tolerated it most of the time.

When Bee helped me to my feet, we were under the watchful eye of the twins.

Busy. Bee. Johnny. Beatrix. So many names for someone so young.

Busy was my favorite. It was burned into my memory the way her eyes twinkled when I had given her the nickname.

"Where are we going?" she asked, breaking the unnerving silence between us.

"*We* are not going anywhere." Cyrus pointed at her. "You are staying here."

My back stiffened, a sour taste erupting in my mouth that I would never see her again. "No," I blurted.

All heads turned my way.

"No?" Sammy chuckled. "Don't think you have a say in this, buddy."

"One, I am not your fucking buddy. And two, I'm not going anywhere without her." It didn't make sense. I knew that. I didn't even know her. But the words tumbled from my lips before I could stop myself.

Busy shifted beside us but I wouldn't meet her stare. Knowing I would only get sucked into her beautiful eyes and probably do things I shouldn't in my current state, I kept my gaze locked on the twins.

"Um…guys, we should probably go before it gets too late. You know Uncle Greyson hates being interrupted after a certain time," Busy said, trying to make light of the situation.

I looked at her then. "Lead the way."

She gave me a small smile and made her way to the front door.

"Start up the SUV." Sammy threw the keys at her without taking his gaze from mine.

Busy muttered a curse. "Then you need to lock up." She gave Sammy her keys, looked at me one last time, and quietly left the house.

Cyrus leaned against the wall with his arms crossed over his chest. "I don't like how you're looking at our cousin."

"Yeah." Sammy's brows narrowed. "What's up with that? You're not going anywhere without her? Really?"

"She saved my life." I shrugged like it was no big deal. "And she'll also stop you two fuckers from finishing the job."

"How do you figure that?" Cyrus pushed away from the wall. "You don't even know her. She could have saved your life as you put it, to take you out or let us finish the job."

It didn't matter. I knew because I could feel it in my bones.

"Whatever." Sammy headed to the door. "Let's get this shit done and over with. I have better things to do."

Cyrus grunted, following his brother to the door. He turned back to me when he saw that I hadn't followed him. "I suggest coming or else what happened tonight, will be the least of your worries."

As much as I didn't want to, I complied and left the house. Finding Busy standing on the porch, it took everything in me not to go to her. I wasn't sure where these new feelings were coming from. I had never been attracted to a woman before. I had sex just for the sake of doing it. It wasn't like I couldn't pay for it but when body parts didn't work, it made it almost impossible to get any enjoyment out of it. So I gave up and took up working out. Running and spending time with…my chest ached, the sudden thought of Trigger sending a wave of grief crashing down onto my shoulders. Closing my eyes, I gave myself a shake. I pushed those thoughts to the back of my mind. I would deal with them later. I didn't need the twins seeing my moment of weakness.

When I opened my eyes, Busy was looking right at me.

Under normal circumstances, I would have been pissed that she saw the vulnerability in me. But instead, I welcomed it. I couldn't dwell on that either, knowing I needed to get this stab wound double-checked, so I could find out everything there was that made up Busy.

SIX

Bee

WHILE WE DROVE AWAY from my house, I couldn't help but wonder exactly where we were going. I suggested the hospital but then remembered that my grandfather used to have a whole operating room set up at his clubhouse. I could only assume that it was still there. I would have suggested it, but I knew that my grandfather didn't like surprise visitors, so I thought better of it.

"Where are we going?" Tanner asked, resting his hand on the bench between us. His pinky accidentally grazed the side of my hand.

I jumped at the unexpected contact.

He rested his hand on his lap, letting out a soft sigh.

I handed him a bottle of water.

He nodded once, his pinky brushing along the side of mine again. That time, it was intentional and definitely not an accident.

A spark shot through me at the soft touch. Quickly pulling my hand away, I dropped it on my lap and cleared my throat.

Tanner smirked, drinking from the bottle of water.

"We're going to see a friend." Cyrus's gaze flicked to mine in the rearview mirror. "Safer than the hospital. Less questions that way."

"We're going to Grandpa's?" I asked, sitting forward. Maybe I should have suggested it in the first place after all.

"Grandpa?" Tanner repeated.

"Your grandfather isn't there," Cyrus told me, ignoring Tanner. "He's away for the weekend, doing who knows what."

"That's who I called," Sammy added. "Figured your uncle owed us a favor."

I snorted. "My uncle doesn't owe anyone favors. Ever."

"Who's your uncle?" Tanner asked, clearly trying to get information.

"Kian Wolf," I told him.

He laughed.

"What's so funny?" I demanded.

Tanner rubbed the back of his neck. "I'd probably be better off if you left me to die in your backyard."

The twins chuckled.

It was like they knew something, an inside joke, that I wasn't included in on. It had been something ever since I was a little girl and it pissed me off. I was the youngest and also the only female. The guys would keep things from me, thinking they were protecting me and because of that, I became naïve. But thankfully, I discovered the internet and I had friends who shed some light on things I wasn't aware of. If it wasn't for Lori and Heather, I wouldn't know anything when it came to the opposite sex.

"Why do you say that?" I asked Tanner, knowing that if I wanted any sort of information, he would be the better one to go to.

"Your uncle has made a name for himself," was all he said.

"Just like you have?" I threw back at him.

Tanner looked away, glancing out the window.

"We're here," Cyrus said before I could apologize to Tanner.

Something told me that he didn't actually like the rumors that had been spread around about him. But I wondered why he never corrected people if they weren't actually true. Or maybe some of them were. Maybe there were too many that he could no longer be bothered to set people straight.

Cyrus pulled up into a large parking lot, my uncle's clubhouse sitting before us. It was a strip club but at the same time, a front for what actually went on in this place. The guys I had grown up with tried shielding me from it, but I wasn't stupid. Also, my mom had told me stories whenever I asked. Like me, she had grown up in the biker life and her father was just as protective as mine. I wondered who was worse. My grandfather wasn't as bad as my dad. Not to me anyway.

"What are we doing here?" Tanner asked, breaking the silence.

"We're going to get that wound in your shoulder fixed." Cyrus left the SUV, not leaving any room for question.

"I suggest hurrying the fuck up," Sammy grumbled. "Don't need your death on our hands." He chuckled to himself, following his brother.

Sometimes I wondered about the men in my life. Especially now. They acted all nice and sweet but there had been something about Tanner that pulled darkness and depravity out of the twins. If the rumors were true, I could only imagine how my father would react when he found out whose life I saved.

(Tanner)

Much to the twins' dismay, Busy walked at my side as we headed into the old strip club. I had heard of her uncle. I even had a run in or two with her grandfather. But that was before my club threw me out and I had a target on my back. Now I was showing up on his doorstep, begging for help and at his mercy.

As soon as we neared the door, several large men started filing out of the club. They wore leather cuts with Mayhem's Revenge on the left breast pocket. I didn't see the president or vice-president anywhere. But I knew they were around. The guys were protecting their own. Which was what my club should have done for me but instead, they went behind my back and listened to that fucker before even allowing me to get a word in edgewise.

"Tell Kian that his niece is here," one of the men told another all while keeping his dark eyes locked on mine.

I was man enough to admit it. I was scared as hell. Not for me. No, I didn't care about my life. With Trigger gone and no longer having my club, not even a family of my own, what was the point? But what I did care about was Busy seeing something that would ruin her for the rest of her life. She was too damn young to be as broken as I was. I was sure she knew her family wasn't perfect. But it didn't mean she actually had to see the evils they did. I made a vow at that point to protect her from the wrongs of the world. I would make it so all she saw was the light inside the darkness. Nothing was going to taint my girl.

My stomach twisted.

She wasn't mine.

BEING US

She would never be mine.

You don't deserve her.

Before I could drive myself crazy with the demons in my head, I took a step back when Kian Wolf exited the strip club.

"Where is she?" he demanded, his eyes scanning the group of guys surrounding him.

Busy laughed lightly, the sound vibrating through me, and rushed into his open arms.

He hugged her tight, his gaze finding mine.

I took another step back when a heavy hand landed on my shoulder.

"Careful," Sammy murmured. "Do something stupid and you won't have to worry about that wound in your shoulder."

I didn't want this. I wasn't backing up to start shit. I was backing up to make sure Busy didn't get involved. But she already was, wasn't she? It wasn't like I ever had a choice really. But this, not being in control, not knowing what was going on, not having any fucking answers, was driving me absolutely insane. The voices in my head were loud. I couldn't silence them, and I knew the longer time went on where I didn't have what I was looking for, the voices would eventually take over.

"Take her inside," Kian told one of his men, releasing Busy.

"What?" Her head whipped around. "No." Her dark eyes flicked my way. "Please, Uncle Kian."

He ignored her and took a step toward me, the men shifting around us.

Busy was dragged into the building, her protests grating over every inch of me.

"What are you doing here, Tanner?" Kian asked, stopping a foot away from me. "Rumor has it that you're running rogue now."

"Not like I had a choice," I told him, my head feeling light. I knew that it was only a matter of time before the wound in my shoulder was either going to make me pass out or kill me. Preferably the latter. I needed liquids and meds. I was sure that Busy did a good job at sewing me up, but she wasn't a professional. The skin around the hole tingled, reminding me of when she brushed her thumb along the damage done to me.

"You always have a choice." Kian reached inside his leather cut and pulled out a pistol.

I was sure that for anyone else, the sight of the gun would make them uneasy. But me? No, it only excited me. It made me realize that I was still very much alive even though I knew at that moment, Busy's uncle would rather kill me on the spot. But he wouldn't. Not when his niece was around.

Kian tilted his head, his dark eyes piercing into me. He was older, probably old enough to be my father, and the president of Mayhem's Revenge. With graying hair and silver sprouting through his dark beard on his strong jaw, I was sure a lot of women would have considered him the silver fox type.

"Checking me out, Tanner?" Kian scratched his temple with the end of the barrel. "I heard you liked all types but sorry, you don't do it for me."

"I don't have a type. I hate people. End of." Until I met Busy at least but I wasn't telling *him* that.

"Interesting." He dropped his arm, aiming the gun at me. "Tell me why the fuck you're here and why my niece is with you." He looked past me. "Are either of you going to explain or do I need to call your president?"

"He showed up at my place."

All of us turned toward Busy who was standing at the entrance to the club.

"Why is she out here?" Kian demanded.

"Have you ever tried keeping her in line? These Wolf women are stubborn as fuck," the man standing behind her said.

"You can thank my mama for that," Busy told him, standing up straighter, before turning back to her uncle. "Tanner was in my backyard and needed help."

Kian's head slowly turned back around. "That true?" he asked, lifting the gun.

"Yes." But I wasn't going to tell him any more when we weren't alone. I didn't trust his men. I had learned rather quickly that any club could have a mole in it. Didn't matter how tight the guys were and pretended to be. If the right amount of money came along, even the strongest and most loyal club member could flip.

"I heard there's a price," Kian added, cocking the gun and aiming it at me.

Busy gasped.

A deafening silence fell over the group after that.

I stepped toward Kian, grabbing hold of the barrel. "Don't tease me, Kian. If you're going to kill me, do it now. And do it quickly because I promise you, it'll be the only chance you'll ever get."

SEVEN

GRABBING HOLD OF THE edge of the barrel, I lifted the gun to my forehead.

Busy gasped.

Bodies shifted around us.

Kian stared at me with his cold, calculating eyes.

"If you're going to shoot me, do it. Stop being a pussy, Kian." I took a step closer to him, going toe-to-toe with him. He was bigger than I was but at that point, after everything that had happened in the last twelve hours or so, I no longer cared if he put a bullet between my eyes. "Do it," I said, egging him on.

Kian pulled the gun back, cupped my nape with his free hand and shoved the end of the pistol against the wound in my shoulder.

"Fuck." The pain shredded through me, my knees almost giving out at the agony.

"Uncle Kian, stop," Busy demanded, but her uncle didn't budge. No, instead, he smirked like the cocky fucker that he was.

"You see," he said, his voice low enough for only me to hear. "I don't need the money. I'll kill you for free. I heard that you've been a bad little boy and have been messing with my brother in-law's family."

"I have no idea what you're talking about," I bit out through clenched teeth. But I did. Busy's father was going to kick my ass.

"Oh, but I think you do." Kian pushed the tip of the barrel into me hard, forcing a muffled groan to escape my mouth.

"Stop!"

All heads turned at the sound of the deep voice booming from the entrance of the club.

Much to my surprise, Nero Wolf, known as Shadow on the streets, came toward us. "What the hell is going on?"

"I thought you were out of town," Kian said, lowering the gun and taking a step back.

"Not that it's any of your business but I was bored, and my granddaughter called, needing help."

"You called him?" Kian asked, spinning on his niece.

Busy rolled her eyes, stepping up beside her grandfather. "None of you guys were listening to me, so I figured you would listen to Grandpa. He's the smart one who actually listens to what I have to say."

Talk to me, beautiful girl. I'll listen to you. I'll listen all motherfucking day. Just give me those pretty eyes.

As if she could hear me, Busy glanced my way, a flush hitting her cheeks.

Her looking at me, eased some of the strain on my body. I wasn't sure why or how, I didn't even care to explain it, but I *did* know that I needed her.

"Tanner, it seems you've caused quite the ripple in my little family." Nero spun on his heel. "Follow me."

Kian looked between his father and me. "Dad."

Nero stopped, raising an eyebrow. "Problem?"

Kian shifted. Even though he was now the president, Nero had built a reputation for himself. Coming from

South Africa and a dangerous part at that, he had to earn his way to the top. Literally. I didn't know what he had to do to survive. I didn't even want to know. I had always kept out of his business. If our paths ever crossed, it was a get in, get out kind of situation. I never asked questions. I highly respected the guy and I knew when to back down, tuck my tail between my legs, and do as I was told.

"Tanner," Nero barked. "You and Beatrix will come with me." He looked past me. "Cyrus and Sammy, if my son-in-law calls you asking for his daughter, you tell him that she wanted to come visit me. Nothing else. Understood?"

"Yes, Sir." Sammy saluted him.

Cyrus grunted, pulled an unlit smoke from behind his ear, and stuck it between his lips.

"I thought you quit," Nero pointed out.

"And I thought you kept your nose out of other people's business," Cyrus threw back at him.

Nero grinned. "Funny." He turned to me. "Tanner, follow me. *Now.*"

My feet carried me forward on their own accord.

Nero Wolf wasn't one you wanted to mess with. I always enjoyed skirting the law and messing with fate, but even I wasn't stupid enough to argue with the guy. He was older and no longer president of Mayhem's Revenge, but he still had a say in what went on in their club. I almost wished I could have been a part of their crew. Or even Hell's Harlem. I had always envied their brotherhood. But I didn't trust people, so it could never work. I didn't even trust myself half the time. As much as I wanted that family type dynamic, I knew once this was all said and done, that I would retire and no longer be a biker. It was only a matter of time before that happened.

"What happened tonight?" Nero asked, pulling me from my thoughts and stopping at the end of the long hall before turning toward me.

BEING US

Busy looked up at me before facing her grandfather. "Tanner showed up in my backyard. Mom and Dad are out of town and I didn't know what else to do. So I helped him."

Nero sighed. "You have a big heart, my darling."

Busy's cheeks reddened.

"What else did you do?" he asked her, pushing open the door.

"I stitched him up after he was stabbed and I gave him a shot of Mezcal." She shrugged like it was no big deal.

But it was. My shoulder still burned from her gentle touch.

"That's probably why you're not dead yet but if you were stabbed, it could have hit something vital. Damaged some nerves. The usual shit," Nero explained.

"I don't need my shoulder to live," I murmured.

Nero's gaze shot to mine. "No. But you could die from an infection. While I give my granddaughter all the credit in the world, she's not a nurse. If you were a car, I wouldn't be wanting to double-check that she did a good job." He turned away from us, leaving no room for question. "Ricky," he yelled. "Prep for surgery. I don't need another death on my hands. As much as my boys would love it, I'm not feeling it tonight."

Thank God for that.

When we followed Nero into the room, my eyes widened. It was like walking into a hospital room. Shelves were stocked with meds and other necessities for fixing wounds and other ailments.

"Tanner?" Nero stepped in front of me. "If you don't want this, you say the word. But you could die if Ricky doesn't check you out."

I swallowed hard.

He was giving me a choice. A choice I never really had before. I wasn't sure why but when I glanced at Busy and saw hope dancing in her eyes, I took a deep breath. Something slid between us. Something new. Something unexpected, especially when I'd only just met her a few hours ago.

She gave me a small nod, encouraging me to fight.

Why? She didn't know me. She didn't know the shit I had done. But to her, it never mattered. Her grandfather was right. She did have a big heart. She was probably the type that would stop traffic to save a spider from getting run over. I bet she even collected worms after it rained and put them in a nearby garden, so they wouldn't get harmed.

I found myself wanting to know more. To know everything that made up Busy.

"Tanner," Nero said gently, pulling me from my thoughts.

I knew what my answer would have been if I had never met her but now that I had, my answer was completely different.

I stood up straighter, looking Nero straight in the eyes. "Do it."

EIGHT

Bee

PACING BACK AND FORTH, I waited in the small office off the room where my grandfather had his medical supplies and where the surgeries happened. I knew he had everything he needed to fix his men when they came back broken and bloody, but I had never actually seen the room before.

The door suddenly opened, revealing my grandpa. He gave me a small smile, the hard lines in his weathered face, softening when his gaze landed on me.

"How's he doing?" I asked, my stomach twisting with the possibility he had died on the table. It had only been a stab wound but I was no medical professional. I didn't know if my sewing him up helped or if Tanner had other wounds he failed to mention.

"He's resting. The surgery went well. You did a good job sewing him up and stopping the bleeding. Luckily nothing vital was hit." Grandpa shut the door behind him and leaned against it. "I need to ask you something."

"Oh." I took a breath, thankful that Tanner was okay but now concerned over whatever it was that Grandpa wanted to talk to me about. "Okay."

"You just met Tanner tonight?"

I nodded.

"And your father doesn't know what happened?"

"No." I shook my head. "It was their anniversary a couple of days ago, so they went away to celebrate. I told them I would only call them if it was an emergency. I was going to call them when Tanner showed up, but Cyrus and Sammy ended up coming over instead and you know the rest."

Grandpa's jaw clenched, his staring making me uneasy.

"What is it?"

"It's not my place because you're a big girl and you need to figure shit out on your own but I'm going to warn you." He paused. "You need to be careful. Tanner is running from something and I have a feeling that it has to do with his club and maybe something else. Eventually, whoever is looking for him, will catch him. I would hate for you to be there when that happens. Also, Tanner is the kind of person who looks out for himself first. I'm sure you've heard some of the rumors."

"Nothing overly detailed." I had lived a sheltered life thanks to the men I grew up with, but I *did* know that Tanner was known to not be a good guy. But that was all I knew.

"If you bring him to your Uncle Greyson's, don't expect a happy reunion."

"I just wanted to help," I confessed. I had seen the men in my life come home damn near destroyed all because they were protecting what was rightfully theirs. I got it but it didn't mean that I liked seeing it at all. While Uncle Greyson tried not to get involved, there were still times where I saw him take my dad and Uncle Catch, leave for a few hours and then when they returned, it was like they had lost a piece of themselves and the only way to find it was by spending some time alone with their wives.

While the biker life wasn't always safe, I knew my uncle was trying to clean up their past transgressions. He had been doing it since before I was born. Since before all of us kids were born. But I was sure he didn't think it would take so long.

"I don't know everything about Tanner. I don't know what he did or why he's hated but he's a human being," I told my grandpa. "I wasn't going to let him die in the backyard. I'm not a monster."

Grandpa grunted, staring at me with those dark calculating eyes of his. "You aren't. But he is."

"How do you know that?" I hated questioning him, but this was starting to piss me off. "Have you seen Tanner in action? Have you seen him do half the shit everyone is saying he's done?"

"Careful how you speak to me, Beatrix," he bit out.

I hung my head, my cheeks burning. "I'm sorry."

"You don't know what he's done. Doesn't matter if I haven't seen it for myself."

I huffed. "I know he's done some bad stuff. But so have all of you. Does that mean you don't have a right to live either?"

"Listen to me, my dearest granddaughter." Grandpa pushed away from the wall and came toward me. "You have too big of a heart." He smiled down at me, cupping my face. "Not everyone has a right to live. Not when they've done things you couldn't even dream about in your worst nightmares. There are monsters out there, darling. Monsters that would make Ted Bundy look like a fucking saint."

My stomach twisted at the thought.

Grandpa sighed, his face softening. "All I'm saying is, please be careful. I'd hate for something to happen and for Tanner to end up losing his life in front of you. I don't want you to see that shit."

"Maybe that's the problem," I mumbled. Not that I ever wanted to see the bad things that went on in the world but maybe if I would have seen at least a little bit of it, I wouldn't be so damn naïve when it came to certain things. I was too trusting. I knew that. Hell, everyone knew that. I just hoped that I wouldn't regret ever saving Tanner's life.

"I know your parents, especially your father, likes to protect you. It's for the better, sweetheart. Trust me." Before he could add any more to that, the door behind him opened.

Ricky peeked his head out into the hall. "We're done in here."

When Grandpa went to follow Ricky into the room, I stopped him. "Why did you want me to come back here with you? You're much bigger than Tanner and he's wounded. It's not like you couldn't handle him yourself if something happened."

"Because I saw the way Tanner was looking at you and the way he was keeping you close. I also know you don't know each other but, Bee, I've been around a long fucking time. He wouldn't have come back here willingly if you weren't with him."

My breath caught at the revelation. Could all of that be true? Why didn't I see it? And how was that even possible?

Before I could ask any more questions, Grandpa stepped into the makeshift hospital room and glanced at me over his shoulder. "Come."

I joined him, my eyes instantly moving to Tanner sitting up on a small single bed at the other side of the room.

Without even waiting, I went to him and pulled up a metal chair. "How are you feeling?" I asked, sitting and crossing my knee over the other.

Tanner's dark eyes slid my way, but he never responded.

"He's still feeling the effects of the pain killers and will probably feel them for a while," Ricky explained.

I pulled the chair closer to Tanner's bed. "You good?"

His gaze took on a glassy look, but he slowly nodded.

A breath I didn't realize I had been holding, left me. "Good. I'm glad."

His lips twitched.

"We'll let him rest a bit and then you can take him to your uncle's place. I'm sure Greyson has some questions for him." Grandpa headed back to the door before glancing at us over his shoulder. "Remember what I said, Beatrix."

I nodded, unsure what to do with the information he had given me.

"I'll be in the office if you need me," Ricky said, and left the room as well, not waiting for me to reply.

When I was alone with Tanner, I expected Cyrus and Sammy to come barreling into the room, demanding to know why my grandfather would leave me alone with him. But when they didn't, the anxiety rushing through me, eased.

"Busy," Tanner said, his voice rough.

I placed my hand on his arm, running my thumb back and forth.

He laid down, closed his eyes, and pinched the bridge of his nose. "Tonight never should have happened."

My eyes popped to his, finding him staring back at me.

"Trigger knew something was off. I should have listened to him but I'm desperate. I need answers," he said, his voice thick. "It doesn't matter." His eyes closed, his breathing soon becoming deep and even.

Something inside of me stirred over the fact that he trusted me enough to be able to fall asleep around me. I finally looked at him then. Really looked at him. There was no gray in his dark hair or in the scruff on his jaw. He must have still been in his twenties or even early thirties. Either that or he had really good genes.

I noticed then how his nose was crooked, maybe from getting in a fight or from being hit in the face one too many times. He was handsome in a rugged, beautiful way but there was something that had happened that kept his heart closed off. I wanted to know more about his dog and Tanner's relationship with him. I also wanted to know why anyone would want to hurt his puppy. Unless it was to prove a point. I didn't know and maybe I never would. But what I did know was that this beautiful broken man currently lying so close to me, needed something. And I vowed to myself that I would be the one to give it to him. Whatever *it* was.

(Tanner)

The pain that was bestowed on my small frail body was something I could never get used to. No matter how many times he came to me during the night or the fact that I no longer fought him off. Even though he liked it when I submitted, he liked it even more when I tried shoving him away.

I woke with a start, sweat dripping down my spine. Ice cold fear that *he* would suddenly appear out of thin air, had me grasping at the blanket and pulling it up to my chin.

"Tanner?"

I jumped, finding a woman, a beautiful woman at that, sitting beside me with a furrowed brow.

Memories of the night came rushing back.

Trigger.

He was killed.

I was stabbed.

Pain. So much damn pain.

Busy.

"Busy," I whispered, my tongue thick.

She gave me a small smile. "Are you okay?"

I looked around me. When I realized that I was no longer that little boy and I wouldn't have to worry about *him* coming to me ever again, I let out a sigh of relief. "Yeah."

"How are you feeling?" she asked, worry evident by the lines set in her forehead.

I shifted my weight, sitting up in the surprisingly comfortable bed. "Like I've been stabbed." I never expected to actually fall asleep. It took a lot for me to sleep in a place that I wasn't comfortable with or when I didn't know if it was safe to do so. But it looked like the night had caught up with me and I passed out without even realizing it.

Busy gave me a small smile. "You were mumbling in your sleep."

"Nightmare," was all I said.

She nodded. Picking up a bottle of water off a table by the bed, she handed it to me. "This might help make you feel better. Although, I'm sure you'd probably rather it be alcohol. I know I would. I remember last summer, I went for a run with Sammy and I tripped over air and sprained my ankle. It hurt like a bitch, but he gave me a shot of tequila later that night and I felt really good after. I also slept like a baby."

I stared at her.

"Oh." Her cheeks reddened. "Sorry. I talk a lot. It's one of my many flaws."

"No. I like it." I found that I could listen to her speak for hours and her talking a lot was definitely not a damn flaw.

"Thank you." She blew a loose curl out of her eyes. "I usually get told to be quiet." She shrugged like it was no big deal. But it was. Maybe not to her but it definitely was a huge fucking deal to me.

"Who tells you that?" I asked, my voice coming out harsher than I intended.

"People." She shrugged again. "I usually only start talking a lot when I'm nervous or bored or trying to make small talk, which is something that I'm not really good at. I find most people want to talk about the weather but who wants to hear about that? Not me. Talk to me about movies or books and I'm all ears." She snapped her mouth shut. "I'm doing it again."

I chuckled. "Don't be nervous around me, Busy. But talk. Talk until you don't want to talk anymore. I like listening."

Her smile grew. "Really?" She stood. "Well, Tanner. You haven't heard anything yet. I'm easing you in slowly."

My chuckle deepened. "I'm looking forward to being eased in completely, baby."

Her eyes widened, her smile falling from her face and her cheeks turning a darker shade of red.

I winked.

Just as I was about to tell her to stay and talk to me, the door to the room opened.

"Ah, you're awake." Nero came into the room and stood at the end of the bed. "Good thing too because I think the twins are losing their minds over Bee being in here with you."

Busy rolled her eyes. "They can get over it."

"Doesn't matter." He cupped her cheek and placed a soft peck on her head. "As much as I love having you here, I know Greyson wants answers."

My stomach twisted, knowing that I wouldn't be able to give him the answers he was looking for. Not completely anyway.

"Fine." Busy went to the door. "Sammy! Cyrus! If you want us to leave, you have to help Tanner to your SUV." She turned back to me and gave me a wink. "I got your back."

Something stirred in me. Little did she know how much I needed to hear that.

"He got stabbed in the shoulder," one of them called back. "His legs work fine."

"Doesn't matter." She scowled. "The pain meds are making him drowsy." She huffed, leaving the room.

While she rounded up the twins, Nero came toward me.

"I'm going to give you a warning," he murmured, low enough for only me to hear. "And I don't give a shit if you don't want it." He pressed his thumb into the wound in my shoulder. "You're lucky you're still alive."

Even though I was on painkillers, the agony that shot through me, forced a rough grunt from my lips.

"I see the way you look at my granddaughter."

Busy looked our way.

Nero waved, digging his fingers into my shoulder.

She smiled and looked away, probably waiting for the twins to hurry the fuck up.

"I don't know what you want with her," Nero continued. "But just remember, Tanner. You have made a lot of enemies over the years for someone being so young. She's led a sheltered life and we want to keep it that way. Do you understand me?" he asked, squeezing my shoulder for added effect.

"Yes," I bit out through clenched teeth. But it didn't mean that I could stop her if she tried anything. He just didn't need to know that.

"Good. Because for whatever reason, I actually like you, Tanner." Nero pulled away and joined his granddaughter at the door.

I stared after him. He liked me? No one liked me. I didn't even like me half the time.

As much as I wanted to ask what the hell he was talking about, Sammy and Cyrus barreled into the room.

"You don't have to help me," I told them, pulling the sheet off of me and swinging my legs over the edge of the bed. I had been alone for so long; I could do everything on my own. It wasn't like I ever had a choice. I also didn't want to be helped by people who didn't want to help me in the first place.

"Bee asked us to help," Cyrus said while his brother stood off to the side with a scowl on his face.

"No, she told us to," Sammy corrected.

Although Cyrus was bigger, there was an air to Sammy that made me uneasy. It was like he was permanently pissed off and just hated life.

Well, welcome to the club, fucker.

My hands clenched into fists at my sides. What I wouldn't give to spar with him. It had been so long since I had a good fight. I had heard of sex being a way to blow off aggression and steam, but it had never been my thing. I could count on one hand how many women I had slept with. If you could even call it that.

"Ignore him," Cyrus said, his voice gentle. "Here." He held out his arm.

I glanced up at him. "Why?"

"Because our cousin likes you and I know when not to go against a woman. No matter how young or sheltered she's been, Johnny is strong as fuck and when she demands something, you do it."

"Why?" I repeated, feeling like a damn parrot.

"Because." Cyrus winked. "I don't want to deal with her mom."

I had never met Zillah Lister, but I knew of her. Her husband. All of them. I had only been lucky enough to meet a handful of the Hell's Harlem crew. But I had a feeling that I would be meeting more of them soon and quickly.

"This isn't right," Sammy muttered, pulling me from my thoughts.

"Doesn't matter." Cyrus glanced my way. "You need our help, don't you?"

"I need to talk to your president." I wasn't letting anyone know how desperate I was without speaking to Greyson first.

"Alright. I'll make that happen, but he won't be happy about it," Cyrus warned. "Now let's get out of here before Johnny has my balls."

Like a good little boy, I listened. Grabbing onto his arm, I let him help me out of the makeshift hospital room. I would have been fine and less wobbly on my feet if it hadn't been for the damn meds. Other members of Mayhem's Revenge stood around, drinking beer, shooting the shit, flirting with the women they had on their arms, and more. It was a typical night for a biker. I had always hated the parties. I was never a social person, but I knew they were needed. It also helped me keep people close so I could watch them. Study them. Have them under my control.

Much to my surprise, we headed out the back of the club. Busy was nowhere to be found but I was looking for her. Even before I knew what I was doing, my eyes scanned the area around me. Needing, hoping, aching to keep her close by. These new feelings weren't normal for me. I never wanted someone to stick around. I shoved people out of my life, made it a living hell for most and I never cared in the least how that happened or if they ever came back. I didn't deserve anything more.

"She went to grab the SUV," Cyrus muttered as soon as we stepped outside.

As if on cue, the twins' large black SUV pulled up in front of us. The passenger window rolled down.

"Hey guys," Busy greeted. "Need a ride?" She waggled her eyebrows.

Sammy grunted.

Cyrus didn't say anything.

And I only stared at her.

I didn't need a ride but I sure as hell wanted to take *her* on one. Every inch of me tingled at the thought of Busy taking my cock deep into her body. Images flashed in my mind of her on top of me, riding me, controlling the thrusts. I pictured her cupping her breasts and throwing her head back with a satisfied moan. I could almost hear myself telling her to give me her beautiful eyes as I took us both past the brink of ecstasy.

"Let's get this shit on the road," Sammy mumbled, forcing me from my unexpected thoughts and opening the back door.

I pulled away from Cyrus, thankful for the assistance but not knowing how to tell him so. I glanced at him over my shoulder, nodding slightly before I sat in the back seat.

Just when I thought he didn't catch the movement, he nodded back and headed around to the driver's side.

Busy took that moment to leave the SUV.

Cyrus closed the door, shutting me in with him.

Sammy stepped in front of Busy, mumbling something to her that made her brows furrow in the middle. Even though she was much smaller than him and definitely shorter, she placed her hands on her hips and

BEING US

stared up at him. Her lips moved over words that I couldn't make out.

"He's warning her against you," Cyrus explained.

"I haven't done anything." Not recently anyway.

"Doesn't matter. We can feel it."

I wanted to ask him what he meant when Sammy opened the passenger door. He glared at me and slumped onto the seat. If he was that worried about Busy, he would have made her sit in the front. I wondered why he didn't.

Busy joined me in the back. Clearly the twins wanted her to have nothing to do with me, but I savored the fact that she was so close just the same.

"Hi," she whispered.

I gave her a small smile. A smile that was meant for only her. "Hi."

"Greyson isn't going to like this," Sammy said, slamming the door closed. "I really wouldn't want to be you right now," he told me.

I rolled my eyes. "I'm sure you're enjoying this anyway."

"Maybe." He shrugged, turning back around to face the front. "You've done a lot of shit, Tanner. And then you just disappear. You've got some explaining to do."

"And I'll explain it all to your president. It's no one else's business." My hackles rose, suddenly feeling like I was being backed into a corner.

"No?" Sammy's head whipped around.

"Leave it alone," Cyrus demanded. "Grey will deal with this shit."

"Fine." Sammy shoved a cigarette between his lips and lit it up, the sweet smoke billowing around us.

I braved a chance and glanced at Busy.

She was staring out the window, munching on her bottom lip.

My eyes dropped to her hand resting on the seat between us.

Reaching out, I ran my pinky along the edge of it.

A sigh left her, the tension on her shoulders dissipating at the small contact between us.

That's it, Busy. Give me that stress. You let me worry about this shit.

A small smile splayed on her lips, almost like she could hear my thoughts.

I took a deep breath, let it out slowly, and closed my eyes, leaning my head against the back of the seat. I tried not to think about what Greyson Mercer's reaction would be once I stepped onto his territory. He was a good man. He had spent years trying to clean up Hell's Harlem messes. I just hoped that he would give me a chance and hear me out or I was good as dead.

NINE

Bee

WHILE **CYRUS DROVE US** to Uncle Greyson's house, also known as the Hell's Harlem clubhouse, I couldn't help but wonder why the twins were on me when it came to Tanner. It wasn't like I had any time alone with him to actually do anything. When Sammy gave me shit, all I could do was stand there and take it. I didn't need it going back to my father before Tanner had a chance to talk to my uncle. I didn't know what he needed help with, but I knew that it was something to do with what happened tonight.

Tanner shifted beside me, his face wincing with each movement.

Much to my surprise, he let out a hard sigh and the next thing I knew, he was lying down with his head on my lap.

My eyes widened.

I caught Cyrus's reflection in the mirror and shrugged.

He shook his head, looking back out onto the road ahead of us.

"He's not safe for you," Sammy said, giving me one of his many lectures that I had received over the years.

"And how exactly do you know what's safe for me, Sammy?" I asked him, placing my hands on my hips.

"Just trust me. He's not the guy you're looking for."

But maybe he was. Maybe Tanner was put in my life because he needed it and so did I.

While Tanner slept, I checked my phone and opened up the group text I had with Heather and Lori. I sent them a quick text stating that tonight was crazy and thanked them for the night out. I also mentioned that we would have to do it again sometime. I knew they would have questions as to why Cyrus and Sammy had pulled me out of the club. They knew I had grown up around bikers, but now, their curiosity was probably piqued even more. But I never told them much. It wasn't like I ever invited them over to Uncle Greyson's place. Not that he would allow it anyway. He was a private man. He even hated the parties that were constantly thrown but for whatever reason, he never stopped them from happening.

"No."

I jumped, glancing down at Tanner.

He shifted, his brow furrowing.

I ran my fingers through the hair at his nape. "Tanner," I whispered.

"Stop," he said, louder that time.

I looked ahead, thinking that the twins would hear him but when they didn't look our way and continued carrying on in their conversation, I blew out a breath of relief. "Hey, can you guys put on some music or something please?"

"Sure." Sammy turned on the sound system and a scream came through the speakers as "Get This" by Slipknot started playing in the background. "Fucking hell, Bee."

I laughed. "It's not my fault you guys don't listen to good music. A girl has to get it while she can."

"You know, this is our vehicle," Cyrus said, shaking his head. "When did you get a chance to play your shit?"

"The last time I drove it, I slipped my CD in there. Not my problem that you guys aren't observant," I teased.

"Women," Sammy mumbled, changing the music to something that suited his tastes. Some rap song came on that I didn't know but it was at least better than some of the shit they listened to.

"I don't think most women listen to that kind of music," Cyrus told his brother.

"True." Sammy shook his head. "You are not normal."

I snorted. "I was raised on horror movies and rom-coms. I'm all kinds of fucked up."

The twins chuckled.

Truth was, I didn't listen to music that others listened to. Not usually. I preferred the underground stuff that never made it to the radio. Or in this case, music that screamed at me. Literally. I couldn't help it. Especially when it came to Corey Taylor. I could feel each word he sang down to the marrow of my bones. To say I was a fan was an understatement.

Tanner shifted, pulling me from my thoughts.

While the twins talked, I focused on the man currently sleeping with his head on my lap. So much had happened in the past few hours, it was like a whirlwind of emotions. I wondered if he had time to grieve over the loss of his dog.

"Bee."

My attention was pulled to the front. The twins were staring back at me. I looked around us, not even realizing we had parked at Uncle Greyson's clubhouse. I looked down at Tanner's sleeping form. My fingers were brushing along the back of his neck. So subtle, but spoke so much through that simple touch alone. Something about this man on my lap called to me and I didn't know why. I wasn't sure if I would ever know. Maybe I wouldn't find out. Maybe this was one of those moments that were just meant to be. It could be one of those moments that didn't need any sort of explanation at all. Damn the consequences.

"Johnny."

I met Cyrus's gaze. "What?"

"We're not leaving you alone with him," he bit out.

I rolled my eyes. "What's he going to do? He's high on pain meds and sleeping." The fact that he trusted me enough to fall asleep on my lap, did something funny to me. It made me feel things I had never felt before.

A look passed between Cyrus and Sammy.

"Guys, seriously." I huffed. "Just go. I'll be fine. He doesn't have any weapons on him anyway." I remembered then how I demanded that he throw his pistol away. "Uh…that reminds me."

Sammy's scowl deepened. "What?"

"I told Tanner to throw his gun away," I told them. "So, it's somewhere in my backyard."

Sammy muttered a curse.

"On it." Cyrus pulled his cell out of his leather cut, made a call, and had a prospect go to my parents' place to retrieve the pistol. At least that was one less thing I had to worry about.

"Thank you," I murmured when Cyrus disconnected the call.

"You need to be more careful. If your dad found that shit…" Cyrus shook his head.

"This needs to stop," Sammy added. "You don't even know him. You don't know what he did or what he could do."

BEING US

"Nothing's going to happen," I said but my voice wasn't as firm as I would have liked. Sammy was right, I didn't know Tanner, but I did know the connection we shared. It didn't matter that we'd only met hours before. My parents had told me about that instant attraction they felt back in the beginning. Uncle Greyson felt it when he met Aunt Eve. Even if not everyone experienced it, it didn't mean that it wasn't possible.

"He's bigger than you," Sammy pointed out. "He doesn't need weapons to hurt you."

"I'm fine," I insisted. It wasn't like the windows were completely tinted. Any issues and someone could see, or I could just leave the vehicle. It wasn't that hard. "I promise I'm fine," I repeated when the guys didn't budge.

Cyrus opened the driver's side door. "Greyson is going to know we're here and come out if we don't go in. We'll give him a few to wake up." He looked at me over his shoulder. "Any trouble, you fucking scream. You hear me?"

"Yes." I waved a hand between us. "Now go."

Sammy grumbled a string of curses but left the vehicle and slammed the passenger door closed.

Maybe it wasn't smart to insist on being alone with Tanner, but he did just have surgery. He needed rest. It would help him give my uncle and everyone else the answers they were looking for anyway.

Tanner stirred but his eyes remained closed. His long lashes fanned out. I was sure most women would love lashes like his.

Running my fingers through his hair, my body reacted to him in ways I had never experienced.

He shifted, wrapping his arm around me and snuggled his face into my lap.

I realized then how close he was to a part of me that no man had ever had access to before.

Tanner took a deep breath, a low rumble following soon after.

"Tanner," I whispered.

That same growl left him again when he pushed his face harder into my lap. His back lifted when he took a deep inhale, a low groan following soon after.

God, he was smelling me. "Tanner," I said, my voice firmer that time. "Wake up."

He jumped, lifting his head. "I...I was dreaming."

I laughed lightly, my cheeks burning. "I bet you were."

His gaze dropped to my lap before looking back up at my face. "It was a very good dream." Something flashed in his dark eyes.

I shook my head, smiling. "We should go inside," I said, pulling away from him.

"Wait." He grabbed my hand, stopping me from leaving the SUV. "I just...I need..."

I looked back at him when he didn't finish his sentence.

His eyes were on his hand that was on top of mine. "What happened?" he asked, brushing his thumb back and forth along a long white scar that covered the side of my hand.

"We were riding our bikes and I was trying to keep up with the boys. I wasn't paying attention and the front tire hit a rock at the perfect angle. I flipped over the handlebars and slid along some broken glass. I needed surgery and I can't feel anything in the tip of my pinky," I explained, wiggling my finger.

Much to my surprise, Tanner brought my hand up to his mouth and brushed his lips along the jagged scar.

My mouth dried.

He kissed the tip of my pinky. "Did you feel that?"

"Tanner," I whispered, my stomach tumbling.

"I haven't had a dream like that in a long time. Actually, I can't remember the last time I had a dream like that. I don't remember what it was about, but I know that it was…"

"A sexy dream?" I answered for him.

"Something like that," he said, but never met my gaze. "Did I say anything?"

"You said no and then stop," I said gently.

He nodded.

I pulled my hand away from him, not needing the twins to catch our little moment. "Something happened."

"Yeah." Tanner sighed, meeting my gaze. "I usually talk in my sleep if I'm medicated or drink too much. Or even when I get high. It's why I don't do drugs or drink really. I have no idea what I'd say, and I don't like losing control."

"And people could try and get secrets out of you or take advantage of your lack of control?"

He only nodded, cupping my hand that was on the seat beneath us.

I pulled my hand out from under his and placed it on top of his but not before I caught the look of panic in his dark eyes. I didn't know what that was about, but I did know that it set off alarm bells. Not because I feared that he would hurt me but that he would hurt himself or someone else.

"How are you feeling?" I asked softly.

"Like hell." His gaze dropped to our hands. "But this…"

A knock sounded on the window, making me jump. I pulled away from Tanner and opened the door. "What?"

Sammy only grunted, stuck a smoke between his lips, and started to walk toward the large clubhouse I had grown up in.

"I guess it's time," I muttered.

"Yeah."

I stepped out of the vehicle, waiting for Tanner to do the same. "You good?"

He looked past me, a dark shadow passing over his face. "Yup. Fucking perfect."

(Tanner)

Truth was, I didn't really care. But I was surprised the guys hadn't killed me already. Especially after everything I had done.

Even though Greyson Mercer was one of the good guys, it didn't mean that he didn't have a reputation to uphold either. Word had it that he had helped bring down a human trafficking ring. I didn't know how he got involved in that, but I respected the guy because of it. As much as I didn't like people, I didn't like bastards who tried throwing their weight and power around even more.

Before we made it into the large house, a tall man followed by Greyson, came out the front door. They stalked toward us.

I stopped.

Greyson had a deep scowl on his face. "I'm only going to ask this once. What the fuck is *he* doing here?"

Busy stepped in front of me.

Sammy smirked, moving off to the side. He clearly didn't give a shit what his president did to me. And Cyrus? He looked between Greyson and me, something flashing in his eyes. Worry? Concern? I wasn't sure. I was about to ask when Greyson closed the distance between us.

"I don't hear anyone answering my question," he said, his voice rough.

"Uncle Greyson, I can explain." Busy crossed her arms under her chest, lifting her chin and staring her uncle down. Seeing her stand up to a man who was twice her size, because of me, stirred something inside of me. The fact that she felt the need to protect me in any way made this attraction I had for her grow into something more. It didn't make sense. Especially when I had only just met her tonight.

"Bee, what the hell is going on?" Greyson asked, his face softening when he spoke to her.

"Maybe we should go inside," the tall man told him. I noticed then that Vice-President sat on the patch above his heart. He was Catch Hunter. I had never met him before. I hadn't met most of them. But clearly my name had gotten around, and I wasn't sure how I felt about that.

"Fine." Greyson spun on his heel and stomped toward the large house.

Sammy cupped Busy's shoulder and led her away.

A growl lodged its way in my throat over the fact that another man was touching her.

I went to take a step forward when she glanced at me over her shoulder, her gaze locking with mine.

"Hey." Fingers snapped in my face.

My jaw clenched. I was met by Catch's icy cold stare.

"I don't know you. I've never had the pleasure of meeting you," he said, his voice monotone. "I don't know why the fuck you're here, but I don't like it. And I especially don't like the way you're eye-fucking my niece."

"I have no idea what you're talking about." What was with these guys and being observant as hell? Although, I couldn't say I blamed them. It would be the exact same reaction I would have if a stranger was on my property.

"Right," Catch said slowly, drawing out the word. "I suggest telling Greyson why you're here. Give him some sob story that I'm sure you've mulled over and then be on your merry fucking way. Got it?"

"I need help," I heard myself tell him. The hairs on the back of my neck tingled, my stomach clenching with each passing moment that Busy wasn't around. My heart started racing. I took a deep breath. I didn't need Catch to see me this way.

So vulnerable. So broken. So torn between doing what was right and what was wrong. I needed help but I needed answers more.

Catch's sapphire eyes searched my face. "Word has it that Nero likes you. He actually called Greyson and vouched for you. Why?"

"I have no idea," I mumbled, going to walk past him when his next words stopped me.

"You touch her, you even think about touching her, and I will do things to you worse than what was done to those dogs you saved."

I was surprised that little fact had gotten around. It had been something good I had done. After saving a bunch of dogs from a dog fighting ring, it had leaked out that I had gone crazy. It wasn't the case. It just pissed me off that the dogs were used in the first place.

I took a breath, ignoring him and walking to the house that could either save me or be my true and final death.

I was betting on the latter.

TEN

TANNER

S SOON AS I stepped into the large house, which I never actually got to truly appreciate, they were on me. I was forced to my knees by Catch with another guy I didn't know, standing on the other side of me. I expected this moment to happen sooner but was thankful it didn't. I didn't want Busy to see her family this way. And I especially didn't want her to see me on my knees. If that ever happened, it would be because I initiated it.

Catch gripped my shoulder, digging his fingers into the muscle.

I winced, being reminded not so eloquently that I had been stabbed only hours before.

Greyson paced back and forth, scratching his jaw. "Where is she?" he asked the twins as they joined our little party.

"In the basement reading," Sammy answered, sticking an unlit smoke between his lips. He smirked when he caught me looking his way. "She says hi."

My jaw clenched but I wouldn't show him how he got to me.

He tilted his head, his smirk growing.

"Alright." Greyson stopped in front of me and crouched. "Tell me why the fuck you're in my home and why I shouldn't kill you right now."

"I need your help," I told him, meeting him square in the eye. I refused to back down. As much as I hated asking for help, this was different. I knew by killing my dog that these fuckers wouldn't stop until they got to me and everyone I knew. It was one reason why I refused to get close to anyone.

Busy.

My stomach twisted. Fucking hell.

"And why would I help you exactly?" Greyson's eyes narrowed.

"I can pay," I told him. It wasn't like I used the money I had anyway. I gave it to local places whenever I bought food and I gave the homeless kid sitting outside my apartment, money every time I saw him. I didn't need fancy things to be happy. I just needed these bastards off my case and my damn dog back. I knew that would never happen, so avenging him would have to do.

"As you can tell," Greyson stood, "I'm doing quite well for myself, so I don't need your money. I also don't appreciate you coming in here and insulting me," he said, walking away. "Kill him."

"No." I shoved out of Catch's grip and jumped to my feet. "I'm desperate. I wouldn't be here if I wasn't."

Greyson stopped, feigning a yawn. "No, you're here because my boys brought you here."

"I'm here because your niece saved my life and her grandfather organized my surgery. I could have stayed in her backyard and died. But I didn't. I'm here." I pointed at the twins. "They brought me here because they have questions. Just like you do. So let me answer them."

"There's some shit going around about you. How you disappeared." Greyson turned toward me, crossing his arms under his broad chest. "Is that true?"

"I have a target on my back. So yeah, it's true."

Greyson searched my face. He turned on his heel, walking away. "I suggest following me."

Catch gave me a shove forward.

When no one else budged, I did as I was told and followed Greyson to a door sitting at the left side of the large room.

He opened the door and went inside before spinning on me. "You armed?"

I grunted. "Yeah, because I keep a Glock in my sweatpants." Nah, it was more like a machinegun. I bit back a sigh. I was losing my ever-loving mind. A mind I couldn't afford to lose in the first place. It was the only thing I had going for me anymore.

"Fine." Greyson moved away from the door and let me enter.

I shut the door behind me, leaning against it. Letting my eyes wander around the vast space, I took in what looked like a room where members of Hell's Harlem met. An old bike hung high on the wall with framed pictures hanging beneath it as well. It took everything in me not to go to them and check them out. Not because I was nosy but because I wanted to know the crew that I was about to beg for help.

"Where have you been?" Greyson asked, sitting at the head of the large wooden table.

"I've been hiding." I turned toward him. "But you already know that."

"I do but what I don't understand is why. Don't you have your club members to protect you?"

I wasn't sure how much information had gotten out or how I should even begin to tell him. Truth was, I had been in the wrong place at the wrong time. When I met up with Meadow Rodriguez, I had assumed I would get what I needed and that was that. I didn't want any trouble. Sure, I liked messing with her and her guys a bit, but I wasn't expecting the place to get blown to shit or for her to lose one of her men.

"I didn't mean for it to happen," I blurted.

Greyson gaped at me. "For what to happen exactly?"

"For Sunny."

Greyson shoved to his feet. "You will never speak that name. You fucking hear me? Because of you, he's dead."

"No." I took a step toward him, not caring in the least that he could very well be the reason I died tonight. "I didn't know that shit was going to go down. I didn't know any of it."

"You didn't?" Greyson chuckled. "Come on. You must think I'm an idiot. Sunny died and then you disappear. You obviously felt guilty and holed up somewhere so you wouldn't be caught. Or maybe you didn't actually feel guilty at all. No. Tanner Horsch has no fucking heart. Isn't that one of the rumors going around?"

My stomach clenched.

"I disappeared as you all keep saying, because my club kicked me out and someone else took over. I lived in the city with my dog. But I was found. I don't know how, and I don't know why. It's been six months. It took six months for them to find me and then they killed my damn dog."

Something flashed in Greyson's eyes. "They killed your dog?"

I nodded. "That's how I ended up in Busy's backyard. I blacked out and just started walking after I was stabbed."

"Busy?"

"Bee." I shook my head. "Johnny. You guys have too many damn names for her."

"I don't like that you've already added a name to that list," Greyson grumbled.

Knowing it was not the time to get cocky, I still couldn't help but smirk. "Oh, I know." It was like these people didn't even know. Tell me not to do something and I was going to do it with a neon sign and glitter. Maybe add some flashing lights and fireworks too. I was a little hurt that they expected any less from me.

"What do you want, Tanner? You disappear for months on end and show up out of nowhere all because your dog died?"

"He didn't just die," I said, my voice raising.

Greyson raised an eyebrow.

I sighed, scrubbing a hand down my face and taking another deep breath. I needed his help. I needed to control this temper for fear that he would kick me out before I could get the answers I needed, before I could see what this thing was between Busy and I. I didn't care that we had only met a few hours before. Something clicked between us. It just felt…right.

"What do you need?" Greyson finally asked, rising from his chair. He went to the bay window behind him and peeked through the blinds. Satisfied that nothing was going to jump out at him, he turned back toward me.

"I need to know why my dog was gutted in front of me. And I need to know why I have a target on my back."

"I heard there's a price on your head." He moved to the table, rested his knuckles on top of it, and leaned toward me. "Should I tell my boys? I know they could use the money."

I swallowed hard. "One. They probably already know about the price hanging over my head. And two. If you were really trying to threaten me, you would have more than just you in here."

"Maybe." Greyson scratched his jaw. "I wonder what my son would do if he were here," he said, more to himself but being the good boy that I was, I answered anyway.

"Jaron would have killed me before I made it out of Busy's backyard." I ran into Jaron once. His father was a kitten compared to him. It had been one reason why I told some of my crew who were in jail alongside him, to leave him alone. But who knows if they actually listened to me.

Greyson smirked. "That's very true." He paused. "Your boys have been leaving him alone."

I blew out a breath I didn't realize I had been holding. "So I've heard."

"I'm a little surprised."

"It doesn't matter if you believe me or not. I respect your son, so I made sure nothing would happen but now I no longer have that control." And that little fact pissed me off even more. "The point is, I need answers and I know you can help me get them."

"Why would I even consider helping you?"

"Because you're a decent human being." Word had gone around that he was trying to clean up the messes of Hell's Harlem for years. I wasn't sure how successful he had been, especially when his son was as bad as I was. Or worse.

"Alright." Greyson started pacing. "Say I help you with whatever it is you need help with, what's in it for me?"

"Answers," I said automatically.

"Answers," he repeated, stopping. "I don't need any answers."

"You want to know why Sunny was shot."

A dark shadow passed over Greyson's face. "He was shot because of you. He died because of you. And if his girl and his partner find out that you're here, it'll be a shitshow. You won't live long enough to give me whatever answers it is you think I need."

"I'm not scared of Shade." And I wasn't. He was bigger and older than I was, but it didn't mean shit. There was a softness to him. It had always been Sunny who was the hothead.

"Oh, I'm not talking about Shade. You pulled some shit, Tanner. A lot of shit actually and we all lost someone because of it. But it affected Shade and Meadow more. You do remember her, right?" Greyson began pacing again. "I'm sure she'd actually like to claim the money that's tied around your neck."

"I didn't shoot Sunny." Even though it was the truth, I knew that no one believed me. I wasn't sure if they would ever believe me.

"You were there. You caused problems. It doesn't look good, Tanner. Did you tell my niece what you did? Besides Sunny getting shot. Did you tell her the other things that happened? Like when you touched Meadow?"

My body stiffened, not realizing he had been told that little fact. I was trying to scare Meadow into giving me information. I was desperate. I had threatened her but would never have acted on it.

Greyson wouldn't look away, but I refused to back down. There had only been one man I ever submitted to. After that, my walls were up and I became cold. If the people who were supposed to protect me didn't care, then why should I?

Greyson chuckled. "Probably not. I know guys like you. I've heard the stories."

"You don't know me." No one did. It was how I preferred it. It meant they couldn't get too close and hurt me. I had already lost Trigger because I let him in. He let me in too and look what happened. He died. Because of me. "I need to know why there's a target on my back," I said, before Greyson could comment even more on how much he thought he knew me.

"Why don't you go crawl back into your hole, Tanner?"

"No, please. I'll do anything. I just need a safe place to hide out at least until I can get answers." I didn't like the desperation in my voice, but I had no choice.

"And how are you going to get answers if you're hiding? You didn't come here with anything. And we both know that cell phones are not the smart way to go if you don't want to be tracked. I don't need a war on my hands and I definitely don't need more shit on my doorstep."

"I know someone. He's helping me and trying to get me the information I need. Please, Greyson. I…" Fucking hell, I was begging. I never begged. I didn't like this. I didn't like this one fucking bit but no matter how much I tried, no one believed me. Served me right for keeping the life I had and for not correcting the rumors that had been spread about me.

Greyson searched my face, his brows dropping to a point in the middle. "Did you shoot Sunny?"

"No." I shook my head. "I know you don't believe me. I wouldn't believe me either, but I didn't need a war. I just messed with them a bit. I know I shouldn't have done that, but I was desperate for information and I have a reputation. Or I had one. Now, I don't give a shit. I don't have my club. I don't have my dog. I don't have anyone. It's just me. That's it."

"What do you want with my niece?"

My stomach twisted at the underlying threat hidden in his voice, but my body still stirred at the mere mention of Busy. "I don't know her. She's been nothing but nice to me and she saved my life."

Greyson nodded. "You will stay in the basement. You won't come out. If this target on your back is actually true, I don't need people coming in here, seeing you, and trying to kill you. The women who live here have been through enough, and as sexist as it may sound, I don't need them seeing any more of that shit."

A breath I didn't realize I had been holding, left me. "Thank you."

"Don't thank me. You can thank Nero." And Busy but he never said it because he knew exactly how I wanted to thank her.

"If I catch you out of the basement before I can make sure your death isn't going to be on my hands, I'll unleash my dogs on you. You feel me?"

"Yeah." I rubbed the back of my neck, feeling like a puppy who had just been scolded for not pissing on the paper like he was supposed to.

Greyson laid down more rules, but I couldn't focus on his words. Memories rushed forth. Bad memories. God-awful ones. I wished with everything in me that they were just nightmares that never actually happened but unfortunately in my case, every single one of these damn memories did in fact happen.

"Tanner, did you hear me?" Greyson's hard jaw clenched, silence falling between us.

"Yeah." I nodded. "I heard you." I didn't. He knew I didn't. But for whatever reason, he didn't press.

A part of me wondered while Greyson may have said it was okay for me to stay in his house, could I be worse off? So many people had come and gone from this place who wanted me dead. But the one person who didn't, called out to me. I needed to find Busy. I needed to know that whatever was blooming between us was something more than just my imagination. I needed to feel a gentle touch. I needed her and I didn't know why.

ELEVEN

Bee

TANNER HAD BEEN TALKING to my uncle for what felt like hours when really, it had only been a half hour at most. But the anxiety rushing through me that Uncle Greyson had taken him out before getting any answers, forced bile to my throat.

I never wanted to leave Tanner alone with him. I trusted my family, but Tanner clearly unraveled everyone and set them on edge. I only wished I could figure out why.

"Hey, Busy."

I glanced up from the book I was trying to read and found Tanner slowly coming toward me with a few items of clothing in his hands.

"Mind if I join you?" he asked, stopping a few feet away.

I looked around him, expecting to see Uncle Greyson or one of the other guys but when I didn't, my heart stuttered that Tanner and I were actually alone.

I shook my head. "How did the meeting go?"

BEING US

He placed the pile of clothes on the coffee table and sat beside me, stretching out his long legs in front of him. "Greyson isn't happy that I'm here. No one is actually." He ran a hand through his dark hair before resting his head against the back of the couch. "But he's letting me stay. I just have rules to follow." He looked at me then. "Which is funny because I've never been the type to follow any sort of rules." His eyes dropped to my mouth.

My cheeks burned. "Well..." I placed my book on the coffee table and turned toward him. "They're good people. I think the fact that you asked for help, works in your favor."

He grunted. "Maybe. I don't know anymore."

"Is he helping you?"

"Yeah. He gave me a burner phone so I can keep in touch with my contact. Cyrus grabbed me some clean clothes as well." Tanner paused. "People want me dead, Busy. And whoever set it in place is willing to pay a lot of money for that to happen."

I swallowed hard. "How much?"

"Five hundred."

"Thousand?" I asked, my eyes widening.

He nodded. "It's why I have to stay down here. For whatever reason, your grandfather vouched for me."

"Grandpa likes people that most don't. I heard he didn't like my dad much in the beginning though." I shrugged. "Who knows why my grandpa does the things he does anymore."

"Your dad won't like me either." Tanner sighed, staring up at the ceiling.

"Have you ever met my dad?" I asked, curious about the man sitting beside me.

"No. I tried to keep my nose out of the spotlight believe it or not. It's not my thing. I paid people to do that shit for me. And then something came up and I had to approach Sunny, Shade and Meadow. And…" His jaw ticked.

"Hey." I touched his arm gently.

Tanner looked at me then. "I'm not a good guy, Busy. But this…I want to be. For you."

My stomach somersaulted. "I'm not changing you. I don't expect that from you anyway."

He looked away.

"Tanner." I squeezed his arm, moving closer to him. "I mean it. I may be new at this but for whatever reason, I like you. Even if it's just to be friends. I got your back, Tanner. I can be your little bodyguard."

He gave me a small smile.

"I don't know why but when you're close, I don't feel like committing murder." He pinched the bridge of his nose, taking a deep breath. There was more to it than that, but I didn't press.

"Um…well, you're welcome?"

He chuckled, dropping his hand to his side.

"How's your shoulder?"

"Hurts like a bitch but it could be worse. It's fucking with my head though because if they wanted me dead, they wouldn't have stabbed me in the damn shoulder."

"Maybe they didn't."

He frowned. "What do you mean?"

"I mean…maybe they didn't want you dead and only stabbed you to get a point across. I watch a lot of movies and I know they're just movies and all but sometimes the bad guys do things just to be funny." I shrugged.

"Sounds like something I would do." Tanner turned his big body toward me, giving me his full attention.

"You like messing with people just for fun?" I asked, raising an eyebrow.

He looked down at his lap. "Yeah. Something like that." He reached a hand out and brushed his finger along my ankle.

BEING US

My breath caught. I had never been this close to a man before. Sure, I was close with the twins and Jaron, but they were family. I was also the youngest. Everyone else was older and treated me like a kid for the most part. But not Tanner. No. Instead, he looked at me like I was a woman. And not just a twenty-three-year-old female who worked a couple of days a week at her mom's auto shop. One who had no idea what she wanted to do in life besides enjoying her twenties at the moment. Even then, I couldn't do that knowing I had the twins breathing down my neck. At least with Jaron, he let me do whatever I wanted but watched me at the same time. God, I missed him. And Piper. I liked Piper.

"What are you thinking about?" Tanner asked, leaning the side of his head against the back of the couch.

"Oh." I laughed lightly. "I was thinking that I like this, and I like how you don't look at me like a kid."

He grunted. "With the thoughts running through my head, I think I would go to jail if I looked at you as a kid."

"Oh…" My eyes widened. "Really?"

Tanner laughed, his shoulders shaking. "Yeah."

"Thank you." I gave him a small smile.

"Nah." He leaned toward me. "Don't thank me, Busy. You just keep being you. That's all I want."

"Tanner?"

"Yeah," he said, his voice low.

"What do you want with me?"

His jaw clenched, his eyes searching my face. "I'm not sure but I do know that I want to be friends. If something more happens, great, but for now, I just need you near me. I don't know why. Maybe I never will. But you…"

"What?" I whispered.

"You calm me in ways I never knew I needed." He cupped my knee, running his thumb back and forth. He watched the movement, almost like he knew he shouldn't be touching me and yet, he was.

I should have pushed him away, but I didn't. I liked when he touched me. Even if it was something small. We may not have known each other for twenty-four hours yet but it was nice having someone around I didn't grow up with. Someone who had an unbiased opinion and saw me for me. Someone who looked past the fact that I grew up with bikers.

"Tanner." I found I wanted more. I wanted to know what it would be like to feel his mouth on mine. Would his kiss be gentle or rough? Would it be firm but passionate? I imagined his hands on me, holding me, touching me, making me feel things I never knew existed until I met him.

His dark eyes popped to mine. He leaned forward.

Just when I thought he was going to kiss me, he gave me a small smirk instead.

A breathless laugh left me.

His grin grew. He closed the last few inches between us, brushing his mouth down the length of my jaw.

I shivered, placing my hands on his waist. "I…"

"Mmmhmm…"

I leaned my head to the side, inviting him to do more. To kiss me. Touch me. Even to just hold me. But we were at my uncle's place. It wasn't safe. Not for Tanner. Not for either of us.

"Someone could come in," I told him, but I still didn't push him away. If anything, I hinted for more. "There are cameras. But most times I think people just say they're around to keep everyone on edge."

"Maybe. Let's test your theory." When his lips found the side of my neck, he sunk his teeth into the sensitive skin.

I gasped, a flush of heat washing over my skin.

BEING US

"Hmm…my girl likes a little pain," he said, his deep voice vibrating against my throat.

"I'm…I'm not your girl." But although I said those words, I liked the sound of being his.

He chuckled, nipping the same spot again. "No one's come to kick my ass yet. Think your Uncle Catch was lying about the cameras?"

"I don't know." But what I did know, was that I didn't want Tanner to stop. At all. I chewed my bottom lip to stop the moan from leaving my mouth.

He swiped his tongue along the spot, soothing the sting. "And Busy, you *are* my girl."

"How? We only just met. You just had surgery." I leaned back, shaking my head. "This—"

"Is perfect," he finished for me. "I don't give a shit that I just had surgery. I don't give a shit that tonight was hell for me and that we only just met a few hours ago. You are the first thing since I brought Trigger home so many months ago, that has been something good for me." He lifted his hand when I went to say something. "Is this fast? No. Being attracted to someone doesn't mean anything. And, baby, I haven't been attracted to someone in a long mother fucking time. If ever at all."

I stared at him. "What does that mean?"

He sighed, his shoulders drooping. "I've never wanted someone. Not sex. Not a relationship. Nothing. Am I a virgin? No. But the few times I had sex wasn't…" A dark shadow passed over his face.

I swallowed hard, my heart jumping. I had seen that look before. Something happened to him. I wasn't sure what. I wasn't even sure if he would ever tell me. Maybe one day.

"Anyway." He cleared his throat. "I've never wanted to just spend time with someone like I do with you."

"You're high," I said, trying to lighten the sudden heaviness in the air.

He chuckled. "I'm not that high."

I smiled. "I think you are. You just met me tonight, Tanner."

"So? Haven't you ever been attracted to someone right away?"

"Not…no, not really." I shrugged.

"But you're attracted to me," he pointed out.

That was when I realized that my hands were still on his waist. I went to pull away when he stopped me.

"No. Don't pull away from me. I like when you touch me."

My cheeks burned. I lifted a hand and ran my fingers gently down the side of his neck before brushing them lightly over his shoulder. "Does it hurt?"

"Not at the moment." He leaned toward me, resting his forehead on my shoulder. "Busy."

"Tanner." I ran my fingers through the soft hair at the base of his neck.

"I know this doesn't make sense." He pushed his face into the crook of my neck. "I know this is new for both of us. I also know there are things going around about me. What I don't know is what's going to happen. Not tomorrow. Not next week. Not even an hour or two from now." He lifted his head, his deep blue eyes searching my face. "But what I do know is that I want you."

"Why?"

"Do I need a reason?" He reached out and cupped the side of my neck. Brushing his thumb back and forth, he leaned forward and placed a soft peck on my forehead and then my nose.

A hot tingle raced down my spine at the soft contact, but it wasn't enough. I needed more and I couldn't explain why.

BEING US

Before I could say anything or even comment on the fact that this man, this beautiful and dangerous man, wanted me, footsteps sounded down the stairs.

Tanner pulled away, quickly grabbing a throw pillow and placing it on his lap.

My eyes widened.

He winked.

I laughed, shaking my head. I had no idea that I could cause that sort of reaction in a man. Especially someone like him. He had to have been experienced. Definitely far more experienced than I was.

Cyrus and Sammy took that moment to come around the corner, joining us in the den.

Sammy had a scowl on his face while Cyrus frowned. They both looked like Tanner was going to do something he shouldn't. Maybe he would have if we hadn't been interrupted. Either way, it would probably be me who would do something I shouldn't first.

"What are you doing?" Sammy demanded, looking between us.

A glance passed between Tanner and I.

"We just finished fucking each other's brains out." I faked a yawn. "I think next time, I should stretch first."

Tanner coughed.

Cyrus chuckled.

Sammy's face turned red. "You are not funny."

"What do you want me to say, Sammy? We were talking. That's it." I crossed my arms under my chest, lifting my chin defiantly.

"You need to be careful," he told me, but his voice didn't come out as sure as a moment ago. "I don't like you, but you need to be careful as well," he told Tanner.

"You keep saying that." I actually yawned for real that time, leaning my head against the back of the couch. "I'm fine. We are fine."

Sammy slumped onto the chair beside Tanner while Cyrus leaned a hip against the edge of it.

"Greyson told me I can stay in the spare room down here," Tanner said, breaking the unnerving silence.

"Yeah." Sammy stuck an unlit smoke between his lips which was something he did quite often. Both him and his brother were trying to quit but I couldn't see that happening anytime soon. "You better keep it that way too."

I rolled my eyes.

"What are you going to do if I don't?" Tanner pressed.

My heart jumped, my body heating over the fact that he was standing up to them. I wasn't sure if he was stupid or bored. Probably the latter.

Sammy's jaw clenched.

"Listen," Cyrus interjected before his brother popped a blood vessel. "Whatever this is between you two, we'll keep it to ourselves. Won't we?" he asked Sammy.

"What the fuck ever." Sammy stood. "I'm going out."

"Tell Red I said hi." Cyrus smirked.

"I'll tell her when she's gagging on my cock," Sammy muttered, stomping away, his heavy footsteps disappearing once he reached the top floor.

"Who's Red?" I asked.

"Someone who wants nothing to do with my brother it seems." Cyrus chuckled to himself. "I guess there's a first time for everything."

I knew that Sammy had gotten around. While alcohol was Cyrus's vice, sex was Sammy's, but I had never seen him bring a woman home to the clubhouse. The other guys had done so but for whatever reason, he didn't. Cyrus and Sammy shared an apartment about an hour away in another city. They kept to the clubhouse mostly to keep an eye on Piper whenever she stopped by. I wasn't sure what was going on there, but I knew with Jaron now being in jail, it was bad. Not that anyone told me more than that.

"It's getting late," Cyrus said, looking directly at me.

"Uh…" I cleared my throat and rose from the couch. "It is."

"Good night, Busy."

"Good night, Tanner." I stopped beside Cyrus. "Be nice to him." Without waiting for a response, I headed up the stairs. Away from the man who told me he wanted me. Away from the man who had been the first I had ever been attracted to. One thing was right. I wanted him as well. But I wasn't sure if that were even possible.

If ever at all.

(Tanner)

"What do you want with her?" Cyrus demanded once we were alone.

"Is your brother going to come back now that Busy went to bed?" I asked, almost expecting Sammy to jump out of the dark corners like the monsters in my head.

"No." Cyrus narrowed his brows. "You leave Johnny alone."

"Why do you call her that?" I asked, curiosity getting the better of me.

Cyrus's jaw clenched and then surprisingly, he sighed and moved to the spot beside me. "She's named after our parents. I call her Johnny because no one else does and it's her middle name. I also know that our dad would have liked having a little girl named after him."

I was momentarily shocked by the confession.

Rumor had it that Cyrus wasn't a talker. While Sammy fucked his way through anything that would open themselves to him, Cyrus was withdrawn and liked to swim in the bottom of a bottle.

Cyrus looked at me then, a slow smile creeping on his face. "You look shocked that I actually answered your question."

"I was told that you're not a talker."

"Yeah and I was told that you're a murderer." He shrugged. "Guess we don't know each other at all and shouldn't listen to rumors, now should we?"

I looked away, the pain in my shoulder pulsing to the beat of my heart. I lifted my arm, trying to stretch and move it as best I could. Wasn't like I had a physical therapist nearby or anything.

"Our mom would have liked you."

My head whipped around.

"And maybe even our dad but he never would have admitted that," Cyrus added. His face was impassive, almost as if he never said anything at all. When he rose from the couch without so much as a word, I wondered if maybe I had been dreaming it.

"Your mom," I blurted.

Cyrus stopped, looking down at me over his shoulder. "Our mom wasn't like everyone else. She saw something in our dad that other women hadn't. I know that Busy sees something in you too. But I promise you, if you hurt her, you will have a war on your hands, Tanner. Is that something you're willing to risk for easy pussy?"

I cringed over his crass words when it came to him talking about his cousin. "She's not easy pussy."

Cyrus jutted his chin forward. "Oh I know that. But do you?"

I stewed over his words. I hadn't even known Busy for twenty-four hours and yet, we almost kissed. "I do."

He cocked his head to the side. "Hurt her and I'll send my brother after you. He's been on edge lately. More so than usual." He sighed, rubbing the back of his neck. "I don't even think sex will make him feel better." He shook his head.

"Red," I muttered, remembering Cyrus talking about this person earlier.

Cyrus grunted. "Pussy that my brother can't have or at the very least, is driving him crazy."

Before I could ask what he meant by that, he left the den, his heavy footsteps sounding up the stairs.

The weight of the night finally came crashing down on me.

Losing Trigger.

Getting stabbed.

Watching my dog get gutted in front of me.

My jaw clenched, bile burning my throat at what I would do once I got my hands on the bastard who killed my boy.

I was a little surprised that Greyson didn't stick his guys on me, so they could watch every single one of my moves.

The burner phone suddenly rang, startling me. Flipping it open, I brought it up to my ear.

"There are cameras everywhere. So I suggest being a good little boy and keeping your dick in your pants."

I frowned at the deep voice coming from the other end of the phone. "Catch?"

"The one and only. I know you were wondering why you don't always have one of us with you. Cameras, Tanner. There are cameras every-fucking-where."

My eyes scanned the room.

"You won't see them." Catch chuckled. "But we'll see you. You know, I'm not a fan of action movies but this is kind of fun."

"This isn't a movie, Catch," I mumbled, leaning back against the couch and pinching the bridge of my nose. Someone needed to get out more.

"Nope. It's not. Remember what I said. And remember what Greyson told you. There are rules and if you need our help like you say you do; you *will* follow them."

My jaw clenched.

I had never been one to ask for help, but I knew that this time, I needed it. Desperately. But when Greyson never asked for something in return, it made me uneasy. He would collect payment. They always did.

I just didn't know when.

TWELVE

Bee

WITH THE MUSIC FLOWING through me, I moved my head in tune with the fast, loud beat. Corey Taylor screamed at me while he sang the words of "Dead Memories." It wasn't Slipknot's heaviest song, but it was one of my favorites.

While I put some food together for Tanner, I moved my hips to the beat of the music. It had been about a week since Uncle Greyson let him start staying at the clubhouse. I hadn't seen much of him and we definitely hadn't almost kissed again since the first time. He had probably just been high on meds and was itching for something. I wasn't sure what or if I was even right but there was no way that Tanner could want me.

He had followed Uncle Greyson's rules and stayed in the basement. I had gone down to the den to watch movies with Uncle Catch and Aunt Sara, but Tanner had never come out of his room. It had been distracting. I couldn't for the life of me remember what movies I had been watching either.

I just wished I could have found the time to sneak off to go see Tanner. I knew Uncle Greyson had one of the prospects bring him food, but I was sure it wasn't the same. They probably just placed the tray on the floor and left. But I actually wanted to talk to him. I wanted to get to know him. Not to change him from the man people were apparently scared of but to find out why they were scared. I wanted him to know that not everyone looked at him like a monster, but a man instead.

"Really, Johnny?"

I jumped, spun around, and saw Cyrus, Uncle Greyson, and a couple of other guys filing into the kitchen. "You need to warn a girl when you're sneaking up on them," I said, turning off the music on my phone. "Why are you guys up so early anyway?"

"Couldn't sleep," Cyrus mumbled, sitting at the large kitchen table. "Sammy came home during the night drunk as hell." He scowled, scrubbing a hand down his face. "It was a shitshow."

"I heard him talking about some chick named Red," one of the newest members, Frankie, said. He rubbed his strong jaw. "Makes me want to meet her if she's gotten Sam's panties in a bunch."

Rounds of laughter erupted through the kitchen.

"It's not like you to be up before my wife." Uncle Greyson poured himself a cup of coffee, ignoring the guys. "Hungry?" he asked, nodding toward the plate of food I was preparing for Tanner.

"Oh. Uh…" My cheeks burned. "I was going to bring food—"

"Got it." Uncle Greyson took his mug and cupped my shoulder before leaning down to my ear. "Not everyone knows he's here. Especially not your father. Let's keep it that way for a little bit longer."

I nodded.

BEING US

He squeezed my shoulder and joined the rest of the crew at the table. A part of me wondered what that was about but I wouldn't press.

Grabbing the plate, I quickly left the kitchen and made my way toward the door leading to the basement. It was funny in a way. I had been through every inch of the house and used to feel so lonely. Especially when the guys went on their runs or was off doing their own thing. But now that Tanner was around, no matter who was home, it was like I could feel him and no longer felt alone.

"Where you off to, Bee?"

My steps halted. Turning around, I saw Sammy coming toward me. "I wasn't expecting you home. Cyrus said you got pretty drunk last night."

"Stop trying to change the subject." He closed the distance between us and picked up a container of yogurt off the plate. "Strawberry. Good choice," he said, placing it back before meeting my gaze. "You don't have to be nice to him just because it's in your nature."

"It's not in my nature."

Sammy chuckled. "Yes. It is. You're nice to everyone."

"Someone has to be nice around here when all of you are grumpy as hell," I threw back at him.

"Language, sweetheart."

My heart leapt to my throat at the new voice coming from behind me.

Sammy smirked, glancing over my head. "Tray, how are you?"

My dad came up to my side. His dark eyes that mirrored my own, glanced down at the plate I was carrying. "Hungry?" he asked, raising an eyebrow.

"Oh." I laughed lightly. "Yeah. I didn't eat a lot yesterday. I was going to read and have this as a snack." I gave him a quick hug and started walking away. "I'll see you later. My book isn't going to read itself," I laughed again, spun on my heel, and rushed off to my bedroom.

Please don't follow me. Please don't follow me.

I chanted the words over and over in my head but of course, my father didn't listen.

"Is something wrong, Bee?"

I swallowed hard but continued walking down the hall toward the room I stayed in while I was at Uncle Greyson's. "No. Not at all. Why would you think something's wrong?"

"Because you're my daughter and I happen to know you." Dad followed me to my room.

I bit back a sigh and entered my bedroom, placing the plate of food meant for Tanner, on my dresser. "Nothing's wrong," I said, turning toward my father.

"You sure?" he asked, leaning against the doorframe.

I nodded. "How was your week?"

"Good." He paused. "Something's wrong. I can feel it."

"No, it's not." I went up to him and wrapped my arms around his hard middle. "I promise, Daddy. Nothing's wrong."

"Alright, if you say so. But if I find out that someone hurt my baby girl in any way…"

I leaned back, looking up at him. "You'll give them a booboo?"

He rolled his eyes. "Something like that."

"You know the guys always have my back," I reassured him.

"Yeah, that's what I'm worried about." Dad cupped my shoulders, holding me at arm's length.

"What do you mean?"

"I mean…" He thought a moment. "I know I've kept you sheltered. I was only trying to protect you. I just don't want you getting hurt but I also know that you need to experience things for yourself so you can learn from them."

I stared at him. "Who are you and what have you done with my father?"

"Ha. Ha." He shook his head. "Just be careful." He kissed the top of my head. "That's all I ask."

"I will. You know that Sammy would be the first to run to you if something happened. You have to know that." And that was why I was trying to keep whatever this thing was with Tanner, on the down low.

"True. Maybe I'll have a talk with him." He winked.

"You do that." I stepped out of his embrace and went to my bookshelf standing against the far wall. I was thankful Uncle Greyson was a reader. Most of the books on my shelves used to belong to him. Even though he had always been careful with them, some of the books were read so much, some of the pages were falling out. Those were my favorite. I loved a good well-read book.

"Oh, before I forget. Your friends called."

I looked at Dad over my shoulder. "Friends?"

"Lori and Heather." He crossed his arms under his chest. "Apparently you went out last weekend and the twins took you out of the club before your friends wanted you to leave."

Sometimes Lori and Heather had big mouths.

"Cyrus and Sammy need..." I snapped my mouth shut. If I said too much, it would all go downhill from there. Things would end before I could get to know Tanner like I wanted.

"Just call your friends and tell them that you're not at home."

"I will." I let out a breath of relief. "Thank you."

There was a moment of silence between us before Dad pushed away from the doorframe. "I'm heading home to your mother. Just wanted to check in on you since I haven't seen you all week."

"Give her a hug for me," I said, trying to ignore how his words forced guilt to rest on my shoulders.

Dad nodded, shutting the door to my room and leaving me to my own thoughts.

Thoughts of Tanner.

Thoughts of how weird it was that he was living at Uncle Greyson's.

Grandpa's friend Ricky had shown up once this past week to make sure that Tanner's shoulder was healing nicely but that had been all I heard about him.

Now it was my turn to make sure he was okay.

My eyes flicked to the plate of food sitting on my dresser. Maybe bringing the food down to him today wouldn't be such a good idea. But when did I ever listen to the rules? Often. I listened to them often. I huffed, mentally scolding myself and attempted to put on a brave face. It wasn't like I would run into anyone. Aunt Eve would be cooking breakfast for everyone who lived in the big house and eventually for others as they rolled in. While her cooking was delicious, I needed to bring Tanner his food and to also see him. To find out if I was crazy or imagining these new feelings between us.

I especially wanted him to know that he had a friend here and that we weren't all his enemy.

(Tanner)

I could sense that I was no longer alone in the room. It had been going on for so long now that I knew before it happened, when it was about to start. I would wake up but pretended to still be asleep. The door would open slowly, the air in my bedroom would shift from comfortable to cool, almost like the devil himself was entering my room. And maybe he was.

BEING US

As hard as I tried to go back to sleep, I never could. Not once he entered the room. Not since I was no longer alone. And especially not when the bed would shift with his weight.

But I still squeezed my eyes shut. I squeezed them so damn tight that pain erupted behind them, giving me a slight headache.

Every time the blankets pulled away from me, I would jump, and he would chuckle. I couldn't help it. The blankets kept me safe. Or so I liked to think. Even though that was never truly the case, they still gave me a semblance of control. They just prevented him from doing what he wanted to do for half a second longer. Not even that.

When rough knees spread my legs apart, the rest of the night would end in a blur.

Pain.

Agony.

Feelings beyond that. Feelings I could never understand.

Why me?

What did I do?

When he finally left my room, all I could do was lay there and hope that death would come take me away. Because I knew that the same thing would happen the next night. And the night after that. And so on. It would continue until I either escaped or died.

I was hoping for the latter.

I woke in a cold sweat. My thoughts were scrambled. Where was I? I looked around the room, nothing recognizable. It was dark but nothing looking familiar.

Where was Trigger?

He usually slept on the end of my bed with me. Sometimes beside me. It depended on how we were both feeling and if the nightmares had consumed us or not.

I sat up, looking around the room when I finally realized that I was no longer in my apartment. Events from the past week came rushing back. Even though I had slept a few nights in this place already, I still wasn't used to it. I was in a stranger's home and it would probably feel like that until I could find a place of my own once again.

Lifting my hands, I watched them tremble. They had never been steady. Not since before the nightmares of my childhood had happened but I just never let anyone see them shake. I had learned over the years how to control the anxiety rushing through me and eventually, how to fight back. I had never been as big as the others in my crew. But having a quick mind and being a tad twisted, had people doing things for me without me having to throw my weight around.

My blood pumped through me but a part of me wished it wouldn't.

I couldn't sit there and feel sorry for myself. I knew that. I didn't have time for it. Already a week had passed, and I was no closer to getting the answers I was looking for. I was waiting for Greyson to come break the door down and demand something that I couldn't give him or else he would throw me out. It made me wonder why he hadn't done that already. He could have killed me. There had been many chances for him to do so or to have one of his prospects do the dirty work. Every time I laid in bed at night, I feared it would be my end. The last of me before I could find out why my club was taken over, why Sunny was killed, and why my dog was a part of it.

But it wasn't like anyone had come visit me. Someone left food outside the door. Maybe they were slowly poisoning me. I felt fine besides my shoulder still throbbing on occasion. They would knock and rush away before I could thank them for the meal. I ended up waiting a few minutes before I opened the door and grabbed the tray of whatever it was they decided to feed me. I didn't want to put them on the spot.

I was in the house of the enemy. I should have been scared for my life when really, I didn't care. I wasn't sure if that was a good thing or not. The only one I could even remotely trust was Busy and even then, I didn't know her. I also hadn't seen her since the night she saved me. Couldn't say I blamed her any. I knew there was a physical attraction between us but that was all it was. Or that was what I liked to tell myself anyway.

Reaching over, I flicked on the lamp that sat on the nightstand and grabbed the burner phone Greyson had so kindly given me.

"You call your club and I will kill you before you take your next breath."

I rose an eyebrow. "My club? What fucking club? They betrayed me and kicked me out. I have no club." I have no one.

Greyson had placed the phone in my palm the first night I showed up and continued going on about things I couldn't remember. That was one thing that had always been my problem. I could never focus and I lost my train of thought. If people were talking to me, I couldn't tell you what they were saying. Usually it was because I just didn't care but something told me that maybe I should have listened to what Greyson had been saying.

I sighed, flipped open the phone, and dialed a number. I waited for it to ring once before hanging up. Ten seconds went by before I called again, waited two rings, and then hung up again. Calling a third time, I waited for an answer.

"Where the fuck are you calling from?" Rowan demanded.

"Nice greeting," I mumbled.

"Seriously, Tanner."

"Yeah, I'm serious too. You should be more polite. Maybe you hurt my feelings."

He grunted. "Right. You have no feelings to hurt."

"True." I shifted my weight, bringing my knee up onto the bed and letting the other one hang over the edge. "Listen, I…" Why was I even calling him? Were we friends and he actually cared about my well-being? Did I care what he thought of me?

"What's going on, T?"

I gripped the phone tight in my hand at the shortened use of my name. He had been the only one to ever call me that. "I don't know."

"I haven't heard from you in a week. You're good? You're safe?"

"Yeah. I am."

"Where are you?"

"I'm at…" I wasn't sure if Greyson wanted people knowing I was there. A sour taste filled my mouth over the fact that I all of a sudden cared. "Have you heard anything from or about Tommy?"

"Nope. And I did some digging and saw the footage from the security cameras in that alley both you and Trigger were attacked in. Looks like the fuckers weren't even prospects. They're with a puppet club. A club who's trying to become part of Devil's Rejects."

"Fuck." It had been one thing I was never interested in. Sure, I let puppet clubs do our dirty work every now and again, but I never actually let them join. None of them were good enough. I had enough shit to deal with within my actual club. I didn't need them adding to that mess. Clearly, I had been right when it came to the shady members in my club.

"Why didn't you get rid of the members you didn't trust, Tanner?"

"I don't trust anyone, Rowan," I reminded him. "You know that."

"Do you trust me?" he asked, his voice taking on a softer tone than I was used to coming from him.

"I don't know."

"Fair enough. I appreciate your honesty." He cleared his throat. "Listen, I have family stuff over the next few days." Which meant that I wasn't supposed to call him.

"I get the hint, Rowan."

"Tanner, I'm not saying that you can't call but—"

"I get it." I hung up before the conversation could become even heavier. I wasn't expecting it to sting when he said not to call. I guess we were closer than I thought.

Turning off the phone, I placed it on the nightstand when a knock sounded at the door.

"Tanner? It's Bee."

My dick jumped at her soft voice coming from the other side of the door. "Come in," I bit out.

The door opened, revealing the only thing in this place that was keeping me from jumping off the edge and saying fuck it to everything.

"Hey." Busy smiled, holding a plate out in front of her. "Are you hungry? I thought you might be. I don't know when you ate last. I know one of the prospects keeps bringing you food, but I thought I would do it this time. I wasn't sure how you've been feeling after the surgery and all. I know it's been a week. Oh God, maybe you're allergic to this stuff. I'm sorry. I should have asked you."

I chuckled, when she finally took a breath. "I'm not allergic to anything."

Her smile grew. "Okay. Good. And I'm sorry for rambling again." Her cheeks reddened.

"What did I tell you?" I demanded, my voice coming out rougher than I would have liked.

She jumped.

Shit.

"Sorry." I cleared my throat. "I just hate that you're apologizing for something that's a part of you." I slid off the bed and went toward her. When I was close enough to touch her, I inhaled, smelling the scent of whatever it was that she put on her skin. "What is that?"

"What's what?" she whispered.

"That smell." I took another deep breath, a low rumble leaving from somewhere inside me.

Her cheeks reddened even more. "It's vanilla and chai. My lotion."

I leaned toward her, lightly brushing my nose down the length of her jaw to the shell of her ear. "You smell..." I paused. "So fucking good."

She shivered. The only thing standing between us was the plate. But a little teasing couldn't hurt.

The scent of her was sweet but not overpowering. The mixture of vanilla and chai, along with her natural scent, unleashed a wave of calm over me. The remnants from my nightmare was no longer there and the anxiety that came along with it, simmered to a dull roar. I lifted my hand, thankful that the shaking was no longer noticeable and took the plate from her. "Thank you." I went back to the bed and sat, placing the plate in front of me.

"You're welcome."

When she went to leave, a thought came to me. "Wait."

She stopped, slowly looking at me over her shoulder.

"Join me?" I hesitated. "Please," I added finally.

She looked from the bed to me, back to the bed again.

"I'll be a gentleman."

Busy took a breath, came deeper into the room, and sat in the chair in the corner.

A breath of relief left me. I didn't want to be alone, but I also had no idea how to actually say that. I was just thankful that she listened to me.

I wanted her closer, but I wouldn't press, so this would have to do. For now.

"I wasn't sure what you liked." She nodded toward the plate in front of me.

BEING US

"This is perfect. I can't repay you enough for this." I looked over the spread laid out on the plate. There was a bottle of water, a small container of strawberry yogurt, a sandwich with lettuce and some sort of deli meat on it, a few baby carrots and a cupcake. I lifted the cupcake first.

"That's left over from someone's birthday. It's about a month old but was in the freezer, so it should still taste fresh."

"Whose birthday?" I asked, inspecting the cupcake. I wasn't much of a sweets guy, but I would eat it. I would eat everything on the plate. Knowing the trouble she went through to prepare this for me, I would still eat everything even if I was allergic to it.

"Mine," Busy said softly.

My eyes shot to hers. "Happy belated birthday."

She chewed her bottom lip. "Thank you."

"How old are you?" I blurted. "I mean…I'm sorry. That's rude of me."

She laughed. "It's okay. My birthday was actually last month. I turned twenty-three."

My dick twitched.

Fucking hell.

No wonder she blushed whenever I was near. She was young.

"H-How old are you?" she stammered.

"Thirty-four." I suddenly felt like a dirty old man. I was eleven years older than her. She probably had guys lined up at her door, ready to sweep her off her feet.

"Really? Not to be rude but you don't look thirty-four."

I smirked. "I've always looked young for my age. Good genes I guess."

She tilted her head. "Why are you looking at me like that?"

"How am I looking at you?" *Like I want to eat you for dinner.*

"I'm not sure," she whispered. "But you're looking at me like you're thinking or wanting something."

"I'm actually thinking how I'm a dirty fucker."

Her breath caught. "Why?"

"Because I'm older than you."

She rolled her eyes then. "Yeah, because you're so old. You're only eleven years older than me and it's not a big deal. My dad's fourteen years older than my mom."

He was going to kick my ass if he ever found out all the nasty things I wanted to do to his daughter.

"But why are you a dirty..."

When her question trailed off, I raised an eyebrow. "Say it."

"Fucker," she said softly.

Before I knew what I was doing, I stood right in front of her. Cupping the arms of the chair, I leaned down toward her.

Her breath hitched. She stared up at me, probably wondering what this *dirty fucker* was going to do or say.

I knew at that point that anyone could come down into the basement and if they checked in on me, they would see their precious little Bee in a compromising position. Even though I wasn't doing anything, and neither was she, we both knew that we wanted to.

I had never believed in this instant connection shit but with her? I believed. I believed fucking hard.

"Tanner." The sound of her trembling voice slid down the length of my cock.

"Do you want me to answer your question, Busy?" I asked, my voice low.

"You...this..." She chewed her bottom lip.

"Nothing to say now? You talk a lot. Which I love by the way. But it seems your words are failing you."

Her brows narrowed. Crossing her arms under her chest, she lifted her chin defiantly. "I have no idea what you're talking about."

A laugh escaped me. "Is that so?"

"Yup."

I towered over her. "Are you sure?"

Her eyes widened but she caught herself and glared at me instead. "What are you doing?"

"I'm going to answer your question." When I was a mere inch from her mouth, I brushed my lips down the length of her jaw toward her ear. "I keep having these thoughts, Busy. Nasty, filthy stuff." I licked her ear lobe, giving it a gentle bite.

She jumped.

"I shouldn't be thinking these things. Not about you. Your daddy would kill me if he knew what I wanted to do to his little girl."

"What do you want to do?" she asked softly.

"I want to fuck you so damn hard; the walls shake." In a quick move, I cupped her throat, pushing her head against the back of the chair. "I want to feel you tremble around me." I brushed my mouth gently against hers. "I want to know what your soaking wet body feels like as I fuck orgasm after orgasm out of you. And then when I'm done, you'll beg for me to start all over again."

Her eyes darkened, her pupils dilating at my words.

But before I lost control and did what I actually wanted to do, I pushed away from her and went back to the bed.

Once I sat on the edge, I took a chance and glanced at Busy. Her cheeks were red, her eyes glassy.

"Tanner." She gripped the arms of the chair.

"Yes?" I took a carrot and popped it into my mouth.

"You...that..." She huffed. "Really?"

I chuckled, finishing off the rest of the baby carrots.

"Tanner," she snapped.

"You asked. I answered." I shrugged like it was no big deal. But in all reality, it was a very big deal. Her family didn't like me and yet, there I was thinking about all the ways I could stick my dick in her. Which wasn't something I was used to thinking. The opposite sex had never appealed to me. Not even the same sex. It used to be frustrating until I found out that it was a normal thing for asexuals. But I wasn't even sure if I could call myself that. I had done research and found out that it could change if you found the right person. And clearly, I had. But it didn't make sense when Busy and I didn't know each other.

"You're frustrating, you know that right?"

"I've been called worse." I moved the plate to the nightstand and went to grab the sandwich when I was suddenly feeling lightheaded, so I went for the cupcake instead. It was chocolate with red icing on top. Maybe sugar would help.

"Tanner? Are you okay?"

Spots danced in my vision. "I think I need sugar." Squeezing my eyes shut, I pinched the bridge of my nose and shook my head.

"Hey." A gentle hand landed on my shoulder. "Do you need more pain meds?"

"No." Truth was, I never took any pain meds to begin with. Not since the surgery. Nero had given me some to take home with me, but I threw them out as soon as I was able. I didn't like the sense of losing control. I had already experienced that as a kid. I would rather suffer through the agony, than to have something else control me.

"Tanner." The bed shifted beside me with added weight.

I took a deep breath and then another. My racing heart finally slowed to a steady beat.

"Hey."

I opened my eyes then, finding Busy smiling at me. "You good?"

BEING US

Before I could stop myself, I pulled her into my arms.

She gasped, her body stiffening, but I didn't let her go. I only held her. I didn't want to ever let her go but I knew that I would have to. Because eventually, someone would come looking for her. And even though the door was closed, it wasn't locked. I was taking a risk by having her in the room, but I needed it. I needed her. I wasn't sure why. I couldn't explain it but touching her, holding her in my arms, calmed the anxiety burning through me.

Tightening my hold around her, I pushed my face into the crook of her neck and inhaled.

"Tanner," she whispered, returning the embrace.

When her hands slid down my back, a shiver followed.

"I just need to hold you," I told her, my mouth finding the soft spot beneath her ear.

"Okay, baby," she murmured.

My heart jumped. I pulled back, moving my hands to her hair. "Say that again."

"Sorry, I…it just came out." Her cheeks reddened.

"Say it," I repeated slowly. "Again."

Busy licked her lips. "Baby."

A low growl escaped me, my hold tightening on her hair.

Something snapped between us.

Just as I was about to push her away, she shoved me back and jumped into my arms. "Busy, what are you—"

"Shut up." She crushed her lips against mine, taking all of my words and breath and making it hers.

I sighed, finally realizing that this was where I belonged. My hands trailed down her back, reaching her ass and pulling her flush against me.

When her center connected with my dick, it lengthened even more beneath her. A soft gasp escaped her.

Reaching up, I cupped her head and broke the kiss. "That's all for you, Busy."

Her eyes darkened, filling with so much lust, it took my breath away. "Tanner, this is new for me."

"It's new for me too. We can take it slow. I just want you in my arms."

She gave me a small smile. "I hope I didn't hurt you."

"Never, baby." I kissed her softly on the mouth. "Never."

She took a deep breath, letting it out slowly before deepening the kiss.

Splitting her lips apart with my tongue, I swallowed her moan.

Before I could take it further with this woman I hardly knew but craved just the same, footsteps sounded down the stairs.

She jumped, her eyes landing on the closed door behind me. She slid off my lap, the air suddenly turning cold around us, and went to the closet door. Slipping inside, she brought her finger up to her mouth.

I nodded.

Busy closed the closet door, hiding herself from whoever was coming down into the basement. I usually didn't care what anyone thought but this was exciting. A part of me enjoyed hiding her while the other part wanted to have her on my arm and show her off. I would eventually. But for now, she would be my dirty little secret.

THIRTEEN

Bee

AS I SLIPPED INTO the closet, I felt like I was a kid hiding the fact that I stole a cookie right before supper. But the hint of mischief flashing in Tanner's deep blue eyes as I hid myself away, made me almost thankful for the interruption. Especially when something was switching between us and fast.

I had never meant to throw myself at him and kiss him. But when I called him 'baby,' the attraction grew. It just slipped out. I was never expecting it to fall from my lips but when it did, it felt almost normal. Like Tanner and I had been dating for a long time. Being with him, spending time with him, felt like it was all meant to be.

"Have you seen Bee?" I heard someone ask, pulling me from my thoughts.

"No," Tanner replied. A part of me wasn't expecting him to actually lie about my whereabouts but I was happy that he had. Even though these people were my family, I knew I would still get issues.

"You sure? She's not in her room. She was grabbing food for you earlier, which I can see that you already have."

I wasn't overly sure who Tanner was talking to. It sounded like Cyrus, but it could have been Sammy as well. As they got older, they no longer looked like twins. Their voices still sounded similar, though Sammy's held an edge of contempt. He just hated everything and everyone around him. I wasn't sure why. No one ever gave me the reasoning behind it. Even his brother wouldn't tell me.

"I don't know where she is. She dropped off the food and then left shortly after."

"Why don't I believe you?"

"I don't give a shit if you believe me or not. You've been on my ass since I showed up at Busy's place a week ago."

My stomach twisted, realizing he was talking to Sammy. It made me wonder if they had a run-in a few other times throughout the week.

"What do you want with Bee?"

"Why do you all keep asking me that? I don't even know her."

But I knew exactly what he wanted because he had told me so. While I appreciated Tanner's honesty, I wasn't expecting him to actually tell me every single dirty detail.

I touched my lips, remembering the fast but intense kiss we had shared. Every inch of me heated, imagining what it would be like to truly be with him. To be with a man who just didn't care about anything else but being with the woman he was attracted to.

"Right," Sammy said, drawing out the word. "I'm not stupid. I've seen the way you look at her and you haven't even known her for more than a week yet."

BEING US

"I haven't seen her all week. I'm sure you all kept her busy to the point she couldn't come see me." Tanner paused. "It's too bad though. I'm sure I could keep her way more entertained than you and your brother. Or is that the problem? Are you jealous? You want her for yourself? Word on the street is that you're a sick fuck, Sammy. I can't say I ever pegged you for the type who got off on degrading women."

My eyes widened.

"You don't know shit about me."

"Yeah, and you don't know shit about *me*."

"You're playing a dangerous game. You're not safe here, Tanner."

"Are you threatening me?" Tanner asked, sounding almost bored.

"No. If I was threatening you, you would know it. I do suggest not letting Shade or Meadow know that you're here though. They wouldn't like the fact that the person who killed the man they loved, was living here."

My stomach fell.

"I didn't kill him," Tanner bit out. "Listen, it doesn't matter if you believe me or not. I don't give a shit anymore. I didn't kill Sunny. I don't know who did, but I will find out. With or without your little club's help."

"Whatever, man. Don't say I didn't warn you." The sound of the door closing a moment later, jarred through me.

The closet door opened, revealing Tanner.

"Hey." He smiled down at me, but that smile never reached his eyes. Much to my surprise, he joined me in the closet and shut the door behind him.

My heart jumped to my throat at being locked in such a small space with him. "Is what Sammy said true?"

Tanner's brows narrowed. "No. Yes, I was there. I saw it all. And I gave your friends a hard time beforehand. So unfortunately for me, it doesn't look good. I understand why they think I pulled the trigger, but I didn't. I promise you that I did not kill Sunny."

"Are there any security cameras?" I asked, switching on the closet light. I needed to see him. "Maybe Uncle Greyson hasn't looked at them yet and—"

"I've already seen them, Busy." Tanner rubbed the back of his neck, his dark eyes locking with mine. "It looks bad. The footage doesn't show much. I should have stayed and worked it out but even I know that wasn't possible."

"How come?" I asked, taking a step toward him.

"Because your uncle would have killed me first before getting the answers everyone is looking for." He chuckled. "Actually, your cousin would have killed me. Greyson? He probably would have slapped me around a bit first. Jaron on the other hand…"

"Would kill you." My cousin had a temper on him. "I remember when I was a kid and I was being bullied by a girl in school. Jaron kicked her brother's ass who was older and bigger than him, since he couldn't hit her."

"Did she stop bullying you?" Tanner asked, leaning against the wall on the other side of the closet.

"Yeah. Her brother ended up slapping her around instead." I grimaced. "It was awful to see."

"I can understand that." Tanner took a step toward me. He reached out, brushing his thumb along my hip. "I didn't kill him, Busy. I need you to believe me."

I searched his face for any sign that he was lying. I knew the basics. Looking away when they said the lie. Blushing. Heartbeat picking up. My dad had taught me how to read people but when it came to Tanner, I couldn't overly tell. There was something inside me, a teeny tiny little voice that said he wasn't lying.

"I believe you," I said softly.

Tanner sighed, his shoulders slumping like the only thing that mattered was my belief in him. "Did you ever play Seven Minutes In Heaven?"

A breathless laugh escaped me. "Oh yeah. Because my dad was totally cool with me going to parties where boys would be."

Tanner looked around him before meeting my gaze. "This closet is big." He took a step toward me, forcing me back.

"That's why I came in here." I backed up until I hit the wall.

He closed the distance between us. "Sammy's worried I'll do something." He lifted his hand, brushing his thumb along the length of my jaw. The touch was so gentle, it sent a flutter of nerves racing through me.

"Should he be worried?" I asked, tilting my head.

"Not sure." Tanner pinched my chin, staring down at me.

"Kiss me," I heard myself say.

His jaw clenched. "I shouldn't."

"I know you want to." I placed my hands on his chest, feeling the beating of his heart beneath my palm.

"Of course, I want to, Busy. You have no idea how much I want to." He tilted my head back, lowering his mouth closer to mine but still never kissed me.

"Please." My body trembled; this need for him unexpected. "Tanner, I want…"

"What?" he demanded, the word coming out as a growl. "Tell me what you want."

"I want to feel you."

"Fuck." He squeezed his eyes shut and took a deep breath. When he opened them, he closed that final space between us, pressing his body up against mine.

I could feel every hard line of him. Every muscle. Every inch.

"You feel that?" He turned my head, licking up the length of my throat. "You feel how hard you make me?"

"Yes," I whimpered.

"You have no idea how perfect you are. What do you want with a broken bastard like me?"

I pulled my head from his grip and grabbed onto his hoodie. "I want you because you don't judge me. You look at me like…"

"What?" His chest rose and fell with ragged breaths. "How do I look at you?"

"Like I belong."

Tanner crushed his mouth to mine, pushing me back. He fisted my hair, holding my head in place as he devoured my mouth.

With his other arm, he snaked it around my middle and held me against him.

The kiss became frantic.

"Tanner," I moaned against his mouth, wrapping a leg around his waist.

He shoved his hips between my legs, pushing himself into me. A groan escaped him, his tongue dancing along with mine.

"Please," I whined, unable to catch my breath but at the same time, I didn't care. I broke the kiss. "I need something. Please give it to me."

His mouth found the side of my neck, his hot breath scorching my skin. "We shouldn't do this in here."

"I don't care where we are. I just need something."

"You want me," he murmured against my throat, his hands running down the sides of my body.

"Yes."

Tanner lifted his head, staring down at me. He ran his thumb along my swollen mouth. "I want to fuck you but not like this and definitely not in a closet."

"We don't have to have sex." As much as I wanted it, I just wanted to feel him. Even if it was something small or just a taste.

When Tanner hesitated, I took a chance and cupped him over his pants.

He shivered, leaning his forehead against mine. "As much as this feels good, we shouldn't." Much to my surprise, he grabbed my hand that was currently touching him and brought it up to his mouth. Placing soft pecks on my fingers, he let out a small sigh.

"Tanner." Did I not do it right? Was that why he didn't want me touching him?

"Thank you for the food, Busy. I appreciate it. I appreciate it more than I could ever tell you." He released me completely and opened the closet door. Turning back to me, he held out his hand.

I looked between his hand and him, hesitating. My heart started racing, my palms became clammy.

"I won't hurt you." Tanner stepped toward me. "What happened just a moment ago, ended because you deserve better than to be fucked in a closet." He pinched my chin, tilting my head back. "You hear me?"

I nodded, chewing my bottom lip.

"No matter what the twins say. Or what anyone says for that matter, I won't hurt you."

"I know."

He smirked, kissing me gently on the nose before stepping back so I could exit the closet. He held out his hand again, waiting.

I placed my hand in his.

Tanner brought it up to his mouth, running his lips along the back of it. "Thank you." He placed a gentle kiss on the back of my hand before leading me out of the closet.

Tanner had an air about him. He was like a tornado sucking me into his grasp. I had no control when it came to him. When he told me that he didn't kill Sunny, I believed him. Even though I hadn't known him for long, I could just see the truth in him.

It may have been naïve of me, but I believed that your soul could recognize the truth in another person, and everyone needed someone to believe in them. I didn't think this man had ever had that. I would be that someone for Tanner and if that made me naïve, then so be it. At least I gave him that much.

There was something about him that I could see. Something deep inside him. He had walls up and didn't let anyone in. But piece by piece, I knew I could break them down.

He just needed to let me.

FOURTEEN

Bee

TANNER HAD BEEN LIVING at the club for almost a month and he was no closer to getting the answers he was looking for.

On one hand, I was sure it was frustrating for him and everyone else involved. But on the other, at least he was safe. Even if he was stuck in the basement.

My dad had been by often, but I was still able to sneak away and spend time with Tanner. I went home every few days, so Dad wouldn't grow suspicious and worked at my mom's shop whenever she needed the extra hands. It had been odd seeing Shade, knowing Tanner was living at Uncle Greyson's.

Whenever I was back at the clubhouse, I would check in on Tanner. I learned quickly that he loved animals. Besides dogs, he loved them all. But we hadn't almost had sex again. We cuddled and stole a few quick pecks here and there, but it hadn't been like the last time. My thoughts traveled back to a week ago when I called him out on it and the aftermath of my outburst.

"Tanner." I opened and slammed his door shut, not caring at all if the people in this damn house heard me. "What the hell is going on? We kiss and then all of a sudden nothing. Did I do something?"

He rose from the bed, placing the plate of food I had brought down for him earlier, on the nightstand. "Come here."

"No." I stood there with my hands on my hips. "You come here. I need to know what I did."

"You didn't do anything." He pointed to the bed. "Come. Here."

"No," I said, lifting my chin defiantly.

Before I knew what was happening, he was around the bed and directly in front of me in a matter of seconds. I jumped, spinning around to open the door when a heavy hand slapped against it.

My heart jumped to my throat, my body coming alive at the mere intensity rolling off of him.

"To answer your question, Busy, I'm trying to be a gentleman. I've never done this before. I don't want to just fuck and that be it." He cupped my shoulders, turning me around to face him. "Look at me."

I met his stare, placing my hands on his chest.

"I want you. I've wanted you since I showed up in your backyard." He brushed his thumb along my bottom lip. "But I also want to get to know you first."

"That hasn't stopped you from kissing me. A few times I might add," I threw back at him.

A slow smile crept on his lips. "That's because I have no self-control when it comes to you." He leaned down, placing a soft, gentle kiss on my mouth.

I wrapped my arms around his neck, deepening the kiss.

He growled, giving my bottom lip a gentle nip. "Stop fucking teasing me."

I giggled, kissing him one last time before pulling away. "Until tomorrow, Tanner."

BEING US

I could still feel his rough mouth against mine. Touching my lips, I smiled at the memory rushing through me.

One night after supper, I gathered a plate of food and brought it down to Tanner. I had brought him food a couple of times, but it had mostly been one of the prospects doing it. But this night was different. Something was in the air. Everyone had been off. Sammy was grumpier than usual. Uncle Greyson's scowl was deeper. And people snapped at each other for no apparent reason. Until Aunt Eve made the instruction that no one was going anywhere, and they were going to spend the evening doing nothing. That was when people started drinking. It eventually turned into laughter, making some of the thickness in the air disappear.

While everyone was unwinding, I headed down into the basement. When I stood outside Tanner's room, I lifted my hand to knock when the door swung open.

I jumped back.

Tanner stared down at me. "What?"

"I have food for you."

In a quick move, Tanner grabbed my arm and pulled me into the room before shoving me up against the door. It slammed shut behind me.

He took the plate from my hands and dropped it onto the dresser.

"Tan—"

"I suggest shutting the fuck up." That familiar tick in his jaw was jumping more than usual.

My eyes widened. "What the hell's your problem?"

"This…you…you are my fucking problem."

"What are you talking about?" I tried shoving out of his grip, but his hold only tightened. "Tanner, what's wrong?"

He released me suddenly, taking a step away from me and started pacing. "I can't do this."

"Do what?" I stepped in front of him. "Talk to me. Tell me what's going on. Did I do something? Did someone else do something? Did you find out answers?"

"No, I haven't found out any answers. And you haven't done anything. That's the fucking problem." His brows narrowed. "You bring me food, which I appreciate, but that's it. I haven't seen you in what feels like years."

My heart jumped to my throat at the desperation rolling off of him. "Tanner, I saw you last night when I brought you your food."

"I…" His shoulders slumped. "I'm losing my damn mind."

"No, you aren't." I closed the distance between us, placing my hands on his chest. His heart was racing beneath my palm. "You're stressed. And you've been stuck down here, so I'm sure time feels a little slower. I also wanted to give you space but…"

"What?"

"I was being selfish and wanted to spend time with you."

His lips twitched. "I want to spend time with you too."

My heart jumped. "I know you need time to mourn, so if you want me to go…"

"No. Never." He cupped my nape, pulled me against him, and wrapped his other arm around my waist. "I can mourn later."

I wasn't sure what was going on with him. I had never had this with a guy before. Was this normal? I needed to call Lori and Heather. Maybe they would know more and give me some advice.

He released me suddenly, putting some distance between us. "I shouldn't do this but not seeing you, threw me off. I know it doesn't make sense. Fuck, I'm losing control." He gripped his hair, pulling at the strands. I noticed then that bags sat beneath his deep blue eyes. Did he have trouble sleeping?

"What do you want with me Tanner?"

He dropped his arm to his side. "I want to be with you in every sense of the word."

"I want that too." I went up to him and wrapped my arms around his middle. "Did you want to watch a movie?"

"I want to do other things, but a movie sounds perfect," he said, kissing the top of my head.

I laughed, grabbing his hand and linking our fingers. "We can watch whatever you want."

He stared down at me, his eyes searching my face. "Yes. I think I'd like that."

(Tanner)

I never thought that not seeing Busy would affect me the way it had. Even though we had gotten to know each other a little more over the past few weeks, not seeing her after getting used to having her around, messed me up. Even though apparently, I had seen her the night before, time was lost on me, and I wanted her by my side at all times.

As the days went by where I didn't have any answers, my anxiety rose.

"I've seen this movie a lot thanks to my Uncle Catch but it's a good one." Busy joined me on the couch and pressed a button on the controller.

When the movie started playing, I was sucked into the storyline almost instantly. It was a romance of sorts but funny and dramatic at parts as well.

"Have you seen this one before?" Busy asked well into the movie.

"No. I haven't seen a lot of movies," I confessed.

"No? How come?"

I looked at her then. I wasn't sure what I was expecting to see but when she looked genuinely curious as to why I didn't watch a lot of movies, I let out a sigh of relief. "I wasn't allowed to watch movies as a kid. Now that I'm older, I just haven't had time."

"Oh." She looked back out in front of her. She inched closer to me and covered my hand that was resting on my thigh. "We can watch as many movies as you want. We can catch you up on all of the classics." She squeezed my hand and gave me a small smile.

When she went to pull away, I caught her hand and brought it down between us, linking our fingers.

Her cheeks reddened.

I made it my sole mission to keep that blush on her skin and that smile on her lips.

While we continued watching the movie, a comfortable silence fell between us. I never had this before. I never had someone who actually wanted to spend time with me. Even my club had left me alone most days. The only time I actually spent any amount of time with them was when we had meetings or went on runs together. Other than that, I was alone. Always so fucking alone.

While Busy laughed at certain parts in the movie, I couldn't help but wonder what would come of this. Sure, we had become close, but it was only because I was living under the same roof as her. Wasn't it? Once this was over, would she toss me aside like everyone else in my life? Animals were the only ones who never betrayed me. They never used me to their advantage or took things from me I never wanted to give them in the first place. It was why Trigger and I had gotten along so well. Both of us had our control taken away at some point in our lives and neither of us trusted the other. Not for a while. And then he was taken. He was ripped from my life before I had a chance to show him how much he meant to me. Most would say that he was just a dog but to me, he was more than that. He was my best friend.

My throat closed up, my chest constricting. I realized then that I had never actually mourned Trigger's death. I told Busy I would mourn later. Now was definitely not the time. Not when I was in a place where my vulnerability could cost me my life. But I couldn't help the grief slamming into me.

I took a deep breath and then another, itching to reach out to Busy and use her to make me feel better.

"What did you think?"

Busy's question caught me off guard. I looked between her and the TV. The credits were now rolling.

"You weren't paying—" She frowned. "Is everything okay?"

I swallowed hard. "No."

She turned toward me. "Did you want to watch another movie or talk or something else?"

Something else. Fuck me, did I ever want to do something else. I had kept her at arm's length, trying to be a gentleman, when I really, I wanted to pull her into my clutches and bask in her innocence.

Taking a chance, I reached out to cup her cheek. "I could go to hell for the things I want to do to you."

The red in her cheeks darkened. "Oh. Well…I think I'd be right there alongside you."

I chuckled, my dick lengthening at her words.

"I'm good with talking, Busy. I just don't want to be alone." I wasn't sure how I felt about being completely honest. It was new for me and something that I wasn't sure I could ever get used to. No matter how much I tried.

"Tell me something happy," Busy said softly, pushing her cheek into my palm.

"I like this girl," I blurted, my eyes dropping to her full mouth.

A slow smile spread on her face, giving me the courage to keep going.

I cleared my throat and continued. "Even though I like her, it's dangerous. She knows some scary fuckers. And that's saying something because I…well I haven't dealt with the nicest people in my life." My uncle being the worst of them all. "But I feel like we were put in each other's lives for a reason."

"Maybe it's to drive the men in my life, crazy." She winked.

"Or maybe it's to help me be a better person." I leaned forward, our lips mere inches apart. Anyone could come down into the basement and catch us, but at that point, I didn't care. Catch had said there were cameras but not once, did anyone come down into the basement and pull us apart. I had a feeling that Busy was right and that he was just messing with me.

I wanted her. In any way that I could have her. Even if it was just a kiss. Eventually, it would turn into more but for now, I would take what I could get.

"Tanner." Busy cupped my cheek, running her fingers over the scruff on my jaw. "I like you too," she whispered, closing the last little bit of space between us.

As soon as her mouth pressed firmly against mine, a growl left me. Cupping the back of her head, I deepened the kiss.

She pushed me back, shuffling toward me and straddling my lap.

I should have told her to stop. I should have pushed her away knowing that we could get interrupted at any moment. But I didn't. I couldn't. Because this was right. She was right. *We* were right.

Busy trailed her mouth down my jaw to my ear, her hot breath sending a shiver down my spine. "I need you. Inside me."

My cock twitched beneath her ass.

When her hands pulled at my hoodie, I grabbed her wrists, stopping her.

"Wait."

She stared down at me, a deep frown between her brows.

"Before you say that I don't want you, I do. You have to feel how much I want you.

"Then why are you stopping?" Her gaze turned hard. "Is there something wrong with me?"

I rolled my eyes. "If I knew that no one was going to come down here and interrupt us, I would take you to my bedroom and…"

"And what?" she asked, breathless.

I took her hand and placed it on my crotch. "You feel how hard I am? All of this is for you. I want to make love to you. Fuck you. Make love to you some more. I'm not stopping because I want to. I'm stopping because…"

"Because the guys in this house could catch us and kill you," she answered for me, her voice monotone.

I chuckled. "Something like that, baby."

Busy huffed, moving from my lap and slumping on the couch beside me. "Fine."

Wrapping an arm around her shoulders, I kissed her temple. "Don't be mad at me."

"I don't know how you have so much self-control," she mumbled.

My laugh deepened. "Lots of practice." Pinching her chin, I turned her head to meet my mouth. "Don't be mad."

"I'm not mad," she said against my lips. "Just frustrated."

"I know." I was too and my cock fucking hurt but I didn't want someone to walk in while I was balls deep inside her juicy body.

A moment went by where we just stared at each other. I wanted to pull her back into my arms but at the same time, I couldn't.

"We can see if something's on TV instead." She started flipping through the channels until she stopped on a show I had never seen before. "This is *The Office*. It's my favorite show," she told me, her eyes lighting up.

"Then I want to watch it."

She kissed my cheek, her smile growing.

All thoughts of us almost having sex for the second time disappeared as she went on to explain that it was an old show, who the characters were and what season we were currently watching. She even gave me a rundown of the storyline. I couldn't remember everything she told me, but I enjoyed listening to her talk. And if watching her favorite show made her happy and allowed me to spend more time with her and get to know her better, I would do it. For her.

Busy ended up grabbing her DVDs of *The Office* and we went back to the beginning and watched it from the start. We got through the first season when she yawned.

Much to my surprise, she pulled the blanket off the back of the couch and laid down, placing her head on my lap. "Is this okay?"

"I think we've moved past asking for permission to touch each other," I reminded her, inching my hand beneath her top.

She laughed, rolling over onto her back and staring up at me. "I know. I just want make sure this is okay."

"I have a beautiful woman with her head on my lap, my cock is fucking hard, and my hand is cupping your tit."

"Your hand isn't—"

I lifted her bra, covering her with my hand. "You were saying?"

She laughed, holding my hand against her. "There's more you can touch."

My dick throbbed. "Fucking hell, Busy. You can't say that shit to me."

She rolled onto her side, her front facing the back of the couch. She took my hand, pushing it down the length of her torso and into the waist of her leggings. "Please touch me."

I pulled the blanket over her, covering her to the point that if someone *did* come down into the basement, they wouldn't see anything.

Slowly inching my fingers beneath her panties, I bit back a growl when they came into contact with her soft but soaked center. "Fuck, baby."

"Please," she whispered.

"Shhh…I'll take care of you." Slipping my fingers deeper between her legs, I slid my index finger into her body.

Busy chewed her bottom lip, her eyes snapping shut.

"Just feel me, beautiful. That's all I want," I told her gently.

She nodded, grabbed my hand that was between her legs, and started rocking against me.

My cock lengthened even more, threatening to explode in my pants.

Pumping my hand slowly against her, I rubbed my palm against her swollen clit. Her body trembled, her legs spreading to give me better access. What I really wanted was to dive my face between her thighs and swallow her orgasm, but I couldn't. Not yet.

"Tanner," she moaned.

Pulling my finger from her body, I started rubbing the tip against her clit.

She gasped, her back bowing.

I bit back a chuckle, watching her come undone beside me. "That's it. Give me that orgasm."

Busy rolled onto her back, spreading her legs.

I took the hint and began rubbing harder and faster.

"Yes." She covered her face, her chest rising and falling. Her thighs shook. "Please. More. God, Tanner. I…"

I stared down at her as she shoved the blanket in her mouth and cried out.

A slow grin spread on my face, but I didn't stop touching her.

"I can't…" Her eyes widened. She bucked against me, tried shoving me away, and erupted into a barrel of laughter.

I chuckled, giving her pussy a light smack.

She gasped; her mouth snapping shut.

"You can." I bent down and kissed her softly on the mouth. "And you will but not right now." I pulled my hand from beneath her leggings and slipped my fingers between my lips. Sucking the essence of her body off of them, I let out a soft sigh at the sweet acidic taste coating my tongue. "Fucking perfect."

She giggled, rolling over onto her side. "What about you?"

"Don't worry about me."

Busy turned onto her stomach, lifting her head. "But I want to return the favor."

"You can. But not right now."

She pouted.

"Come visit me when everyone's sleeping." I brushed my thumb over her bottom lip.

"What will we do?" she whispered.

"Kiss." I reiterated my point by placing a soft peck on her mouth. "Touch. Get naked. Fuck."

"Finally?"

A laugh burst through me. "Getting impatient?"

"I just never met a guy who was…"

"What?" I asked, tilting my head.

"Wanting to get to know someone first before jumping into sex. Not that I have any experience with that, but my friends have told me and even the guys I see come and go from this place…" She shrugged. "I couldn't see Sammy offering to get to know the girl first before sleeping with her."

"Not all of us are the same, Busy."

"I know."

"Listen." I brought my fingers that were just in her body, to her mouth. "This is how much you want me. You smell that?"

Her nostrils flared. "Yes."

"And this is how much I want you." I cupped myself.

Her eyes dropped to my waist.

"When it happens." I pushed my finger between her lips. "And it will happen. It will be so fucking amazing, I probably won't even last long because I know your pussy is going to be tight, wet, and so damn snug, that my cock will explode after the first thrust."

"Geeze, Tanner. Paint me an image why don't you?" She rolled onto her back with a huff. "I'm coming to see you later and you better make good on your promise."

I laughed, slipping my hand back beneath her shirt and cupping her breast. "It's late. You need sleep but I promise."

"Who needs sleep?" She let out a soft sigh, her eyes fluttering closed. Her breathing evened out a moment later.

She shifted, moving to her back and covering my hand with hers.

Blowing out a slow breath, I continued watching the show but never really paid any attention to it. I could still feel her trembling around my fingers. But I would make good on my promise. I wanted her and I didn't think I could wait much longer.

A throat cleared, making me jump.

My eyes popped open, not realizing I had closed them. I must have fallen asleep.

Cyrus and Sammy were staring at us.

Sammy's jaw was locked tight, his face red, while his brother stood there with concern etched on his face instead.

"Busy." I nudged her gently. "Wake up," I said, not looking away from the twins.

"What's wro—oh." She sat up, rubbing her eyes. "Hey guys. What time is it?"

"Hey guys," Sammy repeated. "Do you know what would have happened if your dad would have come down here and found you with him?" he demanded, ignoring her question.

While Sammy went on a tirade, Busy's cheeks reddened and she cowered within herself.

I knew he meant well but I didn't like how he was treating her. She wasn't a child. She was far from it in fact.

The hackles on my neck rose and before I knew what was happening, I was on my feet and in Sammy's face.

His eyes widened for a second before he glared at me and shoved me back. "Get the fuck out of my face." When he looked around me and went to continue yelling at Busy, I stepped in his line of sight.

Sammy raised an eyebrow. "Really?"

"Yes, really." I stepped toe-to-toe with him. "If you want to yell at someone, you yell at me. She has nothing do with this."

"She's just as guilty as you are." Sammy lifted his chin. "Isn't that right, Busy?"

My jaw clenched. "You do not get to call her that." I wasn't sure where this need to claim her as mine came from, but I was the only one who got to call her that. It was my name for her and my name alone.

"Tanner." Busy wedged her way between Sammy and me, placing her hand on my chest. "You need to stop. Both of you do. If my dad did come down here, I would have dealt with it, but I am not a child. As much as you all like to keep me under your thumbs, I'm twenty-three. Just because I'm the only female besides my mom and your aunts, means shit." She lifted a hand when Sammy went to speak. "Now why don't you go run along and play with that redhead who likes to keep pissing you off." Busy tapped her chin. "I really can't wait to meet her though. Especially if she's keeping you on your toes."

Sammy looked between her and me. "If something happens to Bee, I will make you ever regret asking our uncle for help."

Before any of us could say something, he stormed away, stomping up the stairs.

"Ignore him," Cyrus finally said once Sammy was out of earshot.

Busy let out a hard sigh. She had dropped her hand to her side but still kept close. She was so close; I could see the freckles on her nose where the sun had kissed her skin. I could also still see the slight blush in her cheeks from the orgasm I had given her.

"What were you watching?" Cyrus asked, glancing at the TV.

"*The Office.*" Busy crossed her arms under her chest, chewing her bottom lip.

"Good choice." Cyrus ran a hand through his dark hair. "Listen, whatever happens, I have your back. Both of yours. Don't ask me why." He shook his head. "But I approve of whatever this…" He waved a hand between us. "Is."

Busy stepped in front of me. "Why?"

My skin heated over the fact that she was trying to protect me. I was sure a lot of men wouldn't like it. They would feel like less of a man. But I never had anyone protect me before. Not since Trigger. And he died as a result of it.

My stomach twisted. I stepped away from Busy, needing to put some distance between us. My thoughts were scattered as Busy and Cyrus talked amongst themselves. If I lost Trigger because he was trying to keep me safe, I could very well lose Busy too. I couldn't do this. I couldn't put her in harm's way. She deserved better than my broken mess.

Slumping on the couch, I dropped my head in my hands and massaged my fingers into the muscles at the base of my neck.

Another pair of hands joined mine a moment later, making me jump.

"I got you, Tanner," Busy whispered, massaging her fingers into the aching muscles.

I leaned my head against her stomach, taking deep breaths. I wished I could tell her everything. All the shit I had done. All the reasons I had disappeared. Why I ran and hid away for over six months.

"Tanner."

I looked up then, being met by beautiful chocolate brown eyes.

Busy gave me a small smile, stepping between my knees and pushing me back.

"Busy, you…this…" My dick twitched, clearly not caring how dangerous this way. I was just thankful that we were once again, alone. I didn't even hear Cyrus leave.

"I just…" Her teeth found her lip again. That single movement forced a drop of pre-cum from the tip of my dick. "Let me make you feel better."

I shook my head, took a deep breath, and thought of everything but what it would be like to have her hot wet body wrapped around me. "You need to stop."

"I know you want me." She straddled my lap. "You said so yourself."

"Of course I want you." My hands slid down her back, pulling her flush against me.

Busy cupped me over my pants, rubbing me over the fabric.

I groaned, a hot shiver racing down my spine.

"Let me make you feel better," she whispered, kissing my forehead.

I leaned back, watching her.

Her eyes were dark, her mouth set in a thin line.

"Busy," I whispered.

She smirked, pushing her palm against me.

"Fucking hell." I covered her hand, helping her please that ache deep inside of me.

"You're so hard."

A gruff chuckle escaped me. "I wonder why?"

She giggled, placing a soft peck on my mouth.

"You deserve better, Busy," I heard myself say.

"How do you know what I deserve?" Her mouth brushed down the length of my jaw. "I deserve you and you deserve me. That's it."

"Busy." I pulled her hand from my lap.

"Tanner, I know I'm not experienced but I can learn. I want to learn. For you."

Not experienced? Virgin.

She was a damn virgin. She had to have been. She had said she wasn't experienced, but I didn't clue in at just how little experience she actually had.

As soon as I was about to comment on that little fact, the burner phone rang from the bedroom. I gently pushed Busy off of my lap and rushed to it before flipping it open. "Yeah."

"You alone?"

"Kind of," I said, sitting on the edge of the bed. "What's going on?"

Busy stood in the doorway, leaning against the doorframe.

"I was able to dig up some information," Rowan paused. "It seems one of the security videos has you in a compromising position, Tanner."

"And?"

"And that means you need to get out of there. If the people you're currently living with, see this video…" He hesitated. "It looks bad, T."

"Yeah…I figured." When I was in that alley after Sunny got shot, I had seen the cameras. I knew the footage would make an appearance eventually. "Thank you, Rowan." I flipped the phone closed, my stare locking with Busy's. "You want me?"

"I think we already established how much we both want each other, Tanner," she said, wringing her hands in front of her.

Should I tell her about the video? Should I set myself up to fall? Even though Sammy didn't like me, and the rest of the guys didn't either, living at the Hell's Harlem clubhouse for the past few weeks and a bit, had been the safest I had felt in my whole life.

I was no longer worried about someone coming into my room who shouldn't. Even though most of the guys probably wanted me dead, Greyson never told them that I was there. Besides Busy, and I was sure the wives, Catch, and the twins were aware that I was staying in the basement.

"What's going on, Tanner?" Busy's soft voice pulled me from my thoughts. "Who was on the phone?"

"You should go." I went to walk past her when her hand cupped my arm, stopping me. "You shouldn't want me, Busy. I'm not good enough. I'll never be good enough." Before I could stop myself, I leaned down and placed a soft peck on her cheek. "Forget me."

(Bee)

Forget me.

Sure. I'll get right on that, Tanner.

I wasn't sure what his issue suddenly was but whoever was on the phone, gave him some bad news that made him fall into himself. I had watched Tanner's face go pale. He looked like he had seen a ghost, or he had just been told when his life would end.

As he walked down the hall away from me, I couldn't help but wonder how he was as a boy. Something told me that he never had a good childhood. Especially if he wasn't allowed to watch movies. Who didn't let their kid watch movies?

Tanner slipped into the bathroom, the sound of the shower running a moment later.

I looked at the stairs leading to the main floor and back toward the bathroom. I should leave Tanner alone. Something obviously upset him. I should have done a lot of things but instead of listening to that little voice in my head, I listened to the one in my gut. It said to go to him. To talk to him. To show him that I wasn't giving up on us. To show him that he was enough and that he deserved happiness.

My feet took me down the hall and toward the bathroom. The closer I got, the harder my heart raced.

When I stood outside the bathroom, I took a deep breath and slowly opened the door. He was in the shower, his nakedness shielded by the glass door, but I could still see the outline of his body.

He stood up straight, his gaze burning through me. Even though I couldn't see him clearly through the fog of the door, I could sense him. I could almost picture every line of his hard body.

Closing the door behind me, I clicked the lock into place and began stripping. I wanted him to know that this was it. That I was in this for the long run.

Once I was completely naked with my clothes in a pile at my feet, I went to the shower. I had always liked this one and preferred it to the other bathrooms in the house. This shower had two shower heads. One was attached to the wall and the other, you could use to massage every part of you.

Tanner slowly opened the shower door, staring down at me.

I swallowed hard, my eyes traveling down every part of his naked body.

He held out his hand, waiting.

My stomach flipped that he was giving me the option to run. But I would never run. Not from him. I slipped my fingers in his, letting him pull me into the shower with him.

He shut the door, closing me in with him. He looked down at me through hooded eyes.

Placing my hands on his shoulders, I ran them down his torso. His abs jumped under my touch.

Tanner smirked, pulled the showerhead from its holder on the wall, and aimed the running water at my chest. He slowly lowered it down my body, keeping his eyes locked on mine.

My heart raced, my legs spreading on their own accord.

Leaning his forehead against mine, he aimed the showerhead at my center.

I gasped, my head falling back at the unexpected shock of pleasure slamming into me.

With his free hand, he pushed his fingers between my legs, spreading me open to him.

I moaned, digging my nails into his shoulders to keep from falling to my knees. "Tanner." I panted.

He moved the stream of water back and forth over my swollen clit all the while pumping his other hand against me. His fingers slid in and out of me in quick, rough moves.

Wrapping my arm around his shoulders, I held on.

His cock was hard and proud between us, twitching and jerking with every sound that left me.

Circling my fingers around him, I watched his eyes darken as a low groan left him.

"Busy," he whispered. He kissed me softly on the mouth. "Come for me."

"Please," I trembled against him. I lifted my right leg, wrapping it around his waist. It opened my body to him, giving him the invitation to do whatever it was that he wanted to do.

His fingers picked up speed. The pleasure of them thrusting in and out of me, mixed with the water spraying against my clit, sent a shock wave of ecstasy racing through me. The release slammed into me, forcing his name to leave my lips.

When my body calmed down, he hung the showerhead back up on the wall before crushing his mouth to mine.

I kept a firm grip on his cock, stroking it hard. Wrapping a second hand around him, I lined up the tip with my center when a knock sounded on the door.

Tanner muttered a curse.

"Tanner, it's Cyrus, we need to chat," came Cyrus's deep voice from the other side of the door.

"At least it's him and not Sammy," I whispered.

Tanner sighed, placing me gently on my feet. "True." He kissed me softly on the mouth. "It's late. You need to sleep. We can continue this tomorrow."

"Okay." As much as I wanted to argue, I knew that if I didn't go to bed, he would be up all night.

"I'll see you tomorrow when you bring me my food," he said, pinching my chin and giving me another peck.

"Definitely."

"Be out in a moment," Tanner called out.

I released him and went to leave the shower when an arm caught me around the waist.

"Thank you," he murmured into my hair. "Thank you for not giving up on me."

I turned in his arms, cupping his face. "You can try and convince me that you're not good enough, but you are." I kissed him hard on the mouth. "Go see what Cyrus wants but you need to get some rest too. I'll see you tomorrow." I pulled away from him and left the shower.

He shut off the water before turning back to me. "Sleep well, Busy."

"You too." I dried myself off, got dressed and opened the door to the bathroom. "He'll be out in a moment," I told Cyrus, no longer giving a shit that we had been caught. I was done. I was ready for more. My cousins would get over it.

I believed Tanner when he said he didn't kill Sunny. Maybe I was the only one who believed him. Because of that possibility, he needed someone at his side. Fighting for him. Vouching for him. Just being his rock. I was that rock. And tomorrow, I would be his.

Completely.

FIFTEEN

Bee

THE HOUSE WAS QUIET the next morning as I slipped into the bathroom across the hall from my room and took a shower. When I finished, I quickly got dressed and headed back to my room. It was on the second floor and at the end of the hall, past the photos of old and current bikers lining the walls.

When I reached my room, I pulled my phone out of my pocket to check and see if I had any missed texts from Lori and Heather when a throat clearing made me jump.

Aunt Eve and Aunt Sara were sitting on the love seat I had against the far wall.

"You scared me," I said, clutching my throat and trying to ease the racing of my heart.

"Sorry." Aunt Eve stood and went to my bookshelf. "We need to talk."

"What are you doing up so early?" I asked them, shutting the door behind me.

"It's almost ten," Aunt Eve told me.

"Oh. What did you need to talk about? Have you been talking to Sammy? I swear nothing's happened." Not enough anyway.

Aunt Sara laughed. "That's usually what they always say when something's happened or about to happen."

"Maybe I should have gone home when my dad offered for me to go with him," I mumbled.

"Listen." Aunt Sara glanced at Aunt Eve before looking back at me. "We know something's going on. We're not stupid. Catch told me there was a thing but he wasn't sure what it was. But I know. We both know."

"I don't even know Tanner." But I did. Even though we hadn't known each other for long. My feelings for him were strong and they were very real. No matter what he said or how hard he tried pushing me away, both of us felt whatever this was.

"Your dad is going to lose his mind, Bee," Aunt Eve said gently.

It had always amazed me how someone as soft spoken as her was married to my Uncle Greyson.

"We love you." Aunt Sara rose from the couch and came toward me. "We just want what's best for you, but I know that when your dad finds out, he's going to freak out or worse, Bee. We won't be able to do anything about it. I don't even think your mom will be able to calm him down."

"Tanner didn't do whatever everyone thinks he did," I insisted.

"And you know that for sure?"

I met Aunt Sara's gaze. "No. I don't have any proof or anything, but I feel it. I know he's telling the truth." I slumped on the edge of my bed. "I believe him."

They sat on either side of me, taking my hands in both of theirs.

BEING US

"Our guys are bikers. It's a given that they've done some shady shit," Aunt Eve explained. "Did you know that your Uncle Greyson saved my life?"

My head whipped around. "He did?"

She nodded. "We had lost your Aunt Trixie and Jaron was taken from us. We don't like to talk about it. A lot of shit went down and it's hard to relive. Point is, people were trying to separate us. All of us. But we were determined and your uncle's stubborn." She winked.

I laughed.

"I haven't met Tanner. Have you?" she asked Aunt Sara.

Aunt Sara shook her head. "But he seems to have caused quite the stir. I haven't seen my husband this grumpy in quite some time. It's probably why all of the guys are miserable."

"But he hasn't done anything." I huffed. "He's been in the basement and he's not even allowed to come out just in case someone here sees him who isn't supposed to see him."

"We know," they both said in unison.

I rose from the bed. "Thank you for looking out for me but nothing's happened."

Not yet going unsaid.

"Well, we'll leave you alone. Just please be careful." Aunt Eve pulled me into her arms. "That's all we ask. Oh, and just a warning, we won't tell your father any of this but us girls have to stick together."

My heart jumped to my throat. "Are you going to tell my mom?"

"Not yet but if you don't figure out what's going on with Tanner, we'll have to," Aunt Sara said.

I let out a sigh. "That's fair I guess."

"Just please be careful." Aunt Eve held me at arm's length. "Okay?"

"I will." I gave her a quick hug before hugging Aunt Sara as well. "Thank you."

"Always, sweetheart." Aunt Sara passed a glance at Aunt Eve. "Before we go, I just wanted to point out that as much as the guys apparently don't like Tanner, your grandfather seems to like him."

"Probably because it'll piss off my dad." My grandpa had gotten used to the fact that his daughter had married an older man, but she would always be his baby girl. Just like I would always be my father's.

"Probably." Aunt Eve laughed. "Just be careful."

They hugged me again and quietly left my room, leaving me to my own thoughts. I was almost tempted to go downstairs and finish what Tanner and I had started the night before. My fingers itched to touch him again. To run my hands over his hard body.

Letting out a sigh, I flopped back onto my bed just as my phone rang. Rolling over onto my stomach, I reached for my phone but didn't recognize the number flashing across the screen.

"Hello?"

"Is this a secure line?"

"Excuse me?"

"Do you not speak English? I asked you a question. Is this a secure line?" the deep voice repeated, slower that time.

"Uh…as secure as can be I guess." I didn't use burner phones. The only people I talked to on the phone were Lori and Heather and even then, it was few and far between. We were texters or we video chatted on Facebook. Other than that, we didn't really like talking on the phone.

"That doesn't answer my question."

"Well for one, I have no idea who you are and two, who talks on the phone anymore?"

The man chuckled. "True."

"Who is this?"

"A friend."

"Right," I said slowly. "What do you want?"

"I need you to do something for me."

"I think you got the wrong number, buddy." I left the room just as Uncle Greyson was coming up the stairs.

"Nah, you see, I don't. I happen to know who's staying at your house. Although, it's not your house, now is it? You still live with mommy and daddy, but you like to stay at your uncle's from time to time. Isn't that right?"

I swallowed hard, flagging Uncle Greyson down. "Who is this?"

The permanent scowl on Uncle Greyson's face deepened as he came toward me. "Hand me the phone, Bee."

"Yes, Bee. Hand him the phone."

My heart started racing but I did as I was told.

Uncle Greyson stuck the phone to his ear. "I'm listening." His face reddened, his jaw clenching.

I wasn't sure who was on the phone, but it was obviously someone who knew about Tanner. He knew things he had no right knowing.

Suddenly, Uncle Greyson handed me back the phone. "Bee, follow me." He spun on his heel, stomping back down the hall from where he had come from. "I don't suggest making me tell you again or I *will* go to your father."

I bit back a huff and followed him. I was getting sick and tired of being told what to do. It wasn't like I was a child. All I wanted to do was call my friends and chat about nothing at all. Or maybe I would grab a coffee and curl up with a book outside. Or maybe I would leave and go home. But as I followed Uncle Greyson down into the basement, I knew.

I would not be going home anytime soon.

SIXTEEN

Bee

WHEN UNCLE GREYSON AND I neared the room that Tanner was staying in, I was half-expecting for him to knock. But instead, he barged into the room.

Tanner was sitting on the bed. "Good morning." He gently placed a book he was reading on the bed beside him before looking our way. "Problem?"

I wanted to laugh at how casual he was acting and didn't have my uncle ready to rip his head off.

"Yeah, I got a big fucking problem." In a quick move, Uncle Greyson stepped behind me and shoved me forward.

"What are you doing?" I cried, trying to push away from him.

"Tell her," Uncle Greyson demanded, keeping a firm grip on the back of my neck.

"Tell her what exactly?" Even though Tanner's voice came out calm and even, I briefly saw his hand shake before he clenched it into a fist.

"My niece just got a phone call. Tell her who was on the phone." Uncle Greyson loosened his grip. "I'm sorry, Bee," he murmured.

"How would I know who just called her?" Tanner picked the book back up. "If you're done, I'd like to finish this story. I'm getting to a good part."

"Tanner," Uncle Greyson boomed.

I jumped.

"Tell her, who the *fuck* was on the phone," Uncle Greyson repeated, slower that time.

Tanner slammed the book on the nightstand. "He wasn't supposed to call her." He glanced at me. "He wasn't supposed to call you," he repeated, his voice softer. "I promise you."

"Who was he?" I asked before Uncle Greyson ripped every inch of Tanner apart.

"Tommy West."

I looked up at Uncle Greyson. "I don't know who that is."

"He's the president of Devil's Rejects," Tanner answered. "He's the reason I disappeared. He's also the reason I've come here, asking for your help."

"Bee, leave us." Uncle Greyson stepped around me, looking down at me over his shoulder. "Now."

I went to the door, glancing back at Tanner one last time before shutting the door behind me. Uncle Greyson had become gentler and kinder over the years but if that was the case, then why did I feel like I just shut Tanner in with the devil himself?

(Tanner)

Greyson leaned against the door with his arms crossed under his chest. "What does Tommy want and how did he get my niece's phone number?"

"He knows people." I scrubbed a hand down my face. "I don't know what he wants though."

"Tanner."

"What?" My head snapped up then. "I don't know. I swear to fuck I don't know. He wanted my club. He got that. He wanted Sunny's old lady. And he got her. I don't know what else he could want besides..."

"You being dead. That's what the price on your head is for. Is it not?"

"Yes, but I don't know if he set it up. I don't know anything."

"I can't have more bodies on my hands, Tanner. That includes yours. We've already lost too much." Greyson pulled his phone out of his pocket. "What do you want with Bee?"

And we were back to that. "I have no idea what you're talking about." My cock still burned as the memory of her pumping it hard and fast in the shower last night, rushed through me.

"Why don't you try that again and tell me the truth this time?" He took a step toward me.

My heart started racing, my skin became clammy. "Don't. I just..." Spots danced in my vision.

The door suddenly opened, revealing Busy.

"Uncle Greyson, I just wanted to add—Tanner." Busy rushed to me, sitting on the bed beside me and cupping my shaking hands. Her touch, that single gentle touch, calmed the nerves. My hands stopped trembling, my heart slowed, the spots disappeared. "You good?" she asked gently.

I looked at her then. "I am now."

She gave me a small smile.

"Fucking hell," Greyson muttered. "Bee."

Her head whipped around. "I'm not leaving."

His phone took that moment to ring. "Shit." He brought it up to his ear. "What? Oh…sorry, beautiful. What's wrong?" He pointed at Busy. "You behave. Tanner, we'll talk later. I have to make some calls." He left the room but kept the door open. "I'm here, Eve. Sorry, dealing with shit," he explained to his wife, his voice trailing off as he went up the stairs to the main floor.

"I guess I should behave." Busy waggled her eyebrows.

As much as I didn't want to, I pulled away from her and slid off the bed. "Why did you do that?"

"Why did I do what?" She rose to her knees and shuffled to the edge of the bed before sitting back on her heels. "You looked like you were about to have an anxiety attack. I know I haven't known you for long but I'm sure you didn't want my uncle seeing that."

"No. I didn't." I leaned against the wall and shoved my hands in my pockets. "What did Tommy say to you?"

"Not much." She sighed. "But he knows where you are, Tanner. That can't be good."

But I didn't care about me. As much as it made me sound like a dick, I didn't care about anyone in this house either. The only person I cared about was kneeling right in front of me.

Before I could stop myself, I went up to Busy and captured her hair in my fist.

She gasped, staring up at me with those beautiful big brown eyes of hers.

I wanted her mouth on mine. I wanted to taste her tongue, swallow her moans and feel her tremble against me. With her dark eyes begging me for more and that flush in her cheeks, I knew that she felt it too.

"Tanner," she said, placing her hands on my chest. "What are you doing? Uncle Greyson could come back at any moment."

"I don't give a shit about that." And I didn't. The fact that she kept standing up for me, made me want more. The fact that she looked at me as a person and not as a monster, made me crave everything there was when it came to Busy.

I wanted to get to know her. Date her. Be with her. In every sense of the word.

I was like a predator and she was my prey. I wanted to rip her apart with my teeth, run my rough hands over her soft body, and just take us both away until the only thing left was us.

"Tanner," she repeated, licking her lips. "It's not safe...whatever it is you want to do...it's not safe."

"I don't give a shit anymore, Busy. I want to feel you against me." I leaned down toward her, my mouth mere inches from hers. "I want you in my arms. I want to hold you. Kiss you."

"And more?"

I took a deep breath. "Yeah, baby. And more."

She gulped, the sound hitting me square in the dick.

"I've had a hard time controlling myself. Making you come and then pushing you away. That was hard as fuck, Busy. When I met you, nothing else mattered. You were put in my life for a reason."

"We hardly know each other." She cupped my arm, trailing her hand up to my shoulder. "I don't know your favorite food. Or your favorite color. Or what hobbies you have."

"Meatball sandwiches. Don't have a favorite color. And my hobbies consist of reading. That's it."

"Oh."

"Anything else you want to know?"

"Why me?" she whispered. Her voice had been so soft, I wasn't sure if I heard her right.

"Why not you, Busy? You look at me like I'm normal."

"You *are* normal."

"I'm anything but normal." I towered over her, forcing her back. "But I don't want to talk about that shit now."

She fell back on her elbows, her chest rising and falling with ragged breaths. "What do you want to talk about?"

"Nothing." I leaned down, placing a soft peck on her collarbone. "I want your mouth. That's it right now."

Her cheeks reddened. "Tanner."

"Busy." My jaw clenched. "I've had your mouth already. I've made you come. I've seen you fucking naked. But right now, I need *you* to give *me* your *mouth*."

"If I don't?"

I closed my eyes, taking a deep breath before reopening them. "Then I'll leave you alone and never bother you again but, baby, I know you feel this. Whatever this is."

"I do," she said softly.

"Busy," I gritted out. "Mouth. Now. Please."

She tilted her head back. "Take it."

In a quick move, I cupped her jaw.

Her eyes widened.

As much as I wanted to take her mouth for my own, I wanted to cherish this moment more. Slowly lowering my lips to hers, I brushed mine across hers before pressing them firmly against her.

She sighed, opening to me and slipping her tongue between my lips.

I growled, pushing my body into her.

Busy latched onto my hoodie, pulling me closer. We were so damn close, but it still wasn't enough. Even when I finally fucked her, it still wouldn't be enough. I wanted to burrow under her skin and stay there. I wanted to find the deepest part of her soul and curl up in the safety of her warmth.

I knew, fuck, I had known from the moment I met her, that she could be it for me. She could be the safety I had been looking for without even realizing it.

She could be *it*.

It wasn't something that had ever crossed my mind before. It wasn't like I was out looking for someone to spend my life with. But after that phone call from Tommy and Busy standing up for me, I needed to make my move faster than I thought.

"Tanner." Busy broke the kiss, staring up at me. "What is it?"

"Nothing." I went to kiss her again when she covered my mouth.

"Tell me."

A tremor slid down my spine. I took a deep breath and then another. How could I tell her that Greyson backing me into a corner, scared the shit out of me? Or the fact that Tommy knew where I was, and they were all in danger. Or that I was attracted to her more than I ever thought was possible and we had only known each other for just over a month.

"Tanner," she whispered, staring up at me.

I pushed away from her and went back to the door. Taking another deep breath, I closed it and clicked the lock into place.

Glancing back at her over my shoulder, I hesitated. I wasn't sure why. I had always been the type of guy who just went after what he wanted. No questions asked. But now, I was asking every single fucking question. I just had no idea where to even begin.

SEVENTEEN

Bee

SOMETHING WAS OFF WITH Tanner. Maybe it was because of the phone call from Tommy. Or maybe it was from being stuck in this basement for weeks. I wasn't sure. But when he locked the door, my heart skipped a beat and when he turned toward me, my stomach fluttered at the lust in his dark eyes.

Tanner took a step in my direction, stalking me like I was his prey. He grabbed the hem of his hoodie and lifted it up and over his head.

My throat dried.

He was no longer wearing the bandage, the scar of the stab wound, pink and jagged. Other scars lined his abdomen. I had seen them when we were in the shower but never asked him about them.

"What happened?" I asked, itching to touch him. To run my fingers over every faint line and replace those painful memories with happy ones.

"I had to do shit to survive, Busy. Just like the dogs I saved, I had to fight to live."

BEING US

I stared up at him. "You didn't just save Trigger? There's been others?"

He closed the distance between us and crawled back onto the bed. "Yeah, baby. Many others. But I don't want to talk about that."

"Okay." It was clearly a subject for a different time. "Does it still hurt?" I asked softly, tracing the light scar on his shoulder.

"It's tender but I've dealt with worse." He rested his hands on either side of my head, towering over me.

Trailing my fingers down his arm, I reveled in the way his muscles bunched beneath my touch. He wasn't a big guy. Not bulky like Cyrus. But smaller, like he was a swimmer or even a runner. He was lean and hard in all the right places.

"Busy." Tanner blew out a slow breath, leaning his forehead against mine.

I continued running my fingers along every line of his hard torso. I wanted him to take it further, but I also wanted to commit him to memory.

"I feel like you're memorizing me." He kissed my forehead and then my nose.

I laughed lightly. "How did you know?"

"Not sure. Just a guess really." Tanner placed his hand on my hip, pushing his fingers beneath my top and lifting the shirt along with it. "I've never done this before. We've messed around but this…I've never done this."

My stomach flipped. There was no way he could be a virgin. Not with the dirty things he had already said to me. "What do you mean?"

"I mean…" His jaw clenched. "I've had sex. I'm not a virgin, if that's what's going through that beautiful head of yours."

"The thought crossed my mind."

He gave me a small smile. "I just mean, I've never done this. I've never wanted to do this." He shook his head. "I'm not making sense."

"No. You are. I get it. If it helps, I've never done this at all."

His eyes locked with mine, something flashing behind them.

I was a virgin. That much was clear. But he never asked about it. Maybe he would. In time.

Instead of commenting on the matter like I assumed he would, he lowered his mouth to mine. With every stroke of his tongue, the pleasure shot through every inch of me. His hold on me was rough but his eyes told all. He was battling with himself. He wanted to control and dominate but at the same time, he wanted to take it slow and be gentle.

I didn't care which side of him I got. I just wanted him. Not like I had much to go on anyway. I wanted to experience everything with him. I wanted him to show me what he liked. Or maybe he didn't even know. He said that it had been a while and he had never done this before. What exactly he was referring to, I didn't know. Maybe he had sex just to have sex and that was it.

Tanner's hand moved higher beneath my shirt until his fingers reached my chest. He broke the kiss, lifting my shirt and revealing my black bra to his hungry stare. He licked his lips.

My breath caught in my throat, my heart racing.

He lifted his hand to touch me but when it shook, he pulled it back.

I reached out for him before he could pull away completely and linked our fingers. Placing his hand on my breast, I lifted my head and kissed his chin.

He turned his head to meet the impact of my mouth.

I sighed, breathing him in. We had kissed before, but this was different. It was like this was where we were supposed to be all along.

I latched onto his hair, deepening the kiss.

A growl escaped him. He pushed his pelvis into me. A part of him, thick and hard, pressed against my core.

Desire unfurled deep in my lower belly.

"Busy," he whispered against my mouth, trailing his lips down the length of my jaw. He pushed his thumb into the cup of my bra. The rough pad ran over my nipple, igniting a spark of need. Want. Desperation for the man between my legs.

"Tanner, I…" I spread my legs even wider for him, lifting my hips.

His mouth soon found my neck, his teeth grazing over the sensitive skin just below my ear. With a rough move, he lowered the cup of my bra, revealing my full breast. "Hmm…" he hummed against my throat. Lifting his head, he gave me a wink then covered my nipple with his hot mouth.

I gasped, arching beneath him.

Lowering the other cup, he grabbed my breasts with rough hands and pushed them together. He bit and sucked, licked and devoured them completely. By the time he was done, I was panting, aching, needing him in ways I never even knew existed.

Before I could catch my breath, his mouth was back on mine. The kiss turned desperate, like Tanner was losing the very control he had tried so hard to keep a hold of.

He pushed his waist between my knees, rubbing a part of him that ignited a burn inside of me.

Breaking the kiss, I pushed him back on his heels and knelt in front of him.

His dark eyes watched me, following every single one of my movements.

Lifting the shirt up and over my head, I tossed it to the floor. I unclasped my bra and pulled the straps down my arms, letting it drop to the bed.

Much to my surprise, he never moved from his spot. He just continued to watch me the whole time.

Getting a sense of bravery, I hooked my fingers into the waist of my leggings and slowly pulled them and my panties down my hips, leaving me completely bare for him.

His nostrils flared, his eyes darkening even more.

Once I was naked, I tossed the leggings and panties to the side and shuffled closer to him.

Tanner slowly reached out, brushing the back of his hand down the center of my chest to my stomach. A path of goosebumps followed. I had never wanted something as much as I wanted him. I needed us to get lost in each other.

When his fingers reached the apex between my thighs, he began rubbing my clit.

Heat licked my skin. As much as I wanted him to move things along faster, I couldn't help but watch him take his time instead.

His free hand cupped my ass, pulling me against him in a rough move.

I gasped, slapping my hands against his chest.

His lips twitched; his eyes unmoving from mine. He watched. Almost like he was looking into the deepest parts of my soul.

Hooking my arms around his thick neck, I shivered as he continued massaging my clit.

Tanner leaned forward, kissing my chin and giving it a gentle bite.

I sighed, threw my head back, and undulated my hips against his hand.

He chuckled, the sound dark and inviting. "I want to watch you tremble."

"Yes," I whispered.

"I want to watch your thighs shake. I want to be with you. In any way that you'll have me."

I looked at him then, not realizing I had closed my eyes. "I want you. But…"

"What?" He kissed my nose, slipping his fingers lower and slowly thrusting them inside me.

"Is this too fast?"

"My fingers are deep inside you, baby." He pushed his face into the crook of my neck. "We can stop."

"We can?" I leaned back, glancing down at his waist.

He followed my gaze before looking back up at my face. "Just because my fingers are inside you and my cock is fucking hard, doesn't mean anything. You say no and that's it. No questions asked." He pinched my chin. "I won't take you until you tell me it's okay."

"Take me?" I repeated, grabbing onto his wrist and pushing his fingers deeper into me.

"Sex, Busy. I won't fuck you until you give me the go-ahead."

"Well I think we've moved past that." I sighed when he started pumping his hand between my legs.

"I'm trying to be a gentleman but fucking hell, Busy. You make me want to sin."

I laughed lightly. "I like when you're unraveled. And I like when you're not a gentleman."

"With you, Busy." He kissed my forehead. "I will always be a gentleman."

Wrapping my arms around his shoulders, I spread my legs. "Please make me come."

His dark eyes burned into me, his hand picking up speed.

I whimpered, rocking my hips back and forth. "God, Tanner."

"That's it, baby." He nipped my jaw. "Let's get this body nice and wet." He pulled his fingers from my pussy and ran them over the tiny bundle of nerves.

A shock wave of pleasure slammed into me.

Brushing his bangs off his forehead, I covered his mouth with mine.

When he said that he wouldn't have sex with me without me saying that it was okay, it made me wonder if something had happened to him. A heavy weight sat in the pit of my stomach at the thought.

"Tanner." I moaned.

"That's it, beautiful girl." His mouth found the side of my throat. "Christ, you're fucking soaked."

My thighs shook. "Faster."

His fingers pushed and rubbed, sliding back and forth over my swollen clit.

"Please."

Before I knew what was happening, Tanner shoved me onto my back and ran his hand back and forth over my clit in quick moves.

I cried out. "God, yes."

"Fuck, you're beautiful." He cupped my thigh, pushed it against the bed, and held it down. "Come hard, baby."

I gripped the blanket beneath me, tilting my hips up, and up again. I couldn't get enough of the pleasure consuming me. It ripped my soul apart, forced me to see stars, and exploded into a billion tiny particles. I chewed my bottom lip to keep from screaming his name.

As soon as my body calmed down, I was on him.

My mouth slammed down hard on his, I ripped at his pants, needing every inch of him in every inch of me.

He growled, his teeth nipping my bottom lip. Our tongues clashed and danced, trying desperately to control the other.

As soon as I had his pants undone, the phone rang.

"Fuck," Tanner broke the kiss.

"No. Please. You can call them back." We almost had sex several times already. I couldn't wait anymore.

"I need to take this, Busy." He pulled away from me.

I pouted.

Tanner chuckled, doing up his pants. "Trust me, baby. You won't have to wait much longer."

"No interruptions?" I asked, sliding off the bed and getting dressed.

"No interruptions," he repeated, giving me a quick kiss on the mouth. "Promise. But I do have to take this." He slipped his hoodie over his head.

"I'll give you some privacy."

Tanner pulled on the hoodie and went to the nightstand, letting out a hard sigh. "Stay," he said, without meeting my gaze.

I went and sat in the chair in the far corner of the room but much to my surprise, Tanner patted the spot beside him. I took a breath and went to him.

He flipped open the phone but instead of answering, he pressed a button and flipped it closed.

I frowned.

Tanner leaned down to my ear. "As much as I want to be a gentleman for you, I do like when you listen to me. Turns me on and makes me so fucking hard."

A breathless laugh escaped me.

His phone rang again, startling me.

He kissed my cheek, finally answering his phone.

(Tanner)

"You're not out of there yet, are you?" Rowan asked, concern evident in his deep voice.

I appreciated that he was checking up on me but found it annoying just the same. I glanced at Busy, cupped her hand that was resting on the bed between us, and held on. I needed her strength because I knew that I didn't have any of my own.

"No."

"Tanner."

"Listen, nothing's going to happen." I knew because Busy wouldn't let it. Sure, she may have been a female, but Hell's Harlem wasn't like the other clubs out there. They weren't even like Devil's Rejects. They used to be one percenters but had cleaned up quite a bit over the years. Greyson wouldn't go against his niece. Not that I had ever witnessed that gentle, caring side of him, but I didn't need to. I saw the way he looked at her. She may not have been his blood, but she was his family. They were all her family and I envied her for that.

"Are you sure about that?"

I took a chance and glanced at Busy.

She gave me a small smile, curling her fingers in mine and giving them a gentle squeeze.

"Yeah, I'm sure," I told Rowan. "Have you found out anything else?" I asked him, needing to get the subject off of Busy and I. Because honestly, it was no one else's business until I could figure out what the hell was going on between us myself.

"No but whatever Tommy's doing, it's making a wave underground."

My stomach twisted. "What do you mean?" I brought Busy's hand up to my mouth, gave her knuckles a soft peck, and stood from the bed. Releasing her, I began pacing.

"Between him and Roxanne, I'm not sure who's worse. She wanted Sunny but couldn't have him, so she went for Tommy instead. Tommy found out and didn't like that shit, so he slapped her around a bit. It's a mess."

"How do you know this?"

"Tanner, Tanner. I know people, remember?"

I grunted. "Right. Tell me something. Tommy called here."

"He did? How?"

"What do you mean how? That's what I'm asking you, Rowan. He called Greyson's niece. She's innocent in all of this." I stopped by the dresser and leaned against it.

"Is she that innocent though, T?"

My back stiffened. "What the hell does that mean?"

"I mean, if she's with you, she's sucked into this shit just as much as you are. If you want to keep her safe, I mean, if she's your girl and all, then you'd better get out of there."

My gaze snapped to Busy.

She was looking at the book I had been reading for the past few weeks. I had found it in one of the drawers of the empty dresser. It was good. And I was itching to finish it but now, it was like it didn't matter anymore.

"Tanner," Rowan said gently.

"Listen, I need you to find out as much information as you can on Tommy and Roxanne and everyone else involved in this shit. You know what to do and who to contact. Do it. Money is no object, Rowan. You know that. I'll be in touch." I hung up before I said something I regretted. But Rowan was right. Even though I didn't want him to be.

"Everything okay?" Busy asked, placing the book back on top of the nightstand.

Was it? How could I tell her? How could I tell this woman who was my undoing, that I wanted her but feared for her life just the same.

"You want me," I suddenly said, surprised at how low my voice was.

"I think that much is clear." She swung her legs over the edge of the bed, patting the spot beside her.

"Tanner," she said gently. "You're safe with me. I promise."

"I don't know you." But even though I said those words, in all reality, I *did* actually know her. She was sweet and kind. She brought food for me when she didn't have to. She saw something in me that no one else did. She made me feel human instead of the monster most depicted me as. She had been the first woman to ever want to actually be my friend instead of just having sex.

"What's going on, Tanner? One minute you want me and we're almost having sex on more than one occasion and now, you're suddenly closed off." Busy stood from the bed and came toward me. "What's wrong? Did I do something?"

Cupping her cheek, I slid my fingers to the back of her hair. "You could never do anything but being with me is dangerous, Busy," I finally confessed.

"I've grown up with bikers, Tanner. I know that it can be dangerous. But you're a good guy and I know you would do everything you could to keep me safe."

"Of course I would." I kissed her nose, leaning my forehead against hers. "I would give up my life first before I let something happen to you." I realized then that those words had been the most honest ones I had ever said.

"That's..." She swallowed noisily. "That's pretty heavy."

"I have no reason to beat around the bush, baby." Before I could take things further like both of us wanted, I pushed away from her. "I need to talk to your uncle. Something's going on and I don't know what it is and it's driving me fucking crazy. I need to make sure things are calm before we do anything."

"Really?" She laughed. "I think we were about to do something before Rowan called."

"I would have stopped it." But we both knew that was a lie.

"Wow, Tanner. I know I'm not experienced but this back and forth shit is driving me crazy."

"You know I want you, but we have to wait." Not that I wanted to, but I needed to talk to Greyson before Busy and I took it further.

"You mean." She turned slowly toward me. "Before you fuck me."

A shiver raced down my spine. "That's a dirty word for someone like you."

Busy lifted her chin, crossing her arms under her chest. "I can think of many more dirty words to say, Tanner, but clearly you don't want this to happen right now. Maybe not even soon."

My jaw clenched. "Challenging me now, little girl?"

Her brows narrowed. Closing the distance between us, she stared up at me. Her gaze was hard, determined, the lust crackling between us. "Clearly there is something between us." She cupped me over my pants, making me jump. "And I know you want me. All of you wants me." Before I could stop her, she undid the button of my jeans and lowered the zipper. "Tell me different, Tanner," she said, shoving her hand in my pants.

I groaned when her fingers came into contact with my hard cock.

"Tell me." She stood on tiptoes and licked along my bottom lip. "Tell me you don't want more."

In a quick move, I shoved her back against the dresser, the mirror rattling against the wall. "Careful, Busy." I ripped my jeans open all the way, giving her better access to my dick.

Her eyes darkened, her hand pumping me hard and fast.

"I'm being a gentleman when it comes to you but piss me off and I'll make you ever regret saving my life."

Her cheeks reddened but she never let go of my cock. "Prove it, Tanner."

The lust and tension built, billowing into a force that neither of us had control over.

"Prove it," she repeated, pulling me toward her.

I shivered at the hot slice of pain at her grabbing at me.

"Tanner," she whispered.

I brushed a hand over her head, crushing my mouth to hers. Pushing my waist between hers, I rubbed my cock against the fabric of her leggings that covered her pussy. Even though there was a barrier between us, I could still feel how hot she was.

Busy grabbed onto my hoodie, fisting it in her hands and pulling me down hard.

My hips moved back and forth. It didn't matter that I wasn't inside her. The friction forced a low groan from the back of my throat.

"Prove it," she whispered against my lips.

Just when I was about to pull away and carry her to the bed, a knock sounded on the door. "Fucking hell." I couldn't win. It was like the people in this house knew when Busy and I were about to fuck.

"This shit is getting old." She stared up at me. Her lips were swollen, a slight flush hit her cheeks.

I stuffed my throbbing cock away and did up my pants. "Later. I need you fucking later. I can't wait anymore." I kissed her hard, giving her bottom lip a gentle bite, letting her know that I meant what I said,

She pushed me back, jumping off the dresser and cupping me over my jeans. "This is mine."

A hot shiver raced down my spine. "Yes, baby. It's yours. All of me is yours."

She sighed, pushed away from me, and went to the door.

BEING US

I had to give it to her. She challenged me, kept me on my toes and made me damn near happy.

Rowan was right.

But as much as I didn't want him to be, I knew that there was only one way I could make this work. I just hoped Busy forgave me for it.

EIGHTEEN

Bee

WHEN I MADE SURE that both Tanner and I were presentable, I answered the door. Uncle Greyson stood on the other side of it. I expected him to demand why I was in Tanner's room but instead he looked between us, scowled, and walked away.

"Tanner," he barked. "Follow me."

Tanner grumbled a curse and came toward me. "Don't give up on me," he murmured, his fingers grazing my hip.

"Never."

When Uncle Greyson wasn't looking, Tanner kissed my temple and followed him out of the den and up the stairs to the main floor.

I did the same, finding Cyrus and Sammy standing by the door to the room where the club usually held their meetings.

Uncle Catch was sitting on a stool by the bar, talking on his phone.

BEING US

Just when I was about to ask Uncle Greyson what was going on, Shade and Meadow both walked into the house.

My eyes widened.

Roy Allen, known as Shade, had bags under his eyes and graying in his hair. He looked like he had aged years in such a short time. They had lost Sunny over seven months ago. While I was sure they were still mourning their loss, the air around them was no longer thick with a sadness that I felt down to my bones. No, now it was just filled with rage instead.

"I can't believe it." Meadow stopped suddenly.

Shade went to her side. "Fucking hell."

I looked between everyone.

Bodies shifted.

Murmurs sounded.

Mumbled curses followed.

"You said he was here but I almost didn't believe it myself." Shade took a step toward his target.

Tanner.

"What the fuck are you doing here? Have any more members of our family that you're wanting to kill off?" Shade closed the distance between them and grabbed Tanner by the collar of his hoodie. "Do you?"

"Shade." Uncle Greyson went to them but never pulled Shade away from Tanner.

"I didn't kill him," Tanner ground out.

Meadow laughed then. "Right and you didn't put us through hell either. What is it, Tanner? You got what you wanted but it wasn't enough for you. Was it?"

"You have no idea what you're fucking talking about." Tanner shoved out of Shade's grip, pushing him back.

He stumbled a bit, his brow raising.

Tanner was much smaller in size.

Shade had a good fifty pounds on him but the strength rippling from Tanner, clearly shocked him.

"What do you want?" Meadow demanded, stepping up to her husband's side.

Shade brushed his hand down the side of her swollen stomach, staring down the man they had accused of destroying their lives.

Tanner looked my way.

I nodded, trying to give him all the encouragement he needed. Truth was, I had no idea what was going to come of this. I didn't know Tanner's past but my family sure as hell seemed to.

He took a breath and then another and I knew he was on the verge of losing it. Knowing he wouldn't want anyone seeing that side of him, I stepped between him and Meadow.

"What the hell?" she whispered, a laugh escaping her. "There's something going on. Isn't there?"

The back of my neck heated.

"I think we need to chat." Uncle Greyson headed to the meeting room. "*Now.* I won't ask again." He entered the room, not waiting for the guys to follow him.

Shade grabbed Meadow's upper arm and pulled her to the other side of the room, but I could still hear their voices. It wasn't like they were being discreet about it.

"She's fucking him," Meadow cried.

"No, I'm not," I argued. "And even if I was, it's none of your business."

Meadow's head whipped around. Her cheeks turned red. She shoved out of Shade's grip and stomped up to me.

We were about the same height, but she was a little bigger than I was. Also, I had never gone toe-to-toe with a woman before. Or anyone for that matter. But defending Tanner seemed to be my new thing ever since I met him.

"What are you doing?" she asked, her voice thick, "He's the reason we lost Sunny. He was your family too."

"I know that," I said gently. "But Tanner didn't shoot him."

"Do you know that for sure? Can you honestly stand there and tell me that you are absolutely positive that Tanner didn't kill my boyfriend? Shade's boyfriend. Our partner. The father of our baby."

My chest tightened. "Can you tell me that he *did*?"

"I…" She scowled. "I love you like a little sister, Bee. But right now, I'm so disappointed. I just…" Her eyes welled.

The back of my throat burned.

"Shade," Uncle Greyson barked from the other side of the room. "I need you in here."

Shade went up to Meadow and kissed her temple, muttering low enough to her that only she could hear what he was saying. Both of them cupped her stomach, talking amongst themselves.

My chest pained, knowing the baby she was carrying was a result of their love but also a constant reminder that Sunny would never meet his child.

"I'll go sit in the corner like a good little girl. I have a book to finish reading anyway," she mumbled, spun on her heel, and went to one of the tables sitting by the far wall.

"I really hope you know what you're getting yourself into," Shade said, cupping my shoulder. "I also hope you're right." He gave my shoulder a squeeze before joining the guys in the room.

At that moment, I was truly alone. I was stuck between wanting to be loyal to my family and following my heart.

(Tanner)

"You need to tell us what the fuck is going on and why the hell he's here, so I can go back and give my wife something," Shade said, his voice rough.

"You need to remember who you're talking to." Greyson went around to the head of the table.

"Grey, I need fucking answers," Shade demanded.

Greyson's head whipped around.

I almost wished I had popcorn.

"What's so damn funny?" Shade snapped, glaring at me.

"Nothing." I looked at my wrist, pretending to check the time. Not that I had anywhere to go of course but I did have a date with Busy's pussy.

"Tanner, enough." Greyson pointed at Shade. "*You* need to relax. I will give you answers when I get them. Now sit your ass down and shut the fuck up." When Shade slumped into a chair, Greyson cleared his throat. "Anyone else have any issues with how I run things around here?"

Murmured noes went around the room.

"Now, Tanner." Greyson pulled his phone out of the inside of his leather cut and placed it on the table in front of me. "I have news. I'm sure you already know this, but I've come across a video that puts you in a very compromising position. You're lucky I'm in a good mood or else I'd just let Shade rip you apart."

I grunted. "It's not him I'm worried about."

Chuckles sounded around the room.

Meadow had been the only woman to ever stand up to me. Until Busy. I was never attracted to Meadow and she wasn't mine anyway but Busy was single and she didn't want to fix me. Not like everyone else.

"You're enjoying this, aren't you?" He grunted. "You like my coc—"

"Tanner?"

I jumped, finding several pairs of eyes on me.

Shade's brows narrowed but something unexpected flashed behind his eyes. I looked away before I could get caught in his concerned stare. We had nothing in common. Nothing. I refused to have it any other way. Because as much as I needed their help, I would die first before that information got out about me and what I had gone through as a kid.

"Have you seen this video?" Greyson asked, pressing play on his phone. The images on the small screen brought me back to that night. I had asked Meadow to meet me to give me whatever it was my father had left me in his will.

Numbers.

That was all I knew. When she placed the small gold ring in my hand, I almost laughed at how sick and twisted my dad was. Looked like the apple didn't fall far from the tree.

The numbers were to a bank account that held a lot of money in it. I wasn't sure where my father got the money from or why he was giving it to me. That information wasn't in the will. But it wasn't like we had ever gotten along. He never wanted me. Stuck me with my mom until she died, and then I was thrown into the hands of the devil himself.

The video showed Meadow giving me the ring. Other people milling about. And me walking away. As soon as I was almost out of the camera shot, it went to another camera and showed me with a gun in my hand. There was no sound in the video, but I didn't need it. I could still hear the gunshots. The screams. The pain. The damn anguish.

The video switched again, revealing Meadow walking away, me with the gun raised and Sunny walking toward her. I remembered it like it was yesterday. My gun was raised. Sunny went down, pulling Meadow down with him. All because he was protecting her. It looked bad. It looked so damn bad that I wasn't sure how I would ever be able to talk myself out of this one.

A heavy hand landed on my shoulder, the one that I had been stabbed in. Greyson squeezed, digging his fingers into the wound that had healed but was still tender.

I winced, embracing the pain slicing through me because it reminded me that I was still alive.

"You see. This video looks like you were the one who shot Sunny." Greyson placed both hands on my shoulders.

"But I didn't. I never pulled the trigger." Even I wouldn't have believed me if the situation was reversed. How could they? I had a gun in my hand. It was pointed in Sunny's direction, but I wasn't aiming for him.

"Okay, let's say you didn't shoot him." Greyson released me and sat in the chair beside me. "Who did?"

"I don't know." I had a feeling it was either Tommy, Roxanne, or he had hired someone else to do it. Either way, it didn't matter. Because I knew that I had been set up. "But I can tell you that I did not shoot Sunny. I know it looks bad. Fuck, I know that."

"Why should we believe you?" Greyson asked, tenting his fingers under his chin.

"Because it wasn't him I was aiming for," I blurted.

Bodies shifted in the room.

"Who the hell were you aiming for then?" Shade demanded, shoving to his feet.

I looked between him and Greyson. "I was aiming for Sunny's ex."

"Roxanne?" Shade shook his head. "But why?"

"Because I saw her reach into her purse and pull out a gun. I didn't know who she was going to shoot. So I tried getting to her first but shit went down and that didn't happen." That was the truth. They could take it or leave it.

"Are you saying that Roxanne shot Sunny?" Shade asked, his voice thick.

"I don't know. I didn't see her shoot him. I just saw her point her gun in his direction. Other shots started and I left." It didn't make sense. I knew that but there was nothing else I could give them at the moment.

"But why? Why would she go to all this trouble?" Shade began pacing. "I can't tell Meadow this shit. This isn't an answer."

"I don't know. I wish I could give you more. And I know what I di…" I swallowed hard. "It doesn't matter. I will get your wife answers." I was happy to hear that they were still together. I had never met anyone who lived the polyamorous lifestyle until meeting Sunny, Shade and, Meadow. But losing Sunny could have separated them. I was glad to see that it didn't. "You're having a baby," I said, remembering seeing Meadow's protruding stomach.

Shade's brows narrowed. "And?"

"I'll get you answers." It was a promise that I would keep. I had been fucked over many times in my life, it was one reason I had never corrected any of the rumors going around about me. I needed people to think that I was a monster. I needed to know that I was no longer one to be messed with. No matter the cost, I would do anything to make it to the top and be as powerful as I could be. I did this all on my own.

Shade searched my face, but he didn't say anything. He sighed, scrubbing a hand down his face before pushing his fingers through his dark hair.

"How are you going to do that with a price hanging over your head?" Greyson asked, pulling my gaze away from Shade.

"Easy. I'll just go to my—the clubhouse for Devil's Rejects and demand answers from Tommy." It wasn't a foolproof plan, but it was better than what I had a moment ago.

"Tell me something then." Greyson was going to pop my little fantasy. "Why didn't you do this months ago instead of holing up who the hell knows where?"

And there it was. "I only just found out that there is a price on my head. This whole time, I knew there was a mole but that was it. I was just trying to move on with my dog and lay low. I don't know why Tommy had his boys search me out. Things were quiet. It was just Trigger and I. No excitement. Exactly what I wanted."

"So why now?" Cyrus asked, sticking an unlit smoke behind his ear. "Why all of a sudden would he cause an issue?"

"To be funny." I shrugged. "How the hell am I supposed to know?" I wasn't his keeper.

"Because you were close. Were you not?" Greyson pointed out.

"Yeah and I thought I knew him too but clearly I was wrong. Listen." I stood and went to the large bay window. "I don't know what Tommy wants. Besides me dead. But if he knows where I am…" I looked back at the guys who wanted me out of there.

"Nothing will happen." Greyson sat back in his chair, crossing his arms under his broad chest. "After the shit all of us have been through, I upped the security system here."

"That's not going to help you when Tommy and his fucking crew blow up the damn place," I told him.

Greyson chuckled. "You're standing within a fortress, Tanner. There are cameras. Everywhere." He stared at me for a moment. It made me wonder what all he had seen.

I couldn't dwell on that. As much as I needed to confront Tommy and find out what was going on, there was something I had to do. I just hoped Busy wouldn't push me away.

NINETEEN

Bee

MEADOW WANTED NOTHING TO do with me while the guys were talking with Tanner. I couldn't say that I blamed her, but it still hurt. We had grown close ever since Shade brought her home after Sunny had passed. She wasn't much older than I was. She kept Shade on his toes and probably knocked him on his ass just the same. She was funny and said whatever was on her mind, which I appreciated. I just wished she would talk to me now instead of shutting me out.

While I was waiting for the guys to finish their meeting, I went to my room and decided to call Lori and Heather. Since I hadn't talked to them much in the past few weeks, I was sure they had a lot of questions. It was funny how life worked out. I had been upset at the time that Cyrus and Sammy had dragged me from the club but now I was thankful. Because if they hadn't, who knows what would have happened to Tanner.

Letting out a hard sigh, I called the girls through Facebook and waited for them to answer.

BEING US

When both of their faces appeared on the screen, I smiled. "Hi."

"It's about time you called us." Lori pouted.

I laughed.

"She has better things to do." Heather pulled her dark hair up into a messy bun. "How's it going? The twins leaving you alone?"

"Uh...it's going fine. It's been crazy here or I would have called you sooner."

"What's going on?" Lori had been the empathic one between us three. Whenever one of us was hurting, she knew. It was one of the things I loved about her.

"We have a visitor and we're trying to get that taken care of." I wasn't sure how much I should tell them. Even though it was a video chat and we weren't actually talking on a phone line, I had learned over the years that you could never be too careful.

"Oh. Is he hot?" Lori waggled her eyebrows.

Heather rolled her eyes. "Ignore her. She hasn't been laid in a while."

We all laughed.

"But to answer your question." I paused. "He's not just hot. He's nice too and a gentleman. And—" A soft knock sounded on the door. "Come in."

The door opened slightly, revealing...

"Tanner," I whispered. "I need to go." I disconnected the video chat before the girls could ask any more questions. I would explain everything later. "What's wrong?" I asked, placing my phone on the nightstand.

He closed the door behind him, clicking the lock into place. "I wasn't sure if this was your room or not but then I heard you talking."

"I was chatting with my best friends," I explained, suddenly feeling exposed. Even though he had seen me naked already, having him in my bedroom felt like another layer was stripped between us. I never had a boy in my room before. Not even my cousins were allowed in. "How did you sneak up here?"

Tanner went to my dresser and picked up a small stuffed teddy bear my mom had gotten for me during one of her weekends away with Dad.

"Everyone started talking about other shit. Nothing that had to do with me. I'm sure someone noticed that I'm no longer there. Or maybe they thought I went back downstairs." He placed the teddy bear back on my dresser.

"Was anything decided? Or…" I swallowed hard when his dark eyes met mine in the reflection of the mirror.

"There's a video. Greyson showed it to me. It makes it look like I shot Sunny, but I didn't. I know they don't believe me but I…" He turned toward me, leaning against the edge of the dresser. "I need *you* to."

"I do," I insisted.

"Why?"

"You just said—"

"I know what I fucking said, Busy," he snapped, white knuckling the edge of the dresser. "But I need to know why you believe me when you don't even know me."

I knelt on the bed, placing my hands on my knees. "I do know you."

He looked away, his jaw clenching. "I don't trust people. I never have. I was given a reason not to trust anyone at a very young age. People hurt people. It's human nature. It's why I love animals."

"Tanner," I said gently. "Come here." I reached out for him, needing to have him in my arms. To hold him. To comfort him. To just be with him. Everything else could come later. It didn't have to happen now. As much as I wanted him, I could wait for him to be ready. For us both to be ready.

When he didn't move, I shuffled closer to the edge of the bed. "Please."

He let out a slow sigh but finally came toward me.

Rising to my knees, I wrapped my arms around his shoulders as he pushed his face into the crook of my neck.

Sliding my hands down his back, I pushed my fingers beneath his hoodie.

Tanner leaned back and pulled off the sweatshirt, leaving his torso completely bare for me.

Brushing my fingers down the middle of his chest, I traced them over every hard line of him.

"Busy," he murmured, kissing my jaw.

I turned my head.

He took the hint, crushing his mouth to mine.

The kiss wasn't like the others. No. This time it went beyond desperate. It became frantic. To the point that it made my head foggy, and I couldn't think of anything but having him inside me. My body buzzed, that familiar ache between my thighs becoming worse as time wore on. It was like so many things were about to happen that we just needed this time together before we could move on.

Tanner wrapped his fingers around my throat, deepening the kiss. "Busy," he murmured, giving my bottom lip a gentle bite.

I whimpered, my eyes welling as the pain sliced through me.

He licked along the spot he just bit before pushing his tongue back into my mouth.

The pain, mixed with pleasure, forced the ache between my legs to grow. I could feel every inch of him pressed up against my lower stomach. Every hard, thick, and very large, inch.

I broke the kiss, stared at him, and took a breath.

He brushed his thumb along my mouth. "I want to fuck you, Busy. No interruptions this time. You're going to let me, aren't you?"

My heart hammered against my ribs. "God yes."

Tanner grabbed my hand, pulled me flush against him then smacked his other hand against my ass.

I yelped.

His hold on my wrist tightened while his other hand continued raining blows on my rear.

My lower body burned. "Tanner."

He smacked my ass again, rubbing the spot soon after at the same time he sunk his teeth into the side of my neck.

I sighed, tilting my head to give him better access to my throat.

Pulling my wrist from his clutches, I reached for his pants. "I need you."

"You have me, baby." He cupped my ass, pulling my knees out from under me until I was on my back.

A bubble of laughter left me.

He winked, lowering his mouth to my exposed stomach. "You smell so fucking good."

"Tanner," I whined, running my fingers through his hair.

"So good." He licked and sucked, sinking his teeth into my side. Hooking his fingers into the waist of my leggings, he pulled them and my panties off of me and down my legs before tossing them to the side. In a rough move, he cupped my thighs and spread me open at the same time he covered my core with his mouth.

I inhaled a sharp gasp, ripping at his hair and pulling him closer.

He growled, digging his fingers into my thighs. He pushed my knees up, bending me in a way that opened me even more to him.

His tongue thrust inside of me, a low growl leaving the back of his throat.

I whimpered, my eyes rolling into the back of my head at the newfound pleasure.

Tanner shook his head, growling and humming, the happy noises coming from him sending sparks of ecstasy all throughout my body.

He released me with a smack, licking and kissing every inch of me. His tongue dipped lower, reaching that spot that had never been used for any amount of pleasure before. He groaned, his eyes darkening.

"Please, Tanner," I whined. "I need you inside me."

But he wouldn't let up. His mouth moved back to my clit, sucking it between his teeth. He thrust two fingers inside of me, flicking his tongue back and forth over the swollen nub.

"Oh God." I lifted the hem of my shirt and shoved it between my teeth, muffling the scream that shattered through me.

Before I could calm down, Tanner released me and pulled me to the edge of the bed. He ripped open his jeans, pulling out his thick length and beat the head against my mound. I knew this was going to hurt. He wasn't exactly small.

"I need to fuck you." He kissed my jaw, pushing the tip of him over my sensitive clit.

"Oh my," I moaned.

He sunk his teeth into my throat, running the head of his thick length over my soaked center. Before I knew what was happening, he thrust forward, giving me every single inch of him.

"Fucking hell. I forgot a condom."

"I don't care," I panted.

"So damn tight." He crushed his mouth to mine, swallowing my moan. The kiss was soft, but it didn't last long when something switched inside of him and that beast he tried to so hard to keep in check, finally took over. His hips powered forward and back, giving us both what we had been wanting since the very beginning.

I whimpered, arching beneath him and took him even deeper. "Tanner," I sobbed, my eyes welling. The pain of something foreign inside my body, invaded all of my senses. I couldn't focus on anything but the fact that it hurt. So damn much. I broke the kiss, gasping for air. "I…I can't…"

His hips slowed to a stop. He lifted his head, staring down at me. "Talk to me."

"It…" The vision of him blurred. "It hurts."

"It'll get better," he said, kissing me softly.

"No." I swallowed hard. "It really hurts."

He slowly pulled out of me, glancing between us before meeting my gaze. "I made you bleed. I knew you were inexperienced but…fuck, Busy."

I laughed lightly, wiping under my eyes. "I'm not a virgin anymore if that helps."

"Shit, baby." He kissed me hard. "I'm so sorry."

"Don't be." I touched his cheek. "It's not your fault."

Reaching between us, his thumb started rubbing my clit.

I jumped, a spark of electricity burning through me. "Oh…my."

Tanner slowly slid back into me, all the while flicking his thumb over the swollen nub. "Better?"

"God yes." My thighs shook, the pain turning into pleasure.

"That's it." He kissed the spot beneath my ear. "Come all over my cock."

"Please. I…" I lifted my hips, taking him even deeper. The tip of him hit a certain spot deep inside me. It pushed the delicious ecstasy higher and higher until I almost couldn't take it anymore. "Tanner."

BEING US

He leaned his forearm on the bed on either side of my head, staring down at me.

"Faster," I heard myself say, getting lost in his dark stare.

"You sure?"

"Yes, please." A release slammed into me, knocking the very breath from my lungs.

"Fucking beautiful." He removed his hand from between us and picked up speed with his hips.

I brought my fingers to his lips, running them down the length of his jaw. "Please, baby."

His nostrils flared. Something snapped inside of him. He released me and grabbed my hands. Sitting on the edge of the bed, he pulled me into his arms.

Straddling his waist, I lowered back onto him.

He groaned, covering my mouth with his.

Just when I thought I had control, he cupped my ass and began thrusting into me hard and fast.

I held onto him, crying out at the rough way he had control of my body. "Harder."

"Fuck." His hands spread me open.

"Oh God."

"That's it, Busy." He pushed me back, holding me against him. "Ride me. Take everything you want from me."

And I did.

Twice.

TWENTY

BEFORE MEETING BUSY, I had never actually gone down on a woman before. Not that I never came across the chance to do it, but I found that I never wanted to. Women in my life were few and far between. I had heard some of my old club brothers talking about the tasty treats they had and now I understood why. I was instantly addicted to tasting Busy's sweet pussy on my lips. I would fall to my knees every damn time just to have a lick.

Add to the fact that I could taste a hint of the copper after I made her bleed, and I was done.

"Tanner." Busy stared at me with a flush in her cheeks and hunger in her eyes. My girl wanted more.

It was well into the evening and we had been going at it all day. We used each other to take some of the edge off and I had to say, it relieved some of the stress resting on my shoulders.

Hooking my hand around Busy's thighs, I pulled her to the edge of the bed and shoved my face back between her legs.

She gasped, which turned into a laugh followed by a moan.

I chuckled against her swollen flesh. I made sure to be careful. I had already fucked her twice and given her a handful of orgasms, but I found that I needed to still kiss the pain away.

"God." She latched onto my hair, pulling me even closer. She was greedy, hungry for everything I had to give her, and I found I wanted to explore all of this newfound pleasure with her. And only her. My stomach twisted, unsure as to where these new feelings were coming from but at that point, I didn't care. Not liked it mattered anyway.

"Tanner," she whimpered, tightening her hold on my head and forcing my tongue deeper inside her.

My cock lengthened even more, threatening to explode right then and there.

"Please." Her hips thrust up and down, fucking her body on my tongue.

That tiny subtle movement forced a growl from the back of my throat. Cupping her thighs, I pushed her legs apart even more.

Her breathing picked up, her nails dug into my head, and her moans became even louder.

Replacing my tongue with a finger, I slowly slid it into her and gave her clit a hard lick.

She gasped, her dark eyes shooting to mine.

"Come hard for me, baby," I whispered, sliding a second finger into her.

She nodded, chewing her bottom lip.

"Does that hurt?" I asked, not wanting to make the pain worse.

"No."

"Good." I kissed the spot above her clit. "I need to get you prepped for my cock again." I winked.

"I don't know if I can handle any more."

I smirked, glancing down at my fingers disappearing into her body. "You can. I'll make sure of it."

Her thighs trembled, her breathing picking up the longer time went on. She was close, on the verge of breaking for me.

"Tanner," she moaned.

"That's it, beautiful girl." Rubbing my thumb along her clit, I slid a third finger into her, watching the sweet juices from her body, coat them.

"Please, baby, God."

I chuckled.

"Faster," she whispered.

My eyes snapped to hers.

She nodded, chewing her bottom lip. "Please."

Pumping my hand against her hard, I watched her eyes roll into the back of her head. Her body trembled, my name leaving her lips on a soft cry.

Before she could come down from her high, I shoved my face back against her center and drank up the rest of her orgasm.

(Bee)

Tanner was back inside me. I no longer knew what time it was nor did I care. He had the meeting with Uncle Greyson that morning and we hadn't left my bedroom since. It must have been some time in the evening. Maybe even later. Spending the day with Tanner felt right and I wouldn't have asked for it to happen any other way.

He held my hands above my head, keeping his lips on mine. His thrusts were slow, deep, and powerful. Much like the man who had invaded my life from the very first moment I met him. I wasn't sure why or even how, but I knew that we had met when we needed it most. Even though I had a good life and grew up with more family and love than I could ever imagine, it had never been enough. I wasn't sure why. But I knew deep down in my soul that Tanner was what I needed. Even if whatever this was never amounted to more, I would always be grateful for him.

"Busy," he murmured against my mouth, pulling me from my thoughts.

I pulled a hand from his grasp and cupped his cheek.

"Is it better?"

"Yes," I whispered.

"Fuck, baby." He leaned his forehead against mine. "You're so damn wet."

"You took care of me," I told him, lifting my hips. "All day you took care of me."

He slid into me deeper than before. A shudder rippled through him. "I'm an asshole but I don't want to hurt you."

"You're not an asshole." I kissed his chin. "Not to me."

"That's because you don't judge me." He wrapped his arms around me and moved us to the edge of the bed. "And you don't try and change me either."

"Never." My body slid down the length of him. "As long as you're good to me, Tanner, nothing else matters."

"I'll be good to you, Busy." He gave my chin a gentle nip. "I'll always be good to you."

TWENTY ONE

Bee

IT WAS AWKWARD NOW and I wasn't sure why. I was sitting on the edge of my bed, waiting for something extravagant to happen and I was almost disappointed when it didn't.

Tanner moved beside me, taking my hand in his. "Talk to me."

I met Tanner's gaze. I realized then that even though he wasn't much of a talker himself, he liked it when I did. But for once in my life, I really had no idea what to say. What did people do after losing their virginity? Continue having sex?

"What's wrong?" Tanner asked, his voice soft but deep. His hand engulfed mine, his calloused thumb brushing back and forth along the side of my hand.

"I don't know," I confessed. "I feel like this is goodbye. Or that something's going to happen, and I won't see you for a while." I realized then that those words were the truth and that was what my problem was. I was getting so used to having him around that if it were to change, it would hurt.

He looked down at our joined hands.

"I'm right." I turned my body toward him. "Aren't I?"

"I need answers. For myself and for your family. For Sunny's baby. I didn't have much growing up, Busy. But I want to be able to give that to Shade and Meadow at least."

My heart swelled that he would want to do that for someone he didn't know and for people who thought so little of him.

We had spent the day together, wrapped in each other's arms. I had gone to the kitchen at one point to grab us some food but other than that, we never left my bed.

"All of the rumors about you are bad ones." I paused. "Are there any good ones?"

"No one wants to hear about the good shit, Busy." Tanner moved to the head of the bed, patting the spot beside him.

I joined him and leaned my head against his shoulder.

"I've worked hard at getting to where I am," he said, resting his arm across my lap. "I'm not proud of most of the things I've done but unfortunately for me, a lot of it, I really had no choice."

Curling my hand around his bicep, I soaked up his words when he usually didn't say much. I decided right then and there that I would never take moments like this for granted.

"We used to deal with this bastard who made us a lot of money. Mostly weapons but sometimes sex was involved. I never took part in that." He cleared his throat. "Anyway." He cleared his throat again.

I had come to realize that he did that whenever he was talking about something that made him uncomfortable.

"I was sitting at his desk. My guys at the time, stood behind me. He had some men of his own. There were a lot of us in the small office. I remember hearing a scratch at the door. I don't know if anyone else heard it or if they were just ignoring it but I went to check it out and..." He swallowed hard. "There was a beautiful but broken and bloody female pit bull staring up at me. She was supposed to be white, but she was so fucking caked in dirt and grime and dried blood, that she looked brown."

"Oh God," I gasped.

"I remember crouching and running my hand down her back, making sure not to touch any parts that looked painful. Which was most of her, I'm sure. Busy, she..." His voice cracked.

I lifted my head, cupping his hand that was on my inner thigh.

"She was used for breeding. I had heard of that shit on the news but never seen it in person. The fucker laughed about it and told us that he had a breeding rack and he would get the other dogs worked up to the point they would attack her." He shook his head, sitting up and pinched the bridge of his nose. "She licked my hand. It's something I'll never forget. I remember running my hand over her, trying to show her some form of affection, even if it was just a little bit. I wanted her to know that not every human was a monster."

My eyes welled, my throat working over a hard lump.

"She sighed when I scratched behind her ears. When she laid down at my feet, she died almost instantly. She just wanted that one gentle touch before she took her last breath. I told her I would avenge her. I know a lot of people think they're just dogs, but they are the only things that have never hurt me." Tanner's gaze locked with mine, hard and determined much like the man sitting beside me.

Tears rolled down my cheeks at what he was telling me.

"My crew at the time didn't know what was going on with me. Someone had thought it was funny when she died but I killed that fucker. I killed him and laughed. That's who you lost your virginity to, Busy. That's who you just spent the day with. Me. A monster. A killer. I'm just as bad as him."

"No, you're not." I held onto him, pushing my face into the crook of his neck.

His breathing wavered.

"What happened to the bastard who organized it?"

"We stopped doing business with him and I had him killed. I actually fed him to his dogs."

My head snapped back. "You did?"

Tanner nodded. "I think that's what started this whole thing. My crew probably thought I was unstable. Because again, they're just dogs, right? But I paid for the dogs to get the care they needed and the ones that survived, I made sure to get them adopted out to good homes as well. Some of them had to be put down though. They were just too far gone with their injuries."

"I'm so sorry." I wiped under my eyes. "How did you get Trigger?"

"I found him in the alley by my apartment." His shoulders slumped. "He didn't trust me at first and I didn't trust him either, but we needed each other."

I realized then that Tanner was just like Trigger and the other dogs he had saved. He was built to fight and destroy but it didn't mean it was all that he was. Just like the pit bulls and every other dog out there, with the right person, those dogs were loyal, loving, and beautiful. Just like Tanner was with me. There was something about him from the very beginning that I didn't realize I needed until now. He just needed that gentle, loving touch like the dog who died in his arms.

Tanner looked at me then.

My breath caught in my throat.

So much pain and heartache swam behind his dark eyes. He had been shoved aside by so many, shunned by society and had a bad reputation just like pit bulls.

I cupped his cheek, running my thumb over his bottom lip.

Nothing else was said as we sat there staring at each other.

He leaned toward me, placed the softest peck on my forehead, and pulled me into his arms. His hands ran up my back, hugging me tight.

"I'm here, Tanner," I whispered, running my fingers through the hair at his nape. "I'm not going anywhere. Ever."

A shuddered breath left him. "Promise?"

I swallowed past the lump in my throat. "Yes, I promise, baby," I told him, my voice cracking.

He grabbed my hands, bringing them up to his mouth. His shook, indicating the vulnerability rushing through him. I knew that I had been the only one he ever let see this side of him. It didn't matter to me what he had done before. He was a survivor. Even though he felt like a monster, maybe to some he was, but to me, he was my monster. I didn't need a hero. I needed a man who would fight for me, protect me, and love me. I was always partial to the villains in movies and books. Most of the time, they were just misunderstood much like the man sitting in front of me.

"Tanner?"

His deep blue eyes met mine, holding so many questions.

"I…" I braced myself. "I think I'm falling in love with you. Maybe it's not love. But it's definitely feelings I've never felt before. I know this is fast but I—"

In a quick move, he cupped the back of my head, holding it in place. "Say that again."

"This is fast?" I repeated, staring at him with wide eyes.

"No." His nostrils flared. "The part before that."

"I think I'm falling in love with you. In fact…" I gave him a small smile. "I know I have."

He let out a slow breath. "I think I've been in love with you from the moment I almost died in your backyard."

"What?" I gasped. "Are you serious?"

"I saw you. You were breathtaking. I watched you with a glass of wine in your hand. You looked like something was wrong, but I never asked once we finally met. I should have asked. I'm sorry I didn't."

"That's okay." I cupped his cheek. "Nothing was wrong really. The twins had ruined my night and made me leave the club early. But I'm glad they did. Who knows what would have happened to you if I hadn't been home." I paused. "You were brought to me for a reason."

"No, you were given to *me* for a reason." He kissed my nose. "I've never been in love. I wasn't even looking for it. Because I knew that people didn't do it for me. I just wasn't interested. And then we met, and I couldn't focus on anything but having you near me. Not just for sex. That's an added bonus but it wasn't what I was thinking of. I just needed to touch you. Hold you. Be with you. You calmed me, baby. You still do."

I ran my fingers through his dark hair.

"You keep me sane. You're the only one who has seen this side of me." He lifted his hand. It shook, trembling in tune with the anxiety I knew rushed through him.

I grabbed his hand and brought it up to my mouth, placing a soft peck on his palm. "Thank you for trusting me enough to show me this side of you."

"I don't know how this happened. This probably means a war as well. This...what we have, is dangerous, Busy. You deserve so much more than my run-down body and broken soul." Tanner cupped my face, placing the softest peck on my mouth.

My eyes fluttered closed, embracing the feeling of being this close to him. "This might be dangerous like you say." I looked him square in the eye. "But it doesn't mean that it's not meant to be. When my dad finds out, he'll see reason. Everyone will." I looked at the man who hadn't left my side from the moment I saved his life. Besides the time he was in the basement and I was in a different part of the house or working or at my parents' place, we were always together.

"You deserve more."

I huffed. "You keep telling me that but I'm never going to believe you, Tanner."

"Baby." His jaw ticked. "I want what's best for you."

"You, Tanner." I grabbed onto his black hoodie, pulling him against me. "You are what's best for me. I don't care what anyone thinks."

"Yes, you do. They're you're family."

"No." I pushed away from him then, suddenly feeling cold as I slid out of his embrace. "I didn't know who you were when we met. I didn't know that you were once the president of a dangerous motorcycle club. Just like you didn't know that I'm the daughter to Tray Lister. Someone who spent years being a nomad because he could never settle down. Even he felt like he never truly belonged. Not until he met my mom." I knew the stories and the rumors going around about my father. Most weren't true but a lot of them were. Like Tanner, he just couldn't be bothered to correct people. "I love you, Tanner. There's something inside of you that I need. And it's not because you are the first guy to stand up to my family. It's because you may be broken and withdrawn, but I know you love me back."

"Of course I love you back. I wouldn't say those words if I didn't mean them." Tanner took a step toward me. "I needed Trigger in ways that I never knew I needed. His old soul calmed me, but you keep me sane. You've stopped me from giving up and jumping off that ledge so many times. I know we haven't known each other for long." He closed the distance between us then. "And I'm sure there are better guys out there for you, ones who aren't so fucked up, but I promise that if you do want this to continue, I won't make you regret it."

I latched onto him then, pulling him against me. I never wanted to let go. I wanted him to see that he was worthy of love and a family. That he was worthy of me while I was worthy of him just the same.

"This is still dangerous," he muttered into my hair.

"Maybe so." I leaned back. "I'll go to war for you."

"You'll be at my side, baby?" he asked, his voice soft and unsure.

"No. I'll fight the fucking war *for* you."

A dark shadow passed over his face. "I'm not a good guy, Busy."

I cupped his cheek, the scratchiness of his beard tickling across my palm.

He pushed his cheek into my hand, his eyes fluttering closed.

Placing a soft peck on his mouth, I breathed him in. "I don't care."

His eyes popped open then. "But you should. The things I've done…If the right person found out, I could go to jail for a long time, if not for the rest of my life."

Bile rose to my throat at the mere idea of him being taken from me when I had only just found him. "No one will find out." I cupped his face, forcing him to look at me. "And what you did before me, you did it to survive."

He looked away.

"I mean it." I kissed him softly on the mouth.

"Why do you love me?" he murmured, leaning his forehead against mine. "Is it because I'm the only guy who isn't scared of your father?"

"You haven't even met my father yet." I leaned back. "Have you?"

"No."

"Then, do you think that little of me that I would only be attracted to you, lose my virginity to you, fall in love with you, just because you can stand up to the men in my life?"

"What?" Tanner scowled. "No. Shit, baby. Never."

"Then I need you to believe that even if we would have met differently and I didn't have scary men in my life, that we would still end up together. No matter what. And besides, my father was nowhere around when I first met you. Remember?"

Tanner sighed, his shoulders slumping.

"You do remember that, don't you?"

Tanner's gaze slowly met mine. "I do. I remember how determined you were to save my life. A stranger. I could have hurt you. And yet, you let me into your home. It's a wonder your father or anyone else in your family, hasn't killed me yet."

I huffed, pulling away from him.

"No." Tanner reached out for me, tugging me back into his arms. "I just mean...hell, I don't know what I mean anymore."

"Listen to me." I pushed him back toward the edge of the bed.

He sat, staring up at me.

BEING US

I straddled his lap, wrapping myself around him. I had learned rather quickly that it was the only way to keep him calm and grounded. He needed that physical touch. He had told me that Trigger had done the same for him. He kept the voices at bay but with me, my touch, did more than that. They put the demons at ease and silenced them. Not completely but enough that he could go through his day-to-day activities without lashing out at random. I never understood that when we hadn't known each other for long but if what he said was true, I would make sure to touch him as much as I could.

"I love you." I ran my fingers through the hair at the back of his neck. "Sure, we may have met unconventionally but I believe everything happens for a reason. And I don't care what anyone says. The men in my life, the men I've looked up to since I was a little girl, are not perfect. So they can get off their high and mighty thrones. Besides, they're not the ones sleeping with you."

Tanner smirked, running his hands up and down my thighs. "I don't deserve you." He kissed my chin. "I don't deserve any part of you. Not your heart. Not your love. Not your body." His mouth moved down the length of my jaw to my ear. His hands roamed beneath my shirt. "But I promise to make you the happiest I possibly can."

My heart stuttered. "I like the sound of that."

TWENTY TWO

Bee

I**T HAD BEEN A** few days since Tanner and I spent the day in my bed.

Tommy hadn't called again. He never even tried showing up. A part of me wondered if he only made the threat just to put Uncle Greyson and the rest of the guys on edge.

One night after everyone had retired for the evening, I slipped into the basement. Seeing Tanner now after having sex, was almost like I was hiding a delicious secret. In this case, I was. It was scary and exciting.

When I reached the den, I saw him sitting on the chaise, watching a movie. He looked my way, a wide grin spreading on his handsome face.

"Hi." I sat beside him.

He pulled me into his arms, snuggling his face into my neck and letting out a soft purr. "Hi."

I giggled, cupped his face, and kissed him hard on the mouth.

"Hmm..." Tanner ran his thumb along my collarbone, pushing it beneath the strap of my tank top. "I missed you."

"You saw me this morning." My body still burned from the way he had woken me up.

"Doesn't matter." He pulled the strap off my shoulder and down my arm. "I was thinking." He looked down at my chest. "I've told you things that no one else knows." He lowered the tank top, revealing my breast. Licking his lips, he stared as his thumb brushed over my dark nipple.

"What about your friend? Rowan?" I asked, breathless.

"He knows I'm fucked up but no details. I'm not even sure I'd consider him a friend. He's just...there."

"Sounds like a friend to me." My chest tightened, my heart hurting over the fact that there was no one who Tanner could trust. "We're friends."

Tanner's gaze snapped to mine. "I'm in love with you."

"Yeah. But we're still friends."

He cupped my breast, lifting it in his large hand. "I think we've moved past the friends part, baby." He lowered his mouth to my nipple before I had a chance to respond.

I sighed, arching against him. "Have you been waiting for me to come downstairs for this?"

He hummed, lapping at the sharp peak. "I've been hard all afternoon, waiting for you."

Getting a moment of clarity, I cupped the sides of his head. "Cameras, Tanner. Someone could be watching."

"Nah. I actually searched this room and haven't found any. Your Uncle Catch was bluffing. You never answered my question though."

"What question?" My mind was reeling over the possibility that maybe Tanner was right and that there were no cameras at all.

"Don't you agree that we've moved past just being friends?" Tanner asked, pulling the tank top lower until both of my breasts were uncovered.

"Maybe," I whispered, watching him.

He cupped the heavy mounds, pushing them together and sinking his teeth into the flesh. "Do you not agree, Busy? I'm in love with you. You're in love with me. That means we're more than friends."

My mind was a mess as he devoured my breasts. I couldn't think. I couldn't comprehend any normal thought as he bit and sucked, licked and nipped.

"God." I arched against him.

"Tell me, baby. Are we friends? Lovers? Something else?"

"We're friends. God, we're friends. Lovers. More. So much more."

He chuckled, pushed me back, and started trailing light feathery kisses down my torso. Hooking his hand under my thigh, he pushed my knee toward my chest and spread me open.

I was wearing shorts but I was sure he could see how much of an effect he had on me and my body. I wasn't wearing any panties beneath the thin fabric either.

"I can smell you, Busy," he said, his voice hoarse.

I laid back on my elbows, watching him.

"Are you wet for me?"

I nodded quickly.

"So if I swiped my tongue between your thighs, I would taste your cream?"

I swallowed hard. "Yes."

"Take these off." He tapped my hip. "And show me your pretty pussy."

"Take me to your—" Before I could finish the sentence, Tanner jumped to his feet and pulled me from the couch. Tossing me over his shoulder, he charged for his room. He kicked the door closed and tossed me on the bed.

"Now do as I said," he demanded.

Pushing the shorts down and off my legs, I threw them over the edge of the bed.

"Hmm…" His eyes fell to my center. "Look at how swollen your clit is. Maybe I've been too rough."

I followed his gaze. "Never."

He came toward the edge of the bed and grabbed my ankles, pulling me toward him. He placed a soft peck on my hip bone, brushing his thumb over my clit. "A wonder how fast you could come if I keep doing this."

I laughed lightly. "Keep doing that and we'll find out."

He grinned, running his thumb back and forth ever so slightly.

A shiver trembled through me. "God, Tanner."

He kissed my knee. "You're perfect."

I smiled, running my fingers through his hair. "I'm not."

"You are. For me."

My breath caught.

But before he could take it further, I pushed away from him and stripped completely, baring every inch of me to his feasting eyes once again.

In a quick move, Tanner pulled me under him and flipped me onto my stomach.

He sunk his teeth into the base of my neck, his free hand landing a hard swat on my ass.

My body heated.

He shoved me forward, pushing me face first onto the mattress. Keeping a firm hold on the back of my neck, he thrust into me.

I cried out, my body stretching to meet his glorious size that I could never get used to.

He grunted, digging his fingers into my hips and powering into me with so much strength, pleasure shot up the length of my spine.

"Tanner," I whined, not expecting this new side of him but enjoying it just the same.

"Fuck, baby." He towered over me, resting his weight on top of me and holding my head in place.

"Please, Tanner. I need you to move."

He kissed my cheek, linking our fingers and slamming his pelvis against the seat of my ass. "So fucking good."

I whimpered, my legs shaking as a fast but powerful release crashed into me.

He grunted his approval, picking up speed with his hips until I was gasping for breath.

"Please." I was greedy for him. For his touch, his strength but his love even more.

"What do you want?" he asked, his voice low.

"Harder," I whined. "Please fuck me harder."

"That's my good girl." He pulled almost all the way out before slamming back into me.

I shoved the blanket between my lips and bit down.

He chuckled. "Bite it hard, Busy, because I'm not stopping."

I released the blanket, gasping for breath. "Don't stop. Don't ever stop."

He dug his fingers into the cheek of my ass, spreading me open and thrusting hard and deep. "Never, baby. I'll never stop."

TWENTY THREE

Bee

THE SOUND OF THE door opening, sent a shiver tracing down my spine. I was curled on my side, my back facing away from the door. A few nights had passed since Tanner used me good and hard and showed me just how rough he liked it. He had been taking the risk and joining me in bed ever since. Knowing he needed it, I never pushed him away and welcomed him with open arms instead.

A moment later, the bed dipped behind me. A heavy arm wrapped around my middle, followed by a soft kiss to the side of my neck.

Tanner sighed, threw his leg over mine, and held me close.

"Better?"

"You have no idea." He inched his hand beneath my tank top and cupped my breast. It wasn't sexual in the least, but it reminded me how much he needed that human touch. It was like a newborn baby needing skin to skin contact. It was a way to bond with their parent. Was that how it was for Tanner and I? Did it help us bond? Was that a thing once you were past that newborn stage? I wasn't sure but I knew that I would never turn him down for needing to touch me.

"Talk to me."

He sighed again, a low rumble leaving him. It almost sounded like a purr. "We met when we probably shouldn't have. It was unconventional. You saved my life. And even though I know that being together is dangerous for both of us, I like this. I need this actually."

"Tell me why," I whispered, my eyes fluttering closed.

"You calm me in ways I never knew was possible. You keep me grounded and out of my head. You help the rage inside of me simmer." He tightened his hold on me, brushing his mouth just below my ear.

I shivered, pushing my ass into his waist.

His cock, heavy and proud, sat against me. But he never hinted for more. No. He never did when he came to me during the night. I often wondered if sex would help him feel better. But I never asked. I found that I liked this instead. I never had a boyfriend before, so I wasn't overly sure if this was what it was like. The constant touching. The need for the other person, growing with each passing day. I missed him when he wasn't around and I craved him even more when he was.

"How has everyone been treating you?"

"As good as can be expected," he said, his voice low.

"Your nightmares." Every time he came to me during the night, I could feel his heart racing when he curled up against me.

BEING US

Tanner released me and sat up, leaning against the headboard. He ran a hand over his head, through his hair to the back of his neck. He was nervous. He didn't want to tell me, but I could see the weight of his demons resting on his shoulders. We had become closer. I loved him and I knew that he loved me, but we still had so much to learn about each other. He always looked for me, making sure I was close or better yet, at his side. There was something between us that both of us needed.

While I came from a good childhood and had a family who loved me endlessly, something had always been missing. Until I met Tanner, I didn't know what that was. Now that I did, I wasn't letting it go. No matter the cost.

"Hey." I sat beside him, took his hand in mine, and placed a soft peck on his shoulder.

"After my mom died, I went to live with my aunt and uncle. Even though they were technically family, they were far from it. It was fine at first. They yelled a bit. But I was a kid and I had lost my mom. My dad didn't want me. So I got into trouble. A lot. When I got older, around fifteen or so, that's when the shit really started happening." He blew out a shaky breath.

I squeezed his hand, trying with everything I could to give him all the courage he needed to let it out.

Tanner looked at me then. "He raped me, Busy. Repeatedly."

(Tanner)

Telling Busy what had happened to me, brought me back to that dark time in my childhood. A time that no child should ever have to go through. Even though I had been fifteen when it started, I was still a boy.

I could see the anguish in Busy's gaze but what I expected to see that wasn't there, threw me off.

Pity.

Everyone pitied but she didn't. Empathized, sure. But not pity.

"Tanner," she whispered, her voice cracking.

"He would come to me at night," I told her. "It hurt at first. He was a big guy and I was tiny for my age." I closed my eyes, pinching the bridge of my nose. "I...I eventually expected it. Waited for it. I fucking craved it. I wasn't wanted. My mom died. My dad tossed me aside like trash. My aunt didn't care what happened to me. She only took me in to make herself look good. My uncle?" I chuckled, shaking my head.

"Tanner, what happened wasn't right."

"I know." I looked at Busy then.

Concern was etched all over her beautiful face.

I cupped her cheek, brushing my thumb along her bottom lip. "It's funny 'cause he wasn't even gay. He had whores on the side. My aunt knew but she never said anything. You want to know what she did say though? She found out that her husband was fucking a kid and get this shit, she was jealous."

Busy gasped, clapping a hand over her mouth. "What? You were just a boy."

"Yup. And she blamed me for all of it."

"God, baby." Busy's chin wobbled, her eyes welling. She grabbed my hand, holding it tight in both of hers.

"I trusted them to take care of me. My mom trusted them. Her fucking sister and brother in-law. I should have been thrown in the system. It probably would have been better." I pulled away from her and slid off the bed, needing to move. I needed to hit something or go for a run.

"What happened after that?" Busy asked, her voice small.

"I knew it was wrong. What he was doing. But it eventually got to the point where I craved it." I waited, expecting to see Busy's face morph into disgust and when it didn't, I let out a sigh of relief. "I can't explain it. Maybe I'll never be able to. But I was desperate for attention. I was willing to get it from anywhere."

Busy stood from the bed and came toward me. She placed her hands on my chest, looking up at me. "So you were willing to do anything to get it?"

I nodded. "Not at first though. It wasn't consensual in the least in the beginning but…after a while…it's like I had Stockholm Syndrome or some shit." I rubbed the back of my neck.

"God, Tanner." She shook her head. "I can't imagine what you went through. Did he ever get caught?"

My stomach twisted.

Pain. Anguish. Fear.

"My aunt walked in us one night. She lost it and took a fire poker to me. She beat me with it until I finally escaped."

Busy stiffened. "Are you serious? Who does that?"

"She did. I went to the basement and hid. But what's fucked up is when I went back upstairs to see if she had calmed down, they were having sex. In the very bed her husband just finished fucking me in. It was sick. Probably more twisted than what my uncle had done to me." I shook my head, bile rising to my throat. "Something inside of me snapped. I went to the garage and grabbed a can of gas. Brought it back to their room while they were in the middle of fucking and…I lit them on fire."

"They deserved it," Busy said, her voice firm.

"I'm a monster," I murmured.

"No." She pushed away from me. "What they did to you wasn't right. You were a kid. You were impressionable."

"Doesn't make what I did any better, Busy." I pulled her back into my arms. "But I'm not sorry for what I did. They were horrible people."

She turned around, facing me. "Exactly. They got what they deserved. Maybe the way you did it wasn't best but…" She shrugged. "Oh well."

"Oh well?" I gaped at her. "How can you say that?"

"I don't like people who hurt animals and children."

I think I just fell in love with her more. "Most people don't, baby."

"But that's just it. I would have made them suffer a bit," she added softly.

I sighed, realizing I'd just met my match. "I love you."

She poked me in the chest. "And I love you. Don't let those demons tell you any different. Or I'll kick their asses. Got me?"

"Yeah." I placed a hard peck on her mouth. "I got you."

But it still didn't mean that I should have done what I did. No matter how much my aunt and uncle deserved what they got, it wasn't right.

Later that night, while Busy slept soundlessly beside me, I stared up at the ceiling, wondering how in the hell I got someone like her to fall in love with me. I would probably never find out the answer. Instead, I would make it so Busy never fell *out* of love with me. I would be the best I could be.

For her.

TWENTY FOUR

TANNER

THINGS WERE QUIET AND it made me uneasy. After Greyson revealed the video, I hadn't seen or heard from him since. I feared leaving the bedroom I was staying in, not knowing what would happen if I did. No one came to collect me. Not even the twins. I wasn't sure why. It was like the calm before the storm. As cliché as it sounded, it was the only thing that could explain the absolute silence. I didn't even hear any footsteps above me like I did when I first got to the large house.

I didn't know how many days had passed since I spent the first day fucking Busy. I had been going to her ever since. Every chance I had; I was in her arms. If I wasn't, she was coming to my room. She would crawl under the covers, push her naked body up against mine and calm the rage burning through me. I would make love to her, sometimes it would be fucking, and then I would fall asleep holding her. Sometimes we fell asleep while I was still inside her. The connection I shared with her was overpowering. It controlled my actions until all I cared about was putting a smile on her face. Keeping her happy was more important to me than finding out what Tommy wanted.

But even though that little fact was very well and true, it still pissed me off that everyone had been quiet.

I had read the same book at least four times before I'd had enough and slammed it down on the nightstand. I was about to leave the room and storm upstairs in search of Greyson when the door opened.

Busy stepped into the room, shutting the door behind her.

All breath left my lungs at the mere sight of her.

She gave me a small smile, blowing a loose curl out of her eyes. "Hi."

"Hi, beautiful."

Her smile grew.

I slid off the bed and went to her.

"How are you?" she asked, taking a step toward me.

Closing the distance between us, I pulled her into my arms and wrapped myself around her.

"What's wrong?" she asked, not waiting for me to answer her first question. "You're shaking."

"Something's wrong. I can—"

The door suddenly slammed open, revealing a man I had never seen before.

Busy jumped, spinning around. "Daddy?"

Daddy? Oh, fuck me.

I had never met Tray Lister before. I hadn't even seen what he looked like. He was smaller compared to Greyson and even the twins, but he was still bigger than I was. Tattoos lined the sides of his neck, disappearing beneath the collar of his black long-sleeved shirt.

BEING US

Nomad sat on a patch on his leather cut. I had heard that he was no longer a nomad though. Must have been there as a reminder to where he came from.

"What are you doing here?" Busy asked him, completely ignoring the fact that he was staring directly at me. Red faced and breathing heavy, he looked like he was ready to pounce. But I stood my ground. I loved his daughter. I didn't give a shit who he was. I wasn't backing down without a fight.

"Dad," Busy repeated, firmer that time. "What's going on?"

"I didn't want to believe it, but I was told you were here. And you." He glared down at his daughter.

She glared right back, placing her hands on her hips, staring up at him defiantly. "I'm an adult."

"I don't give a shit if you're eighty years old. What the hell are you doing and with him of all people?" he demanded, thrusting his arm out toward me, his voice raising.

Busy laughed. She actually fucking laughed. "You can't honestly stand there and judge me for who I decide to be with. Do you remember grandpa telling you to stay away from mom?"

"I wish she wouldn't have told you that," he grumbled.

"She didn't have to. Grandpa told me." Busy moved to the spot in front of me, crossing her arms under her chest and staring her father down. "I love him."

A shiver raced down my spine at her confession. Even though I had heard her tell me it over and over, I never heard her tell someone else how she felt about me.

"You love him," Tray repeated. He was the one to laugh that time.

"Alright, listen," I blurted, shocked at myself that I had butted in. When Tray and Busy both looked my way,

I went with it. "I came here asking for help. That's it." And fell in love in the process.

"Right. And you came here to take advantage of my daughter too." Tray took a step toward me.

"Oh yeah. That's my thing. Didn't you know that? I make nice with the president of clubs, weasel my way into their house and fuck the youngest female living with them." I feigned a yawn. "I've now added Busy to my ever-growing list."

"Tanner."

I ignored Busy and went toe-to-toe with her father. "I'm sick of this shit. I'm not getting any answers. So do your thing, Tray. Or have you become a pussy as you've gotten older? I heard you used to do some pretty wild shit. Makes me look like one of the good guys."

"Stop this." Busy pushed between her dad and I, placing her hand on my chest. "Back up, Tanner."

"I'm sorry," I told her gently.

She sighed. "You good?"

I was now.

She turned back to her dad. "And you. You need to stop this."

"Oh, I haven't done anything yet." Tray left the room and came back a second later with a baseball bat.

"Dad, seriously!" Busy grabbed the bat from him and threw it on the bed. "Both of you. Out." She pointed at the door. "Now!"

Tray smirked but did as he was told.

I felt like I was dealing with someone my own age and not someone who was old enough to be my father. But if I had a daughter and she was sleeping with the enemy, I would have reacted the same way. I just wasn't going to tell him that.

"This is ridiculous," Busy said just as Greyson came down the stairs followed by Catch and the twins. "Uncle Greyson, tell him."

"Tell him what exactly?" Greyson asked her.

"That he's being crazy and unreasonable." She turned to me. "He is. Ignore him. I've never had a boyfriend before, so he's acting weird."

But I knew. This was it. And there was not a damn thing I could do about it. Not when Catch moved to my left and Sammy moved to my right. Not when Shade came down the stairs and joined our little party. Cyrus walked past us and went into the room I had been living in for almost two months.

When he came back a few minutes later, he shook his head.

Greyson stepped in front of me. "Did you tell her?"

"I told her about the video." But that was it. It was too dangerous to tell her anything else.

"What's going on?" I heard Busy ask but all I could do was stare at a man who had taken me in. Who had given me a roof over my head and helped put food in my stomach. But as his deep blue eyes peered into mine, it made me uneasy. But I refused to look away. I needed him to see that I would win this fight. For Busy. Not for myself but for her. She let me into her heart when she didn't have to. I owed her.

"You're not so scary, are you?" Greyson murmured.

I wasn't sure exactly what he wanted to know or even what he was getting at. But no matter what they wanted; I couldn't do it. Not in front of Busy. "Take her out of here."

"What?" She gasped. "No! You can't."

"Do it," Greyson demanded.

"No! Tanner." She rushed to me, pushing her uncle back and I knew it was only because he let her. "What are you doing?"

I looked down at her then.

Her cheeks were flushed, her eyes wide and unsure. She was scared. For me. For what her family was capable of.

"Don't be scared Busy," I told her softly. "Everything will be fine."

"You don't know that." She latched onto my hoodie, pushing her face against my chest.

I circled an arm around her shoulders, holding her against me. "Whatever you do to me, don't tell her," I told Greyson. I didn't want her having those memories of her family doing something evil and depraved. She trusted these men and if they did what I knew they had been wanting to do all along, this would be a side of them that she would never be able to get over.

She sobbed, holding me tight.

Busy knew just as much as I did that her family could end me. They loved her and looked out for her, but this was bigger than the both of us.

"Promise me," I grit out, holding her against me. "Greyson, damnit. Promise me!"

He looked down at his niece and back up to me.

"Grey." Tray went up to his president, muttering something in his ear.

Greyson nodded. "Fine. I promise."

As soon as those words left his mouth, I shoved Busy away, pushed her out of my arms, and charged into the bedroom.

Muttered curses sounded but I knew that I had at least half a minute before all hell broke loose.

"What the fuck?" someone demanded, the sound of a gun being cocked, flowed into my ears and sent a hot tingle racing down my spine.

Alright, boys. It's time to fucking play.

I jumped over the bed, landing hard on the floor with a thud. I reached under the top mattress and pulled out two pistols. Making sure the bullets were secure in the chamber, I clicked the safety off on both before pushing to my feet. I scratched my temple with the end of one of the guns, waiting for the guys to file into the room.

Greyson came into the room first. "Where the hell did you get guns? Weapons are not free for all here. We have them locked up tight in case someone like you gets your hands on them."

I chuckled. "I have my ways." I took a breath, aiming both guns directly at Greyson. "You're going to let me leave. Aren't you?"

"You came here, asking for my fucking help, Tanner. I should have killed you when I had the chance. What the hell are you *doing*?" He rose a hand when Catch came in with a gun aimed directly at me. "Tell me what you want."

"Busy," I barked.

Catch muttered a curse.

"You asked what I wanted," I reminded Greyson. "I want her to come in here."

"Fuck." Greyson stepped aside and nodded to Catch.

He moved, still keeping his gun aimed at me.

Busy peeked into the room. "Tanner, you...I don't know what's going on right now," she said, her voice strained.

"I need you to come here and get something out of my pocket," I told her.

"No," Tray argued.

"Trust me, old man. I don't want to hurt your daughter. As much as you all think I'm a monster, I *am* actually in love with her. She's the only good thing in my life, so I'm not about to fuck that up."

"That's just it." Tray's brows narrowed. "I don't fucking trust you."

"But I do." Busy pushed past her father and came into the room. "Which pocket?" she asked, closing the distance between us.

"Right one."

She reached into the pocket of my jeans and pulled out a gold ring along with a piece of paper. She held up the ring between her fingers. "It's pretty but I don't know what you want me to do with it."

"There's numbers engraved on the inside of it. It's an account number. The bank information is on the piece of paper," I explained. "Everything in it, is yours."

Her head snapped up. "Really? Why?"

"You know why, Busy."

She looked away, chewed her bottom lip, and slipped the ring onto her middle finger.

I wasn't stupid but I was observant. Especially when it came to her. We had only been sleeping together for just over a month. Long enough for things to happen and for her to miss her period. I saw the pregnancy test in the garbage. It wasn't like we had been safe at all, so I had a feeling that our first time together had gotten her pregnant.

My baby was inside her little body and because of that, what was mine, was hers. I never wanted the money anyway. It was just sitting there.

"I was waiting until we could go to the doctor's to confirm," she whispered.

"I figured as much." I bent at the waist and placed a soft peck on her cheek, not giving a shit that we were being watched. "They won't have to confirm anything though. I know my baby is in this tight little body," I said, low enough for only her to hear.

Her breath hitched.

We would talk about it later. I had questions that I needed answers to first and then I could spend the rest of my life with the woman I loved.

I wrapped an arm around her shoulders and kissed the top of her head. Even though I could feel the bodies shift that were standing in the doorway to the room, they could wait. "You trust me?"

She nodded, her eyes searching my face. "With my life."

"Good." I kissed her one last time, breathing her in. "I need you to be a good girl and go upstairs. Can you do that for me?"

She opened her mouth to argue but snapped her mouth shut instead. When her shoulders slumped in defeat, she pulled away from me and left the bedroom. Once she reached the bottom of the stairs, she turned back to me and blew me a kiss.

When she disappeared up the stairs, I took a step forward, suddenly needing her back.

"Careful." Greyson stepped in front of me. "You've lost your chance to play nice, Tanner. Now tell us what the fuck is going on."

"You need to let me leave," I said, aiming the gun at him again.

"Why now? Why not right when you got here or even before this?" he asked, closing the distance between us. "I know you won't shoot me. You wouldn't want to hurt Bee that way."

I swallowed hard. "I need answers. I can't sit here and wait anymore." As soon as I saw the pregnancy test, I made a vow to myself that no matter what the outcome was, I would leave and get the answers myself. I had been holed up for too damn long. Rowan did what he could, and I appreciated his help, but this was now on me.

"I need to leave. I need answers." I felt like a damn parrot.

"Why should we do that?" said Catch, asking the question that I was sure everyone was thinking.

"Because I'm not getting anywhere by staying here. I shouldn't have been here this long anyway." But I was and had fallen in love in the meantime. Who knew that a man like me would even be capable of such a thing?"

"And then you started sleeping with my daughter," Tray added.

"I didn't start sleeping with her when I first got here," I corrected him.

"But you wanted to," Sammy interjected. "I saw the way you looked at her. We all did."

"It doesn't matter. That shit is between Busy and I. No one else. I don't give a flying fuck who you are or what your relation to her is. What happens between us, stays between us." I raised both arms. "Now, are you going to let me leave or not?"

"Everyone, out, now!" Greyson's deep voice boomed through the small room.

"Grey, we're not leaving you in here with him." Catch nodded toward me. "The fucker's unstable."

Truth was, I had never felt more stable in my life. And Busy had everything to do with that little fact alone. It was all her. My emotions. My strength. My fucking power. It was because of Beatrix Lister. I didn't just love her. I breathed her. Lived for her. I was everything. For her. My feelings had come on hard and fast. Maybe it was because I had been alone for so long. Or the fact that she wasn't experienced. Either way, we would learn and explore together. Once I got the answers I was looking for, after all of this, I would take her out of here and build a life with her. Just us and our little family.

"Leave," Greyson repeated, coming around the bed and stepping directly in front of me. "He won't shoot me. He doesn't want to hurt Bee." He had said that twice. While that all may be true, if *he* hurt her, I would end him before he had a chance to hurt another. That was the only reason he was still standing. Because of Busy, it was the only reason I hadn't blown up the place yet.

I lowered my arms, dropping them at my sides. "I need answers."

"I know," he said gently. "Leave us," he told his crew. "I won't say it again."

The guys shuffled out of the room.

"And shut the damn door," Greyson ordered.

Sammy shut the door, doing as his president directed.

"Tanner."

"I need to leave," I murmured.

"How did you get the guns? One of my guys give them to you?"

I met Greyson's gaze then. "What do you want?"

"I want answers just like you do. I also don't want my niece getting hurt in the process. So, what are you doing to do, Tanner?"

Everything. I was going to do everything. And I didn't give a shit who I had to go through. I just prayed that I would see Busy again after this because if I didn't, then what was the point?

(Bee)

I was pacing.

Back. Forth. Back again.

I had slipped the ring I had taken from Tanner's pocket and put it on my middle finger of my right hand. I didn't know who it had belonged to. Or even what exactly was in the account. I could only assume it was money. A lot of money.

Also add to the fact that Tanner knew I was pregnant. Stupid me. Of course he did. It wasn't like I had gone out of my way to hide the pregnancy test. I wanted him to find it. I had imagined at the time how he would react. Would he be like some of the guys I had heard about and be turned on by it? Or would he be like the heroes in my romance books and become more of an Alpha male knowing their baby was in the woman they loved? When I thought about all the ways that he would react, nothing prepared me for how calm he had been. Maybe under different circumstances, he would have reacted the way I expected. Maybe he still would. But for now, all I could think about was keeping my baby safe and having Tanner back in my arms.

"Bee?"

I spun on my heel, finding my mom coming into the main area where the bar and tables were. Uncle Greyson had thrown get-togethers there quite often, I could still hear the noise from the last party and feel the music deep in my bones.

"Mom?" I rushed to her and threw myself into her arms.

"What's going on, sweetheart?" she asked, hugging herself around me.

"I don't know," I cried. "Something's wrong and I don't know how to fix it or what to do." My throat burned, my eyes welling with unshed tears. I just wanted to take Tanner and get out of there. But the other part of me, the rational part, knew that could never happen. Not until he got the answers he needed.

The door leading to the basement, opened with a bang, making both Mom and I jump.

Dad was first while the rest of the guys followed him into the room.

"Where's Tanner?" I asked, rushing toward Dad. I looked around him but didn't see Tanner or Uncle Greyson anywhere. "Daddy, please tell me where he is."

He looked down at me, that familiar tick in his jaw becoming more pronounced as time went on.

"Tray." Mom came up behind me. "What is it?"

"You should probably go to your room," he told me.

"No. What happened? What did Uncle Greyson do?" I gave Dad a shove when he wouldn't answer me. "Tell me!"

"Johnny, you need to calm down."

"Would you calm down?" I demanded, spinning on Cyrus.

Voices sounded around us, but I couldn't make out who was saying what. No one was giving me any answers. I feared the worst, unsure as to what exactly Uncle Greyson was capable of doing. I only knew that he would do anything to protect his family.

"Bee."

My head turned slowly as Aunt Eve and Aunt Sara came toward us.

"What's going on?" As soon as Aunt Eve asked the question, her husband came up the stairs from the basement.

Tanner followed behind him, his head bowed, his shoulders hunched.

"Tanner." I rushed to him.

His dark eyes met mine.

"Please talk to me. Tell me what's going on. Please." I continued asking the same question, but I still wasn't getting anywhere.

Tanner placed a soft peck on my forehead.

My breath caught, my eyes welling at the gentle touch coming from someone like him.

"I love you, Busy," he whispered. "I'll come back to you and our baby. I promise." He kissed my cheek, grazing the back of his hand over my lower stomach. "Wait for me, beautiful. Don't fucking stop waiting."

"Never," I said, my voice wavering.

"That's my good girl." He gave my hand a squeeze before stepping away from me. "So, how about that ride?"

"Where are you taking him?" I asked the twins as they followed Tanner out of the house, but they wouldn't answer me. "Uncle Greyson."

"Greyson," Aunt Eve said gently. "Where are the twins taking him?"

He looked between us both before coming up to me. "I need you to trust me." He cupped my face. "I know you have questions. I promise they'll get answered but I need you to have patience."

"Just tell me where he's going," I pleaded. "Please. That's all I want to know."

Uncle Greyson sighed. "Home, Bee. He's going home."

TWENTY FIVE

TANNER

I WAS VIBRATING. **ADRENALINE** rushed through me, giving me that strength I had taken advantage of from the very beginning. I had always known not all of the wires in my brain were crossed right but I never knew just how bad it was until that night.

Heat licked my skin, the glow from the fire in front of me, making the hairs on my small body, tingle.

The flames danced.

The screams died.

The smell of charred flesh burned into my lungs.

I grinned as I watched my aunt and uncle die at the hands of the fire I started.

My uncle had spent the better part of a year, raping me. While my aunt only beat me, she never stopped her husband from doing the unspeakable things he did. Even after she caught him on top of me.

It only made sense for them to die while fucking. Served them right.

"This isn't going to end well," Sammy said, pulling me from my thoughts. He stuck a smoke between his lips, lit it, and inhaled before blowing out large smoke circles.

"How do you know that?" Cyrus asked, his eyes flicking to mine in the rearview mirror before looking back out at the road in front of us.

"Just do. This fucker has enemies." Sammy nodded toward me.

I ignored them and went back to staring out the window. It had been a couple of hours since we left the Hell's Harlem clubhouse. We had been driving for a while and it was now later into the night. While most were getting ready for bed on this side of the world, others, like me, were only just starting their day.

"Do you have a plan, Tanner?" One of them asked but I wasn't sure who.

"Yeah, to get back to Busy." It was the only plan I cared to follow through on.

"We're here." Cyrus leaned forward, pulling the SUV down an alley and shutting off the headlights before the vehicle came to a complete stop. "I think we are, anyway."

"About fucking time," Sammy mumbled. "Are you sure this is the place?"

I took a breath, leaned my head from side to side, and let the crack that rippled through the tendons in my neck, slide over every inch of me. "Oh yeah."

Before the twins could ask any more questions, I jumped from the vehicle.

The driver's side window lowered. "You be safe. You have a girl to get back to."

I looked between Cyrus and Sammy and nodded.

BEING US

The instructions were that they would drop me off and leave. I didn't need something to happen to them. I had already caused enough trouble in their little world.

Knowing what I would have to do, I walked down the alley toward a large metal door that I had used so many times over the years, I lost count.

I looked behind me, no longer seeing the twins' SUV. Taking a breath and then another, I mentally counted to ten and told myself that I could do this. That I *had* to do this. Not just for me. But for Busy and our baby. For her family. For Meadow, Shade, and Sunny's baby. For all of them.

For the first time in my life, I no longer wished I was alone but used that to my advantage nonetheless.

Being at the club now, seeing it for the first time in months, left a sour taste in my mouth. Knowing the things that had been done beyond this door was far worse than what had been done to me as a boy. But it never affected me the same way. I didn't trust these people. I never had. Never would. But I had trusted my aunt and even my uncle at first. They were supposed to take care of me. Love me. Keep me safe from the evils of the world. But they didn't. They were worse than evil. They were the very reason I didn't sleep at night. I was far more terrified of them even though they were dead and gone, than the people who put a price on my head.

Sucking in a deep lungful of air, I adjusted the collar of my hoodie. My gaze flicked to a rusty steel pipe standing in the corner against the brick wall. While I had the two pistols in the back of my jeans, this was better and would be far messier.

Grabbing the pipe, I slapped it against my open palm, itching for the taste of blood.

Tugging open the door, I pulled a pistol from my pants and stepped inside. The scent of depravity slammed into me. I almost forgot what it smelled like. It was death mixed with copper. Add a dash of sugar and you had yourself a recipe for evil.

"Honey, I'm home," I called out, banging the steel pipe against the wall as I walked down the long hallway to what was once considered my office. I had every intention of bringing the club back to the way it was. But I wouldn't be president. I didn't want the job anymore. When I had that title, it wasn't as satisfying as it would be for most. No, instead, it made me moodier than usual.

The further I walked down the hall, the more eerie the place felt. I was a little disappointed that I didn't have anyone greeting me.

The door at the end of the hallway opened, revealing Tommy West. A guy I used to bounce ideas off of. A guy I had considered possibly even a friend. Or someone I could put up with anyway. We had a mutual understanding. For whatever reason, we trusted each other but not enough. Something had happened where he needed more. He was greedy for power. Hungry for people to do his bidding. And I stood in the way of that.

"Miss me?" I asked him, resting the end of the pipe on the floor and leaning my weight on it as if it were a walking cane.

"What are you doing here?" he demanded, his brows furrowing in the middle. He looked back into his office. "Where the fuck are my men?"

I ground my teeth together. "Aww. No welcome home party?" I pouted. "Too bad."

"What do you want, Tanner?" he asked, looking past me.

The hairs on the back of my neck tingled, that familiar rush trembling through me at what was to come next in only a matter of seconds.

Wrapping my hand around the pipe in a firm grip, I spun around, landing it against the side of someone's head.

BEING US

The body dropped to the ground in a bundled heap.

"Didn't you know it's rude to sneak up on people?" I asked, nudging the unmoving body with my boot. When it didn't move, I stretched my arm out in front of me, pretending to check out my nails. "I'm surprised you don't know what I want," I told Tommy. "You see. A friend told me that there's a price on my head." I started pacing, giving the three remaining standing guys who had joined our little party, a wave. "Five-hundred grand. Really, Tommy?" I placed the pipe on my shoulders, resting my forearms on top of it. "I'm a little offended that you thought you couldn't get more for me."

"What the fuck are you going on about?" Tommy shut the door to the office and started walking toward me.

"What the fuck am I talking about," I repeated, laughing. I glanced at the guys who stood a few feet away. One was a prospect. He had only joined the club a few weeks before I was forced out of it. What was his name again? "Rat, it's been awhile. How's the arm? They let you play with guns yet?"

The skinny fucker glared at me. He had given Shade a hard time for being gay. Even though that was true, the way Rat went about it, had pissed me off, so I broke his arm.

"Do any of you know what I'm talking about?" I asked the guys. I didn't recognize the two larger men standing on either side of Rat.

One actually shook his head.

"Didn't think so. I appreciate your honesty." I continued pacing. "You see. I don't know if you know me." I looked at them and waited. When they didn't say anything, I let out a sigh. "What are you teaching these guys?" I asked Tommy. "No matter. I'm happy to tell you. You see, I was the president of Devil's Rejects. Before Tommy. Actually, while Tommy was gathering all of you to be his little minions, I was still running this club. Or I thought I was anyway. But while I took care of a personal matter, little did I know that Tommy here was convincing all of you to kick me out."

When the guys shifted, I grinned.

"Looks like you know who I am now." I stopped in front of them. "Isn't that right?"

"We've heard of you," the larger of the group said. Tattoos lined the side of his buzzed head, traveling down his neck and disappearing into the collar of his black long-sleeved shirt. He was a big fucker. His piercing charcoal eyes looked directly at me. He rose an eyebrow. "Checking me out, Tanner?"

"I think he likes you."

My gaze flicked to the smaller guy standing beside him. Something about him was familiar but I couldn't make out exactly what it was. He was younger. Baby faced. I would give him early twenties at the most.

He chuckled. "Maybe he likes me too."

The bigger guy scratched his jaw. "Hmm...I'd be willing to share." He made a point of letting his eyes roam down the length of me. "Although, he's a tiny one. I'd probably break him."

I coughed, shaking my head. "Sorry, buddy. You don't do it for me."

"Trust me." His eyes snapped to mine. "I do it for everyone. Doesn't matter if you're a man or a woman. I can make anyone bend to my will."

"Maybe he has someone at home," the baby-faced guy said, stepping closer to his friend.

I frowned. "Now I really feel like I've met you before."

The smaller guy laughed, resting his arm on top of his friend's shoulder. He ran his tattooed fingers over his mouth, his smile widening. "I think we'd both have fun breaking him."

"Are you done?" Rat asked, grimacing.

"You know, I seem to recall you being a little homophobic." In a quick move, I swung the pipe and bashed it against his knees.

He screamed, falling to the ground beneath him.

"That's right. On your knees like a good little boy." I crouched, grabbing a fistful of his hair and pulling his head back. "Next time you will think twice about insulting anyone for their sexual preferences because remember, I know where you live. I know where your parents live. I even know where that pretty little sister of yours lives."

Rat's face paled. "You wouldn't."

He was right. I wouldn't. But no one needed to know any different. The rumors had gone on for so long, might as well let people believe them. As long as Busy didn't, that was all that mattered to me. I tried for so long to correct them that I just finally gave up. There was no point.

I rose to my full height, looking back at Tommy who had been watching the whole ordeal play out before him. "I have questions. And you have answers. I know you will give them to me because you want to watch me squirm and beg for what I want."

Tommy's brows narrowed.

"He's actually right," one of the guys murmured behind me.

"Where's the rest of the crew?" I asked no one in particular.

"Around. Some of them are in the actual club, doing who the hell knows what. Some are on a run. Some are probably even sitting on their thumbs, doing fuck all."

I looked back at the younger guy. "Really?"

He shrugged. "Everything's gone to shit since you've left, Tanner."

"It wasn't like I had a choice." But before we got into that, I stepped over the body on the ground who still hadn't moved and backed up down the hall. "Can I trust you?"

"We're not with Tommy, if that's what you're wondering." The bigger guy and the one who was clearly into anything that gave him the go-ahead, gave me a curt nod. "We're not who you think we are."

I didn't know what he meant by that but instead of asking, I walked toward Tommy. "Office."

"Why would I do that?" Tommy pulled a pistol from the waist of his jeans and aimed it at me. "You shouldn't be here."

"If you wanted me dead, you would have had me killed a long time ago, Tommy." I shoved him back when he didn't budge. "Office. Now."

"Fine, Tanner. Go into the office. But you won't like what you see." Tommy opened the door for me and pushed me into the small room.

I stumbled a few steps, my eyes landing on a woman kneeling on the floor. Everything gave out from beneath me. All breath left my lungs as I stared at the one person who had become the only reason I no longer wanted to do something stupid. Besides Trigger, she was the very reason I was still alive.

My chest tightened.

I fell to the ground as my knees gave out from under me. "Busy."

TWENTY SIX

A **DARK SINISTER LAUGH** sounded from behind me. It slid over my skin, digging into every nerve racing through my body. It had reminded me of when my uncle would laugh every time I cried. Or every time I screamed when my aunt wasn't home, and he took things to a whole other level of depravity.

"Busy," I repeated, my voice hoarse. I dropped to my knees in front of her. I never wanted this. She deserved so much better than the wrath and destruction I brought with me every single time I got close to someone.

A white cloth was shoved in her mouth, tied at the back of her head in a knot. Her hands were bound behind her by rope that was digging into her skin.

Pulling the cloth from her lips, I kissed her softly. "I'm so fucking sorry."

"Don't be," she whispered. "Just kill him. Do what you do best, baby."

"Are you hurt?" I asked, running my fingers over a dark bruise forming on her cheek. I could only imagine what happened for her to earn this mark. A mark that I would kill Tommy for. A mark that I would replace with my loving ones.

"I'm fine, Tanner," she insisted, staring up at me with hard eyes. *He had Trigger killed,* she mouthed slowly.

Rage burned through me. I kissed her again before pushing to my feet. "How the hell did you get her here before me?"

Tommy was leaning against the wall beside the door with his arms crossed under his chest. "How do you think, Tanner? I have someone within Hell's Harlem. It seems Greyson has upped his security, so I had to pay someone really well to get in there quietly. I knew you were on your way, so I figured you wouldn't talk unless your little Bee was here. Also, my boy knows a short cut but showed up here shorty after you did."

My head whipped around.

"They're fine. Everyone is fine," Busy told me. "A little beat up but I promise, they're alive," she bit out through clenched teeth.

My blood pumped through me at the vicious edge in her tone. I didn't like it but at the same time, I did. She was gentle. Kind. Not a villain. She wasn't me. *I* was the villain. I was the monster under the bed. I was the damn anti-hero in the books who everyone loved to hate and hated to love at the same time.

"Where were you?" I asked her.

"I was in my room. Frankie…" She shook her head. "He's a prospect and works for him." She nodded toward Tommy.

"You took her from her bedroom?" I asked Tommy.

BEING US

He grinned, scratching the scruff on his jaw. "What are you going to do, Tanner? Do you believe that your new little family is all fine and well with you being with their precious little Bumble Bee?" Tommy pushed away from the wall. "Why would they care what happened to you? You're not wanted. You were never wanted. Not even by your own club. But they wanted me." He punched his chest. "*Me*, Tanner. And I gave them everything they wanted. Money. Power. Women. Drugs. Sex. So much fucking sex, they didn't even know what to do with all the pussy they've been getting."

"One, Hell's Harlem is not my family. We have a mutual understanding. They leave me alone. I leave them alone." It was one thing Greyson and I had discussed privately. "Second, *she* is my family," I said, pointing at Busy. It took everything in me not to pull her into my arms and take her out of there, but I couldn't, knowing that this shit with Tommy wouldn't end until I got rid of him for good. "But you already knew that or else she wouldn't be here. Isn't that right? There's just something I don't quite understand though."

"Oh?" Tommy raised a dark eyebrow. "And what's that?"

"Why? You could have started your own chapter. You didn't need to take over mine. If you would have come to me and told me you wanted to be president…" I realized then how stupid that sounded. Tommy never wanted to be the president of his own club. He wanted to be the president of *mine*.

A slow grin spread on his face. "Lightbulb just go off?"

"What do you want? Besides all of this which you seem to have already gotten. Are you wanting more?"

Tommy rubbed his jaw. "There is something else that I want. Besides your club. Which surprisingly, was really easy to take over. And Sunny's old lady?" He chuckled. "She didn't even belong to him for long. Seems he was hung up on his partner the whole time. She was just a hole to be used. She actually wanted a man who would do anything to make it to the top in the club that he's in. Sunny was a pussy. He liked being Greyson's little bitch. They all do."

"And yet, you don't seem to care if these bitches as you call them, do work for you? Am I right?" This wasn't the Tommy that I knew. He always had an air about him that made me uneasy. It was why I kept him close, so I could keep an eye on him. But he never hinted that it wasn't enough.

"I couldn't give a shit if they do work for me because I know that I could always find someone who will." Tommy took a step toward me. "Do you want to know what else I want?"

"I already asked you, but you seem to be delaying your answer." I feigned a yawn. "This is boring. How about I just take my girl and leave."

Tommy chuckled, his eyes dropping to Busy. "You see, your dog's death was just a treat, but I think she would be the perfect parting gift."

Busy whimpered.

I backed up, standing directly in front of her. "You had Trigger killed. Why?"

"Why not?" Tommy shrugged. "He was old anyway. I did him a favor. It actually wasn't my idea though. I just ordered the hit."

"Who killed him?" I craved his death, whoever the bastard was that stabbed Trigger.

"The guy you hit with your pipe. I was surprised he showed his face."

I made a mental note to make sure the bastard stayed down. "Why do you want Busy? She's used up. Why would you want my sloppy seconds?" Bile rose to my throat at the vile words leaving my mouth.

"Oh, I wouldn't use her. I'd toss her to my dogs." Tommy started pacing. "That's what you used to do, isn't it, Tanner? When you finished with a woman, you would throw her to your men and let them feed on her until they were good and full."

"Whatever happened before has nothing to do with what's going on right now," I bit out, gripping the pipe in my hand like it was my lifeline when something bumped against my calf.

I took a deep breath when I realized that it was Busy's forehead. How stupid was I? She was my damn lifeline. Always had been.

"What do you want, Tommy? Is it money? I have money that I can give you. Not like I need it."

Tommy stopped pacing. "Money's nice and all but I want to take everything you've ever owned. I already took your dog. Now I'm going to take your girl too."

Red clouded my vision.

"I know you have a thing for animals. Do you make your bitch beg too? I bet she's a fucking screamer." He looked around me. "Aren't you? I could get a lot of money for someone like you." He stood up straight. "But while she would be fun to play with, it isn't enough. It'll never be enough."

Something inside of me snapped.

I shoved the pistol into the back of my pants and moved the pipe to my other hand. I started tapping it on the ground. For most, it would be considered annoying and I was sure that it was. But for me, it was a countdown.

Ten.

I craved his blood.

Nine.

He would die for thinking he could get rid of my dog and that be the end of it.

Eight.

He would die for thinking he could get my girl. My Busy.

Seven.

Tap. Tap. Tap.

Tommy stopped pacing, his brows narrowing in the center.

Busy's breath hitched. She knew. She might not have known me for a long time, but it didn't matter. I was a monster. *Her* monster.

Six.

Five.

Tap. Tap. Tap.

"What the fuck are you doing, Tanner?" Tommy raised the gun. "Have you finally lost it?"

Ignoring Tommy's questions, I was vaguely aware of Busy talking. Whatever she was saying was giving me the strength I needed to take this motherfucker out.

Tap. Tap. Tap.

Four.

Three.

I didn't give a shit that he had a gun aimed at me. I didn't give a shit that we were in his clubhouse. A clubhouse that used to be run by me. I could only hope that some of the guys still trusted me and were willing to follow me out from under this fucker's clutches and join a president who deserved that title. If they weren't, they would die.

Tap. Tap. Tap.

Two.

Just like my aunt and uncle.

Just like the bastards who ran the dog fighting rings I stopped.

"You want to dance, boy?" he growled, cocking his gun.

I laughed. "You think that's going to stop me? The only way you're going to get out of this, is if you kill me.

Which by the way." I checked my wrist. "You better make it quick. I have a date."

Tommy's face turned red. "You know, I heard you were sick in the head. But the whole time I knew you, I never understood those rumors. Until now. It's like you just don't care."

"I don't." I did but I never used to. Not until I met Busy and actually had a reason to live now. Add to the fact that she had my baby in her belly and nothing else mattered. Which reminded me to up his pain for hurting my girl who was growing something that belonged to me.

When I went to take a step forward, a commotion sounded on the other side of the door.

Tommy and I glanced at each other before we both did what the other had been thinking the whole damn time. We charged for the other, not caring what was going on outside of the office. We had one goal in mind and one goal only.

Death.

TWENTY SEVEN

TANNER

TOMMY HAD AT LEAST twenty-five pounds on me and some inches in height, but I was faster. When his fist connected with my cheek, it knocked me back a bit and forced a metallic taste in my mouth, but it was like this newfound awareness had taken over.

When he went to swing again, I ducked and swung the pipe against the side of his head. The end connected with his temple, but the big bastard didn't go down like I had hoped.

An animalistic sound escaped him when he charged for me.

Not thinking twice about it, I grabbed the pipe with both hands, pulled it back and swung it forward with all the strength I could muster.

BEING US

The pipe penetrated Tommy's throat, the end coming out the back of his neck. Blood splattered my face and hands. His eyes bulged, his breath leaving him in short bursts of air.

"You should have shot me while you had the chance." I pushed on the pipe until he slid further down it. "I warned you. You never mess with a man's dog or his girl."

As the life left him, I pulled the pipe back, ripping it free from his throat. Watching him fall to the ground in a crumbled heap, I nudged him with my Shit Kicker. I waited for any sign of life. When he only laid there, unmoving, it was like a weight had been lifted off of my shoulders.

"Do you still love me?" I heard myself ask.

"Yes," Busy answered without even hesitating.

"You still want to be with me?" I nudged Tommy again because you could never be too safe.

"Tanner."

My head whipped around. "I asked you a question."

Her lips pursed, her eyes going hard. "Yes, now come over here and untie me, so I can touch you."

I looked down at my hands. They were coated in Tommy's blood.

"Tanner, please."

Ignoring her, I rushed around the room, needing to find something, anything, to wipe off the blood that would forever taint my soul. When I couldn't find anything, an idea came to me.

Fuck it.

Wiping my hands on my jeans, I got them clean enough where not a lot would touch her, but it didn't matter anyway. I would never be able to scrub myself clean enough. I would always see the blood.

"Tanner."

I wiped my face with the bottom of my hoodie. When I lowered the fabric, Busy was staring up at me.

"Untie me, baby."

I rushed to her and dropped to my knees before untying her wrists and ankles.

She pulled the gag from around her neck and over her head before tossing it to the floor.

Once the fabric fell, I was on her.

(Bee)

Everything happened so damn quickly tonight, my head was spinning. But I focused on the fact that Tanner was back in my arms. Sammy and Cyrus had driven him hours away. When they had left, all hell broke loose. Tommy's crew had shown up and tried shooting up the place but Uncle Greyson was ready. I was just never prepared for Frankie to come take me.

"I have questions," Tanner said, pushing his face into the crook of my neck. "But I need to get you out of here first."

"We can talk later."

He nodded, rising to his full height and held out a hand.

I took it, letting him help me to my feet just as the office door swung open.

Tanner pushed me behind him, shielding me. "What the hell are you doing here?"

I looked around him, my eyes widening at seeing Uncle Greyson and… "Daddy?"

Both Dad and Uncle Greyson looked between each other before they glanced back at Tanner and I.

BEING US

"We'll explain everything but we need to get out of here," Dad said, leaving no room for argument, his dark eyes landing on Tommy's still body.

"Did you have some fun?" Uncle Greyson asked, nudging Tommy with his boot.

I braced myself, almost expecting Tommy to jump up and get his revenge. But when he didn't, I let out a slow breath.

Tanner looked down at me, his brows narrowing.

"I'm good," I told him. But I wasn't. I knew Tanner had a dark side to him. He warned me of that. But seeing it in action made me feel almost…I wasn't sure how I felt. But when I realized that I wasn't scared of him and almost proud of what he did instead, it sent a sour taste to my throat. I should have been scared of him, shouldn't I? He killed Tommy in front of me. I understood why he did it. I got it. He saved my life and avenged Trigger and everyone else who Tommy had hurt, but it still didn't make it right.

Tanner brought my hand up to his lips, brushing his mouth along my knuckles. "Tommy had Trigger killed and took my girl." He looked back at Uncle Greyson. "He deserved more than what he got but I didn't have a lot of time."

Uncle Greyson nodded.

Tanner looked back down at me. His eyes were dark, stormy. They pleaded with me not to give up on him. On us. I wouldn't. But I had questions. He had told me that he killed his aunt and uncle. A part of me wanted to ask how many others he had killed. But then at the same time, I also didn't want to know.

"Come." Dad headed to the door of the office before turning back to us. "You okay?"

I nodded. "I am."

"She's lying," Tanner blurted.

My head whipped around. "I am not."

Dad grunted. "Probably. Her mother would do the same thing." He shook his head. "Women."

"Ganging up on me now?" I asked Tanner, raising an eyebrow.

"Nah." He kissed my cheek. "Just making nice with your old man."

I cupped his face, searching his eyes for something that indicated that he wasn't alright. But when I couldn't find anything, I brushed my thumb along his bottom lip instead. "Take me home."

He nodded, grabbed my hand, and led me from the office.

But once we stepped out into the hall, we were stopped short by Uncle Greyson standing with a few of the members of Devil's Rejects. When I looked harder, I realized that they weren't wearing leather cuts. So maybe they weren't actual members. I recognized the one big guy as the driver who brought me to this place with Tommy.

"Tanner." I tugged on his hand.

"What is it?"

"He was there." I nodded toward the large guy who stood with a smaller one. Tattoos lined the side of his head and thick neck. Something was eerie about him. About both of them. But I couldn't quite put my finger on exactly what that was.

"You take my girl?" Tanner let go of my hand and charged for the guy who only stood there with his arms crossed under his chest.

"Nope. I was just the driver. I would have told you that earlier, but you seemed preoccupied." He feigned a yawn. "But she's fine. Is she not?"

"That's beside the fucking point," Tanner growled, pushing him. When the guy didn't budge even a step, Tanner shoved him again.

BEING US

"Listen." The bigger guy grabbed Tanner by the collar of his hoodie and shoved him up against the wall. "I didn't hurt her. I'm not the one who hit her. That was Tommy. But you already took care of that. Didn't you?"

"Stop." I rushed to them but of course, neither of them would budge. "I'm fine. I promise that I'm fine."

"See? She's fine." The man released Tanner, readjusted his hoodie and patted his cheek. "I like to think I had a little hand in keeping her safe."

Tanner scoffed.

"Um...he did actually," I said, still not overly sure what the hell was going on but was glad that we were finally moving forward.

"How?" Tanner grabbed my hand and pulled me into his side. "Tell me."

"My mouth got away from me and I told Tommy off. I called him a pussy for having a prospect do his dirty work and I told him that he should have taken me if he wanted to show how big of a man he was. He hit me and this guy here, told me that if I kept my mouth shut and did as I was told, I wouldn't get hurt. He also got me some ice for my cheek when we got here. Tommy was only trying to scare me, and it worked. But it pissed me off even more. The only thing he wanted was to take over your club. He said he didn't care about Sunny's ex-wife. She was just a means to an end. The power, money, and everything else were an added bonus I guess." I shrugged. "But I promise, I am fine."

Tanner searched my face before looking back at the men surrounding us. "Why don't I know you?"

"The name's Bryson Rain but most call me Bear." He stuck his hand out as a smaller man came up beside him. "And this scrawny fucker is Kitson Moore. Or Kid but you already knew that."

Tanner shook his head. "Wait, what?"

"It's like he's psychic," Kitson said, resting his arm on Bear's shoulder. "I've always been called Kid and you didn't even know that."

"We need to go," Uncle Greyson said, coming toward us. "We'll explain on the way home. Don't make me fucking repeat myself." He spun on his heel and headed toward a door at the end of the hallway. "Bear and Kid, that means you too."

"I hate being told what to do," Bear mumbled.

"Really?" Kid's eyes lit up. "It's not that bad." He winked, waggling his eyebrows.

Bear chuckled, shaking his head. "I'll remember that."

"Kid," Tanner repeated. "I know you."

"Maybe you do. Maybe you don't." Kid turned and started following Greyson out of the club. "I guess you won't find out until later."

"Tanner." I kept his hand firmly in mine and led him outside and to the twins' SUV. "We need to go."

"Hold on. There's something I have to do." He kissed my forehead and pulled away from me before heading back to the entrance of the club. When he disappeared into the building, I thought that maybe this was it. That maybe he had truly lost himself and allowed the demons to finally take over.

For good.

(Tanner)

"Tanner, where are you going?"

I ignored Greyson and headed back into the office where I had left Tommy's body. But once I entered the room and saw that it was completely empty, I laughed. "Wow. That was fast."

Greyson clapped my shoulder. "I know people. Your club wasn't as trusting of Tommy as he led you to believe."

"Why?" I asked, when a few of the guys I had grown up in the biker life with, started coming toward us from down the hall.

"Where the hell have you been?"

"It's been way too fucking long, brother."

The words started blending together, coming from each and every one of them.

"Tommy said you died," Bud Nolk, a long-time member of Devil's Rejects, added. His rough voice sounded like he had just gargled with shards of broken glass.

"I guess I did in a way," I answered. And I was reborn when I met Busy.

"Where have you been?" Donny Waver, another member who had been with me in the club ever since I took over, cupped my shoulders. "We need answers, Tanner."

"I had to hide. I thought or Tommy made me believe anyway, that if I stuck around, I'd end up dead. By all of you. I couldn't take the chance, so I disappeared."

"Do you not know us at all?" Donny flinched like I had just smacked the beard off his face. "We've been with you since the beginning. Long before Tommy came around. You were a shithead kid who forced his way into our lives, and we had no choice but to let him in. Fuck." He walked away and began pacing.

"I…" I swallowed hard.

"He's right." Bud leaned a shoulder against the wall. "But I get it. Tommy had a way of making people do things for him. Things they didn't want to do either. Sure, some of the guys might have done it because they wanted to follow him and not you, but I can guarantee you that Donny and I are not like that. And Bear and Kid who you just met? They have their moments, but you can trust them too."

"I don't know what's going on right now," I mumbled.

Bud pushed away from the wall and came toward me. "We're family, Tanner. Where you go, we go. Hell, if you don't even actually want to be president anymore, that's fine too. But we do need a leader."

"Who's the vice-president now?" I asked.

"I am."

I turned at the new voice.

A stocky guy came toward us. He was shorter than my six-three but wide around the middle. He was built like a wall and I knew then that I did not want to meet him in the middle of a dark alley.

"Heard you had a run-in with my boys. They killed your dog and left you for dead." He grimaced. "I've done a lot of shit but hurting an animal just to prove a point? Nope. Not my thing." He stuck his hand out. "The name's Sky. Sky Paiva. And yes, that's my real name." He walked past me. "Seems I've become president without even wanting it."

"But you're vice—"

"I am." He lifted a hand. "Your VP was killed by the way."

My chest tightened.

"He was given a funeral. You know, so Tommy could cover his tracks and all." Sky shook his head. "I don't get it. I probably never will."

"I don't want to be president," I said, voicing something that had been weighing on my mind for quite some time.

"You know you can't just give up that role, right? You either retire or you're killed. You know too much."

BEING US

Donny came back toward me, staring me down. "You do know that. You made the fucking rule, remember?"

I rolled my eyes. "Yes, I remember. Thank you for the heads-up. But I don't want to be president. So you," I nodded toward Sky, "get to be it instead. It's your lucky day."

Sky reached into the inside of his leather cut and pulled out a pack of smokes before sticking one between his lips. He lit it, puffed a couple of times, and inhaled. Letting out a deep breath, the spicy scent of his smoke billowing around us. A grin suddenly spread on his face. "I did always like being in control."

TWENTY EIGHT

Bee

WHEN **TANNER HAD GONE** back inside the club, I went to run after him when Sammy stopped me. I had struggled against him and even kicked him in the shin but that didn't stop him.

"I don't give a shit how hard you kick me, Bee. I'm not letting you run after him."

I knew he wasn't doing it to be mean and that he was only looking out for me, but it still didn't make me any less mad that he was stopping me.

Now I was sitting in the back seat of Cyrus's SUV, waiting. "I don't know why you won't let me go in there. It's not like I would do anything. I just want to make sure he's okay."

"Tanner is a big boy. He can take care of himself," Cyrus said, leaning an elbow on the windowsill.

BEING US

"You know. I'm getting sick of being your damn babysitter."

My head whipped around. "Excuse me?"

Sammy glared at me. "You heard me."

"I never asked for this. I never asked for any of this."

"Sure." Sammy slipped out of the vehicle and lit up a smoke.

I stared after him. Even though Sammy had always been the hothead between them, it still hurt to hear him say how he really felt.

Instead of dwelling on it, I opened the door.

"Johnny, I don't suggest doing that."

I didn't listen to Cyrus and left the SUV, slamming the door shut behind me.

Sammy chuckled but he didn't look my way. He just continued puffing on that damn smoke while leaning against the hood of the vehicle.

"You know." I stepped in front of him. "I hope you find a woman one day who drives you absolutely crazy." I placed my hands on my hips. "I hope she gets in so deep under your skin that you can't do anything about it. All you can think about is her. And I also hope that she slaps that stupid smug grin off your face."

Sammy raised an eyebrow, something flashing behind his eyes.

Cyrus had briefly mentioned someone he referred to as Red. It made me wonder if Sammy had already met the woman I wished on him and that was why he was all of a sudden grumpier.

I searched Sammy's face, looking for a sign or any sort of indication that there was someone, anyone, who could knock him down a peg or two. He was a cocky fucker. I loved him dearly. He was family. But he needed to leave me alone.

Before he could say anything like I knew he wanted to, the door to the back of the club opened.

Tanner stepped out of the building, followed by a couple of other guys I didn't know.

"You love him," Sammy said suddenly, stepping up beside me.

"I do." With more than I ever thought I had to give.

"If he hurts you, I'll end him," Sammy said, his voice so low, I wasn't sure I heard him properly.

"I know." I knew it was his way of apologizing.

Much to my surprise, Sammy kissed the side of my head. "Go to him."

Doing as I was told, I headed toward Tanner.

One of the guys clapped him on the back and pulled him into a hug.

My heart warmed at the sight before me.

The big guy who had driven me from Uncle Greyson's place to this club, went up to Tanner and gave his shoulder a squeeze before walking toward me. "You good?"

I shrugged. "Is he?"

"He's as good as can be expected. But I'm sure you'll figure out a way to make him feel better." He stuck out his hand. "Bryson Rain but you can call me Bear."

"Are you a biker?" I asked him, returning the handshake.

"No." He winked, keeping hold of my hand. "I work with bikers from time to time, but I have never been, nor will I ever be, a biker."

"How come?" He was a big guy. Seemed like he would fit the role perfectly.

"Not my thing." Bear released my hand. "You ever need extra protection, you call me." He reached into the inside of his leather jacket and pulled out a small business card. Handing it to me, he gave me another wink and started walking back to the club. He joined Kid and a few other guys. I noticed then that he stepped up close to Kid, their hands brushing against each other.

Bear looked my way, giving me another wink.

Kid followed his line of sight, a slow grin spreading on his face.

I swallowed hard. I wasn't sure what was going on there. Not like it was any of my business, but I was curious just the same.

Finally looking down at the card in my hand, I turned it over. It held a picture of a bear's head on one side and that was it. The other side was blank. How the heck would I be able to call him if I didn't have his number? I shook my head, stuffing the business card in my back pocket.

"Bee?"

I spun on my heel, finding Uncle Greyson and Dad coming toward me. "I thought you guys left."

"We were going to and then we saw Tanner head back into the club," Dad explained. "Wanted to make sure that you were okay first."

"How did you know that I was here?" A cold draft suddenly wafted around me, sending a shiver down my spine.

A look passed between them before they glanced back at me.

"I headed to the clubhouse just as Tommy's boys showed up," Dad told me.

Uncle Greyson crossed his arms under his chest. "I knew we had good security now, but I had forgotten for a moment just how good it was."

"You know Lucas would never let you have any different," Dad reminded him.

Uncle Greyson chuckled.

"Who's Lucas?" I asked, never hearing that name before.

"A friend." And that was all that Uncle Greyson said about it.

"What was done with Frankie?" I asked, knowing it would be a sensitive subject but needing to find out more just the same.

Frankie had grabbed me from my bedroom. It was like a scene right out of a horror movie. I went to bed to read for a bit and he came out of the closet like a monster. Everything had happened so damn fast. I never even had a chance to scream when he tackled me and covered my mouth with a cloth soaked in chloroform.

"Unfortunately, I trusted him when I shouldn't have." Uncle Greyson sighed. "But he's been taken care of and that's all you need to know."

My stomach twisted.

Uncle Greyson rubbed the back of his neck, leaning his head from side to side. "I need a drink, my wife, and a damn vacation."

"I hear you, brother." Dad pulled me into a hug. "You good?"

"Yeah, Daddy. I am." But I wasn't.

"You sure?" he murmured, squeezing me.

"Yup." Another lie.

He released me, giving himself a little shake. "I need to see your mother. I'll wait until you leave and then we'll follow."

I nodded, watching him walk to his bike with Uncle Greyson at his side. They straddled their machines and waited. Having them there relieved some of the tension resting on my shoulders, but it still wasn't enough.

"Busy."

My breath caught in my throat.

Warm arms wrapped around me, pulling me against a hard body.

My heart jumped, my stomach doing flips at having Tanner so close once again.

"Hey." Tanner brushed his nose up the length of my throat. "You're good. You're safe, baby." He kissed the spot beneath my ear, running his fingers over my lower stomach. "We're good."

A shiver rippled down my spine. "We're safe," I whispered, turning in his arms and wrapping myself around him.

"We are." He kissed the top of my head. "I promise. I won't ever let anything happen to you."

"You can't promise me something like that. Frankie took me. Tommy hit me. You…I…" I pulled away from him.

Tanner grabbed my hand. "Stop."

"It's true." A lump lodged its way into my throat. I knew that this was not the time to be having this discussion, but I couldn't stop the words from leaving my lips. "We need to go."

Just as I was about to grab his hand and lead him to the SUV, a scream sounded from somewhere inside the building. The back door banged open, revealing a red-faced woman.

"Who did it? Who fucking killed him?" Tears streaked her cheeks, her hair a mess around her face. Her clothes were winkled and unkempt.

Tanner pulled me behind him. "What the hell are you doing here, Roxanne?"

My eyes widened. This was Sunny's ex?

"I asked a question. Was it you, Tanner?" she seethed. "I know you've always been jealous of him."

"You have?" I whispered.

"She's crazy, baby," he mumbled. "I have no idea what you're talking about, Roxanne. He was like that when I showed up."

"Right." She sniffled, roughly wiping at her cheeks.

A couple of guys came up behind her, including Bear and Kid but she was none the wiser.

"You expect me to believe that." She charged forward.

Faster than I ever thought was possible, Sammy ran past us and blocked her from getting to Tanner.

"Get out of my way," she screamed.

Sammy sidestepped around her and grabbed onto her shoulders.

"Stop!" She reached behind her, her hand coming back with a large butcher knife in it.

He grunted, grabbing her wrist. "You shouldn't bring a knife to a gun fight, sweetheart." He squeezed until she winced, dropping the knife.

It shattered to the ground at her feet, her sobs becoming harder. "I just wanted Sunny to love me. I wanted Tommy to love me. But I wasn't enough. For either of them. I'll never be enough." She sniffled. "It was never supposed to be Sunny. I never meant to kill him."

My heart jumped to my throat. "It was you? You killed Sunny? This whole time, everyone believed it was Tanner."

"I have no idea who you are." She wiped her face. "Tanner never killed him. He never even had a hand in it. Tommy wanted him to do it though. Didn't he?" she asked Tanner. "But you're a pussy."

"I had no reason to kill him. Tommy never even mentioned it to me, so I have no idea what kind of shit he was feeding you." Tanner moved beside me. "Now you're standing there, telling us, that you were the one who actually pulled the trigger?"

Tears started streaming down her face faster. "I was trying to kill Shade," she sobbed.

Bile rose to my throat. Holy shit.

"Holy shit," Tanner murmured.

I had known through just overhearing the guys talking about it, that Roxanne had a hand in Sunny's death but hearing her say it, made it seem almost unbelievable.

BEING US

"We have to tell Shade and Meadow," I told Tanner, grabbing his hand and trying to lead him back to the SUV. I just wanted to get out of there and go home. I wanted him. I wanted to start a life with him and not have to worry about keeping him hidden. I wanted to go to the doctor's together and have this pregnancy confirmed. I wanted to move on.

"Why go through all of this?" Tanner asked. "What's in it for you?"

Roxanne stopped sniffling. It was like something switched in her. She went from a grieving widow to a psychopath in a matter of a second. "You took something from me, so I had to return the favor."

"What the fuck are you talking about?" Tanner shook his head. "This doesn't make any sense."

"You took Tommy from me!" she screamed. "He was so fucking focused on ruining your life, I needed to take something from you that would hurt just the same. That's why he had your dog killed. That's why your girl was taken."

"They were innocent in this!" Tanner yelled, his voice cracking.

"Tanner." I tugged his hand, not wanting him to be seen by anyone else when he finally broke.

"Well as much as this has been fun, I think it's time we all call it a night."

All heads turned to a large man leaning against the brick wall by the door.

Sammy released Roxanne. "She's all yours."

The man grinned. "Good. I've been itching for blood." He snapped his fingers.

Bear and Kid stepped forward. Without even being told, they grabbed for Roxanne before she could bolt. She started screaming when Kid grabbed the back of her neck and spun her around. His fingers locked onto her jaw, silencing her.

He leaned down to her ear, his eyes meeting mine. He mumbled something to her, keeping his gaze locked on me. There was something about him that I didn't like. He had seemed nice enough at first but now, it was like he was a contradiction. While he had a smooth face and looked around my age, his eyes told a different story.

With his fingers digging into her jaw, he pulled her toward him.

She whimpered.

I swallowed hard, backing up a step.

His lips moved over words I couldn't hear but understood just the same. I only imagined what he said to her. Threats. Promises of what they would do to her because she had done things she shouldn't have.

"Busy?"

"I…" I shook my head, continuing to back up. "I don't want to be here. We need to go. We really need to go." I didn't want to see what they would do to Roxanne. I had heard stories of women betraying bikers and how they had disappeared. It wasn't the disappearing part that freaked me out. It was everything before that. What was done to them. What they went through. The pain. Agony. Sheer terror as they probably wished for death but knowing it would not come until the men were good and ready. They continued to live out their time in a way I wouldn't wish on my worst enemy.

"Hey." Tanner's voice washed over me, but I couldn't focus on him. All I could see was Roxanne being man-handled by Kid who probably told her things I couldn't even imagine in my worst nightmares.

Roxanne somehow had gotten a little brave and shoved out of his grip.

He chuckled, the smile falling from his face a second later when his hand landed against the side of her head. The force knocked her to her knees.

A gasp escaped me.

Both Kid and Bear looked my way.

Tanner stood in front of me, blocking their line of sight. "Look at me and keep backing up. Do it, now, Busy."

I looked up at him and did as I was told.

"Only a few more feet, baby. Look at my face."

I did. I let my eyes roam over every hard line of his features. His dark beard had grown in some. His nose was a little crooked. I had never asked him how it got that way. Maybe it was from getting punched.

"Almost there," he said gently.

"What's going on?" Cyrus asked from behind me.

"Busy saw something she shouldn't have," Tanner explained, keeping his gaze on me. "But to be fair, it wasn't like they went out of their way to keep that shit hidden."

"Fucking fucker." Sammy stormed past us. "I hate people who beat women just for the sake of showing their power."

"But you like it other times?" Tanner asked.

"Hey, if she wants to be slapped around and degraded because that's her kink…well…" Sammy pulled the passenger door open and slipped into the SUV. "But before you judge me, I've only met one woman who wanted that shit."

"What did you do?" I asked, not realizing that was a thing. God, my naivety was showing.

"I didn't say no." He winked, shutting the door behind him.

"Ignore him." Cyrus walked past us. "Let's go home before your dad throws a fit."

I turned, finding Dad and Uncle Greyson still sitting on their bikes.

Tanner opened the back door, letting me slip inside before he joined me.

Once I had my seat belt done up, he wrapped me in his arms.

"I'm sorry," he murmured, kissing my temple. "I am so fucking sorry for everything. For all the shit I've put you through in such a short amount of time."

I let out a sigh, my breath wavering.

"I mean it, Busy." Tanner kissed my cheek, leaning his forehead against the side of my head.

I cupped his knee, giving it a light squeeze but I was unable to get the image of him killing Tommy out of my head. It made me uneasy and I feared that it would ruin Tanner. "Are you okay?" I finally asked him, looking up into his dark eyes.

"Don't worry about me." He kissed my nose, sitting back and looking out the window.

"I guess Bear and Kid aren't coming with us like Greyson wanted," Cyrus pointed out.

"Nope. They're preoccupied. Which is funny 'cause Kid doesn't look like the type who would do that shit." Sammy huffed. "Bee, don't look out the window."

Tanner shielded me from whatever was happening outside the club.

Cyrus pulled the SUV out of the parking lot with a screech of the tires. Uncle Greyson and Dad followed behind us. As soon as we were away from the club, I was finally able to breathe.

"Do you think we got all the answers we needed?" Sammy asked from the front, re-directing the conversation.

"I don't know." Cyrus scrubbed a hand down his face. "I really don't know."

I leaned my head against Tanner's shoulder, thankful that we were finally back together and that the events of tonight were finally over.

"I love you, Busy," he mumbled. "Don't ever doubt that."

BEING US

I didn't but I also wasn't sure if it was enough.

TWENTY NINE

TANNER

BUSY DOUBTED ME. NOT that I blamed her really. We needed to talk. Especially about what she saw me do. I didn't want to talk about it. I didn't want to talk about anything. No, instead I just wanted to hold her and have her tell me that everything would be okay and that she wasn't going anywhere. She had called me her monster and she didn't judge me for the shit I had done. But now I wasn't so sure.

Once we arrived back at the Hell's Harlem clubhouse, Busy and I slipped out of the back of the SUV. She muttered something about going to take a shower and I only nodded like a damn fool. What was I supposed to do? I didn't want to force myself on her but at the same time, I needed her in my arms. Not for sex. Just to touch her and soak up all of her love that I didn't deserve but craved just the same.

BEING US

When I was about to step into the house, Tray stopped me. He came toward me, forcing me back a step.

The hackles on the back of my neck rose, tingling with a warning that something bad was about to go down.

Cyrus came into my field of vision from the right. Sammy came up on the left. They were following me. With every step they took, I took one back.

I lifted my hands involuntarily; thankful they weren't shaking.

"You saved my daughter," Tray said, finally stopping a foot away. "You got rid of the bastard who ordered her to be taken. From her damn bedroom."

I only stared at him. Was he going to give me shit for killing the bastard in front of Busy? "I didn't want to do it front of her."

Tray nodded, his shoulders slumping. "I get that. There's been a lot of shit I never wanted to do in front of my wife, but it happened. We talked about it and we moved on. Although, Bee is like her, they do things themselves and they never ask for help. I also saw the shiner on her cheek."

"She told him off."

"You took care of it?"

I nodded.

Tray shook his head. "Damn women. Drive me fucking crazy but I love them just the same."

"Me too," I blurted. "I mean…"

Tray tilted his head. "You *do* love her. Don't you?"

"I do." Never having to deal with the father of someone I was sleeping with before, I wasn't sure what the rules were. Were we supposed to hug it out? Bump fists? Grunt like cavemen?

"Why are you looking at me like that?" Tray asked, crossing his arms under his chest.

"I just don't know what I'm supposed to do now," I confessed.

"How about you go make my daughter happy and take whatever this is between you two, one day at a time?" He clapped my shoulder. "I don't know you. But I've heard things. Horrible things about you. But I've seen the way you look at Bee, even though it's been a short time that you've been together. As long as you keep that smile on her face and tears out of her eyes, you and I won't have a problem. We clear?"

"Yes, Sir," I muttered.

"Good." He released me and headed back toward the house. "Greyson wants to chat about what went on tonight. We need to give Shade and Meadow some closure. And then you can go to Bee." He looked at me over his shoulder. "She's going to need you."

I took a deep breath and gave him a slow nod. Truth was, I was going to need her more.

(Bee)

When I entered the house that had been a second home to me for as long as I could remember, I felt a sense of peace wash over me. It was like the walls knew that the stress of the evening was finally over, and they could breathe a sigh of relief.

I had every intention of going to take a shower, but I was stopped short by both Meadow and Shade.

They both stared at me like I had a dick protruding from my forehead.

"You're making me nervous," I finally said.

"Fuck it." Meadow threw herself around me, knocking me back a step.

BEING US

My eyes widened. I was stiff, my arms at my side like I had no idea what to do with them.

Shade chuckled, shaking his head.

"I'm sorry," Meadow said, her voice cracking. "I just wanted someone to blame. That wasn't fair of me."

"I…" I returned the hug, squeezing her. "I'm sorry too."

"No." She leaned back, holding me at arm's length. "I don't like Tanner. Maybe I never will. But that's not your fault. And…" She sighed. "But I know he didn't shoot Sunny."

"You do?"

I jumped at the deep voice coming from behind me.

Tanner stopped at my side, brushing his fingers down my arm.

My heart skipped a beat. Linking our fingers, I reveled in the way we both relaxed just because we were touching. Finally.

"Greyson told us that even though that video makes it look like you shot him, Roxanne admitted to killing him herself." Shade shook his head. "We heard about your dog too. I'm sorry."

"Thank you," Tanner whispered.

"I understand people being jealous but that shit…that's a whole other level."

Meadow wrapped her hand around Shade's arm. "We have answers now, baby."

"Finally." He kissed her forehead and cupped her stomach. "I just wish Sunny was here to have them."

"I kind of feel bad for Roxanne," I blurted.

Heads whipped around.

My cheeks heated. "I mean." I cleared my throat. "She was obviously in love with Sunny, but that love took a darker turn when she realized that it was over between them. She probably thought that if she took Shade out like she had hoped, Sunny would go crawling back to her and she could console him. When that didn't happen, she snapped. More than she did in the first place. And now, who knows what those bikers are going to do to her." I shivered, my stomach twisting at the thought.

"I'm not sure I want to know." Meadow grimaced.

"Greyson." Shade stood taller. "You guys good?"

"Yeah." He came up to us with my dad in tow. "Couple things. We're not having a meeting tonight. We can talk tomorrow." He looked at Tanner. "I also wanted to talk to you about Kitson or Kid as you call him."

Tanner frowned. "I know him."

"You do," Uncle Greyson said. "He was the homeless kid you gave money to every time you left your apartment."

I gaped at him.

"So this whole time, you actually knew where I was?" Tanner chuckled, rubbing the back of his neck. "Wow. You guys are good."

A cheeky grin spread on Uncle Greyson's face. "Wasn't my idea."

"It was mine."

All of us turned as Sammy and Cyrus joined our little group.

"When Sunny was shot, I couldn't get it out of my head how you just disappeared," Cyrus explained. "I became obsessed."

"He did." Sammy nodded. "It was annoying."

"I met Kid a couple of years ago. Every now and again, we'll meet up, ask favors of each other, the usual shit," Cyrus said, ignoring his brother. "He's a good guy but like you witnessed tonight, he has…" He coughed. "Issues. Anyway, I paid him to search you out and to lay low when he did. He knows people. Apparently, it's someone you know."

Tanner's jaw clenched.

"Looks like you had several people looking out for you." Cyrus's brows narrowed. "But you didn't know that."

Tanner's phone rang at that point. He pulled it from his pocket and flipped it open. "Yeah." He paused. "It seems you have your hand in a lot of shit." He held the phone out to Cyrus. "He wants to talk to you."

"Who is it?" I asked Tanner when Cyrus took the phone from him.

"Rowan," he told me.

"Your friend?" I had no idea that Cyrus knew him as well.

"Yup. Apparently, Cyrus and he go way back." Tanner sighed. "I had no idea."

While Uncle Greyson and Dad went and joined Cyrus while he was talking to Rowan, Meadow stepped up to Tanner. She crossed her arms under her chest, staring up at him. "I don't like you. You caused a lot of shit. But you love Bee. And she's my girl. She's family. If you hurt her, you won't have to worry about the boys in this house." She raised an eyebrow. "We clear?"

"Crystal." Tanner brought my hand up to his mouth. "Very crystal."

My breath caught at the heat in his dark eyes.

"Well that was interesting," Uncle Greyson said, rejoining us. "I didn't know you were friends with Rowan."

"Do you know him?" I asked, taking a step closer to Tanner's side.

"Yeah. I'm friends with his parents." He looked at Tanner. "You got a good friend in Rowan. Don't fuck that up. Our threats are little compared to what he would do to you."

Tanner grunted. "Oh, I know. His pretty face means shit."

"Oh a baby-faced bad boy." Meadow waggled her eyebrows. "I like it."

"Careful," Shade murmured.

Uncle Greyson chuckled. "Listen, I just wanted to add that now that Roxanne is no longer an issue, we can move on. You can start healing."

"We have our baby for that." Meadow smiled, cupping her stomach.

Shade's face lit up. "I can't wait to meet our little one. I think Sunny would have loved being a father."

Meadow's eyes shone. "I agree." She sighed. "We should go and take advantage of the fact that we're alone. Before the baby comes and all."

Uncle Greyson grunted. "I remember when Jaron was born, I didn't get alone time with Eve at all."

"That's because I liked making you wait," Aunt Eve called out as she walked by with a case of water bottles.

We all laughed.

"Well, in that case." Uncle Greyson spun on his heel, followed his wife and took the heavy case from her.

A squeal sounded a moment later, followed by laughter. "Stop. We're not alone."

"Woman, I'll do whatever the fuck I want to you. I don't give a shit where we are and who's around," Uncle Greyson's deep voice boomed.

"You're so grumpy." Her laughter followed behind her as both her and Uncle Greyson headed to their part of the house at the back.

Tanner wrapped his arm around my shoulders. "You good, Busy?"

No. But I would be. "I need to take a shower." I pushed away from him before he could protest and jogged up the stairs to my bedroom.

When I reached my room, I quickly stripped, throwing my clothes in the laundry hamper, and headed into the bathroom. I wasn't sure what my issue was, but I knew that I needed to wash tonight off of my skin. I also needed to feel Tanner. To be with him. Hold him. Have him hold me just as much. I needed him to tell me that everything was fine now and that we were going to be okay.

I cupped my flat stomach, still unable to believe that I was pregnant. I wasn't sure how my parents were going to take it, but I would tell them after Tanner and I went to the doctor's.

When I stepped into the shower, I turned on the water and let it rain down over me.

"Busy?" The bathroom door shut.

I turned as Tanner stepped into the shower with me. He was beautiful. Every hard line of his body twitched under my scrutiny. His flaccid cock jumped, making heat spread between my legs.

Clearing my throat, I looked away but not before I caught the grin spreading slowly on his face.

"You good?"

"You keep asking me that, but I have no idea how to answer you." I spun back around.

"Baby." He came up behind me, wrapping his hands in my hair. "I'm sorry for what you saw."

I let out a hard sigh. "Is that what you're worried about?" I turned in his arms, placing my hands on his chest. "Are you worried that because of what you did, I'll leave you?"

Tanner leaned his forehead against mine. "A little bit."

"Tanner." I cupped the sides of his neck. "You saved my life. How could I leave you because of that?"

"You saw me kill Tommy. You saw that part of me that I've been trying to keep hidden for so long. I just...I'm a monster. I really am."

"No." I stood on tiptoes and placed a hard peck on his mouth. "You are not a monster. Sure, you're a little bit sick and twisted but who isn't?"

He rolled his eyes. "Busy."

"Listen to me." I cupped his face. "I love you. I am in love. With you. I am carrying your baby. Yes, I know we didn't meet under conventional circumstances but who gives a flying fuck?"

His lips twitched.

"I want to spend my life with you."

Tanner let out a slow breath. "You do?"

I gave him a small smile. "I do."

He ran his fingers along my cheek. "Does it hurt?"

"A little bit but I think what you did to him, hurt him more."

Tanner pushed away from me. "You can't joke about that shit, Busy."

"Hey." I grabbed his arm, pulling him back toward me. "I'm not trying to make light of the situation, but the guy was a bastard."

"I know he was but he...I thought..."

"You thought he was your friend," I finished for him.

Tanner nodded. "I guess I'm not as scary as people think."

"Oh, I've always known you weren't as scary as people say you are." I winked.

He chuckled. "Have you washed your hair or anything?"

"No. I just got in here when you joined me."

"Good." He pulled me in front of him and pushed me gently under the water. "Let me wash you, Busy."

My heart jumped.

His hands pushed through my hair, getting it wet before reaching for the shampoo. "Tonight, scared me. I thought for sure I was going to lose you when I'd only just found you."

"I've seen a lot of movies thanks to my parents being horror fans but when Frankie was in my room…" I shivered. "I don't know if I'll be able to sleep in my own bed again."

"I know, baby." Tanner squeezed out some shampoo into his palm. "But you won't have to worry about that anymore."

"What do you mean?" I asked, turning around so he could wash my hair.

"I mean." He tugged my head back. "I'm going to have a house built in the middle of fucking nowhere, to keep you and our baby safe."

"And you," I added.

"And me." He kissed my forehead.

"I'm not sure my parents would like me living in the middle of nowhere, but I do think my dad would like the fact that it's safer. I don't know."

"I will give your dad all of the information once I have it but the first step, is choosing a location." Tanner moved his hands through my hair, massaging and kneading, pressing the tips of his fingers into my scalp.

A shiver raced down my spine. "God, that feels good."

He chuckled, pushing his waist into my ass. "Does it?"

A breathless laugh left me when I felt his erection pressing up against me. "Yeah, baby, it does."

"Hmm…" He kissed the spot beneath my ear. "I missed you, but I don't want to pressure you or anything."

"We can shower and then go from there." I looked up at him. "Okay?"

"Okay." He gave me a small smile.

"So, what happens now? I mean, now that Roxanne confessed to shooting Sunny and then you taking Tommy out. Are you going to become president again?"

"No." Tanner pushed me under the water and helped me rinse my hair. "The vice-president, Sky, is going to take over. I'm done. I'm retiring."

"Really? Can you do that?"

"You can." He pulled me back into his arms once my hair was rinsed completely. "And I'm doing it. Because I want to spend my life with you too, Busy. I want to raise this baby." He brushed the back of his hand over my lower stomach. "I want to fuck more babies into you. I just...I want you. That's it."

I cupped his face and placed a hard peck on his mouth.

His hand moved to the back of my head. He deepened the kiss, slipping his tongue between my lips and taking every ounce of control from my very body.

"Tanner." I panted.

"Sorry." He gave my lip a gentle bite.

I jumped, the pain shooting right to the spot between my thighs.

"Sorry," he repeated, sliding his hand down my back before cupping my ass.

"You don't need to apologize but..."

In a quick move, he pushed me up against the cool tile of the shower. "I want to wash the rest of you." He sunk his teeth into the base of my throat. "Will you let me do that for you, Busy?"

My chest rose and fell with ragged breaths. "Yes."

"Good girl." Tanner grazed his fingers over my hip, slipping them to my lower stomach. "I promise to give you the best life I possibly can."

My breath caught. I wasn't sure if he was telling me or our baby but either way, I welcomed his sentiment with open arms.

BEING US

"I love you, Busy." His mouth moved up the length of my neck. "I will spend the rest of my life showing you just how much. Every day that passes, I fall more and more in love with you too. You see me. The real me. Not the man I let everyone else see. You see my anxiety, my fear, but you also see my strength as well."

"And your passion," I added.

His fingers moved ever so slowly back around to my hip, over to my tailbone and lower. They slipped between the crack of my ass, running over a spot that had never been given to anyone but for his to claim.

"This is mine, isn't it?"

I swallowed hard, pushing into his touch. "Yes."

"You're going to let me take it one day, aren't you?" His mouth brushed over the shell of my ear, sending a shiver down my spine. "Aren't you?" he repeated, his voice raspy.

"God, Tanner. Yes. I'll give you everything."

He chuckled. "I shouldn't be doing this. Not right now. Not after the night you've had but I…"

"Don't stop," I panted, tilting my hips. "Please don't stop."

"Hmm…" His fingers dipped lower, running over my hot center. "I should be making love to you. Not wanting to fucking rip you open."

I didn't care anymore. I just needed him inside me. I knew we had a hell of a night, but I also knew that connecting with him, sharing this moment, with him, would make us both feel better. It would be our own version of therapy. I knew the other guys in the club were the same way. I wasn't stupid. Whenever Uncle Greyson said he needed his wife after they went on a run or had a hard night, he would search her out and we wouldn't see them again until the following day. Sometimes longer. Depending on what had happened.

"Tanner, I need you inside me," I heard myself beg.

In a quick move, he kicked my legs apart and pushed me face first into the wall of the shower.

It was on the tip of my tongue to demand for more when I felt the tip of his cock running over my swollen center. I pushed back against him, taking him into my body.

"Fuck," he said, his voice raspy.

I whimpered, my body stretching around him. From this angle, it felt like he was going to rip me in half and put me back together all at the same time. It hurt but felt so damn good, it messed with my head.

"Please, Tanner," I whimpered, trying to move but reveling in the way he had control of my body just the same.

He released my hand, trailed his fingers down my spine and grabbed onto my hips with a firm grip. "I'm going to ride you so fucking hard, you're going to forget how to walk."

Placing my hands against the wall, I waited. "Do it. Please."

When he pulled almost all the way out, I waited with bated breath. And as he slammed back into my body, I broke.

(Tanner)

I had no intention of fucking her. Not at least for a little bit. But I was on edge. Had been since I got Busy back in my arms. Seeing the bruise on her cheek and the fear in her eyes, drove me absolutely mad.

I needed to erase the awful memories of the night and replace them with thoughts of me. I wanted to use

BEING US

her, fuck her, and make her beg and plead for everything I had to give her.

Getting a good grip on her ass, I began thrusting hard and deep. I watched as my cock slipped in and out of her heat, her body clenching around me as I powered into her.

Her sounds of pleasure enveloped me in a blanket of bliss.

She whimpered, moaned, even cursed under her breath. But she never told me to stop. She took everything I had to give her. Everything that made up me and me alone. I wasn't a good guy. Hell, I was considered a villain to most, but this woman wrapped around me, saw something in me that no one else had ever seen before.

She loved me.

She accepted me.

And she never tried to change me. Not even once. Not even before we actually knew each other and were nothing more than a mere name to each other.

She never believed the rumors. Some were true. Some were not. It was hard to differentiate between the two anymore.

Busy never asked about the things I had done.

She wanted to start new memories and made me want to do the same as well.

With my baby in her belly, I would make her see that this was more than just a fast relationship. She was my life.

Beginning.

Middle.

End.

She was it. She had always been it.

Those thoughts were the driving force behind my thrusts. My hips moved on their own accord. My movements were brutal, violent, but she welcomed it. Her body sucked me in even deeper with each powerful thrust.

Her whispered words encouraging me to fuck her as hard as I wanted, but love her even more, pulled me forward.

When my teeth found her neck, she trembled against me. Her thighs shook, a soft cry leaving her full mouth.

My hips slowed but I never left the safety of her body. If I could stay like this forever, I would. I had never felt more at home. She calmed me. Kept me sane and the anxiety at bay. She was the piece of me that had been missing my whole life.

"I love you, Tanner," she murmured, her cheeks flushed from the orgasm I had just fucked out of her.

"I love you, Busy." I covered her hands leaning against the wall. "More than I could ever tell you but promise to show you just the same."

"Love me and our baby," she murmured. "That's all we need."

THIRTY

Bee

AFTER OUR SHOWER, TANNER wrapped me up in a large terry cloth towel. He pushed me toward the edge of my bed, keeping his hands on me and his mouth locked on mine.

"I can't get enough of you," he whispered against my lips.

It was like as soon as everything had happened tonight, knowing that we could finally move on and live peacefully, had something inside of him switching. He had always been nothing but gentle. Never really hinting until I made the first move. But now, it was all on him.

With my arms wrapped around his shoulders, the towel fell away from my body and landed on the floor at my feet.

He released my mouth, staring down at my naked body. His eyes darkened, his jaw clenching with that familiar tick I had come to love.

Tanner lowered to his knees, placing a soft peck on my stomach. His lips moved lower, sending tingles racing through every inch of me. His nose brushed over the spot just above my clit. "I can smell your need for me, baby," he murmured, his voice low.

"I always need you." Even though he had fucked me in the shower, it wasn't enough. It would never be enough.

"Hmm…" He brushed his nose lower, moving it over my swollen clit. "You smell so damn good."

"God." I shivered, my knees shaking.

With a quick swipe of his tongue, he flicked it over the nub, sending a surge of wetness between my legs.

"So good," he repeated. "You smell like sunshine and rain all rolled into one."

I laughed lightly. "Sunshine and rain?"

He grinned, staring up at me. "Yeah. I love sunny days but actually prefer it when it rains. It makes everything smell…fresher and it gives life to everything that needs to grow." His eyes dropped to the apex of my thighs. His thumbs brushed over my folds, pulling them apart. "Hmm…I think your pretty little clit wants some attention."

A laugh escaped me. "Yeah, it wants you to make me come."

"You did that in the shower, baby. Hard too. I could feel your cunt squeezing my cock. I thought you were going to break it off." Before I had a chance to comment, he brushed his thumb to my center, pushing it into me.

I latched onto his hair, trying to pull him closer but letting him have the control he needed just the same.

"Feel good?" he asked, looking up at me through hooded eyes.

"Yes," I whispered. "Oh yes."

"Good." He pulled his thumb from my body. "Turn around and bend over the edge of the bed."

I did as I was told, resting my hands on the edge of the bed when I felt his hot breath between my legs.

BEING US

"I'm going to devour every inch of you, Busy." He gave the cheek of my ass a gentle nip. "You're going to love it. Crave it. Need it." When his palm connected with my ass, I cried out, arching into his swing. "Tell me I'm right."

"You're right, Tanner. God, you're so fucking right."

"Good girl."

When his mouth covered my hot center, all thoughts were lost as he consumed me completely.

(Tanner)

While Busy and I walked into the main area of the large house, I held her hand tightly in mine.

She looked up at me, gave me a wink and brought our joined hands up to her mouth. Her rosy cheeks reddened even more when she kissed my knuckles. She had a glow about her. One that I had put there myself.

It had been a few hours since everything had happened at my old clubhouse. And even more since Busy and I took out the events of the night on each other.

My muscles were sore, my dick felt like was it was raw and going to fall off. Even she was walking a little slow. But the pain was worth it in the end.

"Marry me," I blurted, running the towel over Busy's hair. We had taken another shower and now I was drying her. Truth was, I just used it as an excuse to get my hands back on her body.

She turned toward me. "Really?"

"Yes. You have my baby in your belly. You love me. I love you. It seems like the next step."

"How about we move in together and go from there?" she suggested but I could see the excitement flashing in her eyes.

"No." I pinched her chin, fusing my mouth to hers before giving her bottom lip a bite. "I want you as my wife. Not just my girlfriend or fiancée. Or lover," I purred that last word.

She shivered.

"I want it all, Busy. I'm greedy when it comes to you. I want my ring on your finger." I lifted her hand and pulled off the ring that my father had engraved the account numbers on. I never even realized she continued to wear it until now. "I meant what I said when I told you that the money in the account is yours."

"No." She shook her head. "It's yours. Or it's ours if we do get married. But...really, Tanner? Is that what you want?"

"Why wouldn't I?" I placed my hand on her stomach. "You've given me so much in such a short amount of time. You've given me a gift. You've given me love, passion, friendship." I kissed her shoulder. "And more. More that I can ever say because I don't know how."

Busy cupped my nape, pushing her fingers through my hair. "Okay."

My head snapped up. "Okay?"

She smirked. "I'll marry you."

I jumped off the bed, causing a bubble of laughter to escape her. Before she could ask me what I was doing, I shoved her back and dove my face between her legs.

She cried out. "Tanner."

"Say it," I growled against her pussy. "Say you'll marry me."

"Yes, baby." She tugged at my hair, pulling me closer. "God, yes. I'll marry you."

That had been over an hour ago and I couldn't help but feel almost proud in the way I had her screaming my name in a matter of seconds. I made a mental note to buy her a ring but we both agreed, thankfully, that we didn't want a long engagement.

"We have to tell my parents," Busy said, just as her parents came into the room. She gave me a quick peck on the lips and joined her mom and dad.

BEING US

I stood back, watching Busy interact with them and everyone else around us. She was the light in the darkness that had invaded my life for so long, I almost wasn't sure how to move on from it. She would look at me every now and again, give me a small smile, blow me a kiss and continue talking to her family.

"You're going to marry her."

I didn't say anything as Cyrus came up to my side.

"I'm right. Aren't I?"

"Yes," I finally said.

"Good." He clapped my shoulder, giving it a squeeze. When he went to pull away, I grabbed his arm, stopping him.

"I…" I pulled my hand back, letting my arm drop to my side. "Thank you for helping me and making it so I could leave."

"I have no idea what you're talking about." He winked and joined his brother at the bar.

"I need your help," I told Cyrus when no one else was around and I could finally get him alone.

"Why would I help you?" The question may have been cold, but his tone wasn't. Cyrus liked helping people. He wasn't his brother. He didn't hate everyone and feel like the world owed him something. No. He was kinder. Softer. But ruthless when he needed to be.

"Because I'm in love with Busy and I'm willing to do anything to make her happy and keep her safe."

Luckily for me, Cyrus was a romantic at heart. He just never told anyone that and swore me to secrecy. Couldn't ruin his rep and all.

"I'll be the one to check out your room," Cyrus explained, pacing back and forth in front of me. "And you're going to act like you're losing your shit. When you come into the room, you'll find everything you need." He stopped, his brows narrowing. "Don't make me fucking regret helping you or I will tell my brother

everything and put him on your ass. He's grumpy and moody as fuck. I'm sure he's itching for a little taste of blood."

I owed him. I owed all of them. With my life. Literally.

"Hey." Busy came up to me, a huge smile on her face. "You good?"

I pulled her into my arms, placing a soft kiss on her forehead. "I am now."

"Good." She snuggled her face into my chest.

Looking out at the group of people I had come to know over the past few months, I realized that I could get used to this. I never had a family before. Even with my club, I wouldn't consider them family. It was more of a job and now that it was in Sky's hands, a weight had been lifted off of my shoulders.

Bud, Donny, and I had exchanged numbers since I got a new one and we made a point to keep in touch. They had been the only good thing to come out of the club. They never judged me when I went in guns blazing and took out dog fighting rings. Having dogs of their own, they understood.

"How does it feel to have a family now, Tanner?"

My body stiffened. "What?"

Busy smiled, standing on tiptoes and kissed my cheek. "You have a family now."

"I have you," I corrected her.

"Yes, you do." Her smile widened. "But you have everyone else too and I know over time, they will come to know you like I do."

"No." I pinched her chin, tilting her head back. "No one will know me like you do. And that's how I intend to keep it."

Her eyes darkened. "Okay, well maybe not exactly like I know you, but they'll still know you better and not from what the rumors said."

"I can live with that."

"Good." She moved in front of me, standing with her back to my front and wrapping my arms around her shoulders. "Thank you."

"No." I kissed the top of her head. "Thank you."

I would probably end up thanking her for the rest of our lives, but she was right. I did have a family now. One that wouldn't hurt me. One that would help me, especially when it came to Busy. Her dad accepted me. I didn't know her mom, but I would. I wouldn't let any of them down and show them just how much I loved their daughter. They wouldn't regret letting me into their family. I would make damn sure of it.

While everyone talked amongst each other, Busy and I stayed back. With her in my arms, the anxiety that I had been so used to having over the years, diminished. It was still there at times, tingling beneath my skin and reminding me that I would never fully be in control. But with Busy's help and her love for me, I would at least learn to accept it.

EPILOGUE

Bee

"**D**ID YOU LOCK UP?"

"Of course, Daddy." I unlocked the door and clicked the lock back into place just to be sure.

"Good girl. How long were you gone for?"

"Three hours. That includes a half an hour each way it takes to drive back into town."

"Anyone follow you?"

"No." Although my father and I had the same conversation ever since Tanner and I moved to the middle of nowhere, literally, it still made me uneasy. I was waiting for one of these days for my answer to be yes instead of no like it usually was.

"Good. Remember what I told you if you do catch someone following you?"

"Yes. Don't go home and keep driving. Call you or Uncle Greyson and head to the safehouse." It was Cyrus and Sammy's parents' cottage and was a few hours away. The twins hadn't been there in years but someone in Hell's Harlem was always there. I never knew about it though until Tanner and I had moved in together. Both of us had a key. If we were ever separated for any reason, we agreed to meet there.

It was to keep us safe, my dad had said, when really, it was a decoy. If someone was following us, I would head there and whoever was there, would take over and stop the person tailing me. Which meant, they would kill them.

It was hard at times being with a man like Tanner, knowing who he was and what he had come from. His club had given him a retirement party. Sky Paiva took over as president. They removed the patches from Tanner's leather cut and hung it up in their office. He wasn't allowed to join another club and if he did want to get patched back into the Devil's Rejects, he would have to start over and be a prospect just like everyone else. I wasn't sure if that was how it was done in most clubs, but Tanner agreed to the terms, so I never questioned it.

Tanner continued to look over his shoulder whenever we were out in public. Most would probably tell him not to worry but I didn't. I worried with him instead. He feared that more people were after him but my love for him went deeper than that. I had dug myself into his heart and I refused to let him handle this on his own. Much to his dismay of course. He felt the need to take it all on his shoulders instead of having me worry with him.

"Your mom misses you," Dad said, interrupting my thoughts.

"I miss you guys too." I would see them in two weeks when Tanner and I went for a visit but until then, we would stay home. I only ever left to grab groceries.

"I also ran into Heather and Lori the other day."

"Oh? That's nice. I spoke to them yesterday." Even though I hadn't seen them as much as I used to, I talked to my best friends almost every day. I explained to them in not so much detail, everything that had happened. When Tanner and I had gotten married, they were both my maids of honor. The wedding was small but perfect. I wouldn't have wanted it any other way.

"What time is it?" Daddy asked.

I checked my watch. "Almost three in the afternoon." I kicked off my shoes and pulled off my sweater before hanging it on the hook by the door.

"Three hours for you to do everything," Dad grumbled. "I hate that you go into town by yourself."

I rolled my eyes. "We have this conversation every day, Daddy. I can't speed or else I'll get pulled over and then that would draw more attention to us. I already get weird looks when I go to the grocery store." Not that anyone knew who I was, and Tanner wasn't seen often in town.

"I know." Dad sighed. "Alright, sweetheart. Call me on Wednesday."

"I will." We said our goodbyes and I stopped in front of the fireplace. Brushing my fingers over a small golden urn sitting on top of the mantel, I smiled. "Don't worry, Trigger, your dad will never forget you." Rowan had gifted Tanner the urn on our wedding day. Memories of holding him while he cried into my shoulder still haunted me but I was thankful at the same time that he trusted me enough to let himself go like that.

Heading to the door that led to the basement, I pushed it open and stepped down the stairs until I reached the large room, we were planning on using as a playroom for our kids.

Tanner was pacing. He had a deep scowl on his face and if I didn't know better, it looked like he was trying to wear a hole in the carpet with all of his walking back and forth.

"Tanner," I said gently, shutting the door behind me.

BEING US

Tanner stopped pacing, his stiff body relaxing when his dark eyes landed on me. "Finally, you were gone way too fucking long."

"You're as bad as my dad. I wasn't gone that long."

He came toward me, cupped my cheek and my belly, and placed a soft peck on my lips. "How's my boy?" he asked, ignoring me.

I laughed lightly. "Growing and kicking his mama much like the first one you put in me." I covered Tanner's hand that was on my swollen stomach. We had found out it was a boy right as soon as we were able.

Tanner chuckled.

We were due any time with our second son.

"Mama!"

I smiled, crouching low as our firstborn ran toward me and threw himself around my legs. "Hi, baby boy. Did you have a good afternoon with Daddy?"

Manuel Horsch had been born first and now we were blessed to be giving him a baby brother.

"Yes!" he exclaimed.

My heart swelled. Running my hand over his dark head of hair, I picked him up into my arms. "I actually have a surprise for you." I grabbed Tanner's hand and led him up the stairs to the garage.

"You do? Baby, you know I don't like surprises."

"Trust me." I patted his arm. "You'll like this one." When we reached the door to the garage, I turned to him. "Ready?"

"No," he grumbled, a deep frown settling between his brows.

I laughed.

Pushing open the door, I stood to the side and let Tanner enter.

"I don't know what I should be looking for," he said, pushing a hand through his dark hair.

I smiled, checking out my husband. We had married rather quickly. Uncle Greyson called up a minister and we were married within a couple of months of everything going down.

Letting my eyes roam over Tanner, I still couldn't get over the fact that he was now mine. Officially. He was beautiful and breathtaking. No matter how many times he told me that he didn't deserve me, the broken mess of a man dropped everything for me and our son and soon-to-be second son. He had told me in the beginning that he did some things that he could go away for. That he *should* go away for. But no matter what he did, I was able to look past that and see the true man in front of me. He was trying. He was trying so damn hard to right the wrongs he had made.

A soft woof pulled me from my thoughts and brought me back to the present.

My smile widened, my heart jumping to my throat over the surprise I had for him.

Tanner's head whipped around, just as a puppy came around from the other side of our car. He sat, planted his butt on the pavement, and stared up at Tanner. His tail wagged back and forth, his tongue lolling out the side of his mouth.

"Who's this?" he asked, looking down at the puppy.

"This," I moved Manuel to my side and picked up the little ball of fur with my other arm, "is Rex. He's an American Staffordshire Terrier. His dad died in a dog fighting ring and his mom was hit by a car. Or that's what I was told anyway but I think she died by something worse than that." I cleared my throat when a dark shadow passed over Tanner's face. "Anyway, he's a rescue and he's yours."

"Really?" Tanner swallowed hard. He ran a hand over the puppy's head, giving him a scratch under his chin.

I placed Rex in his arms and hugged Manuel to my chest, watching Tanner. "He is. I know how much losing Trigger hurt and it's never been the right time to get a new puppy. I also know you like older dogs, but I found him online and thought he was perfect."

Rex licked Tanner's face, making him chuckle. "Where did you get him?" he asked, his voice thick.

"I came across an ad asking for help. They had interviewed hundreds of people, but no one fit what they were looking for. They wanted to make sure Rex would be in a good home. So, I emailed them and told them what happened to Trigger. We met up at a coffee shop in town and ten minutes later, I was driving home with him."

"That's where you went this afternoon?" Tanner asked, lifting Rex in the air.

Rex's tail wagged back and forth, his tongue moving up and down like he was trying to lick Tanner's face. He snuffed, grunting when he realized he couldn't reach.

I laughed, running my hand over his small but chubby gray body. "Yeah. I would have told you, but I really wanted it to be a surprise."

Tanner lowered Rex and hugged him to his chest.

Rex licked his chin, curled in his arms, and let out a soft sigh. It was like he had just met his person. His protector.

"Thank you," Tanner whispered. "Thank you so fucking much, baby."

"You're welcome," I said, my voice coming out shaky. "You're not mad that I never told you?"

"No." He shook his head. "You...this..." He kissed the top of Rex's head. "I can never repay you for this."

"You don't have to." I stood and placed a soft peck on Tanner's cheek. "Or you can repay me later," I whispered, waggling my eyebrows.

Tanner grinned, the thickness in the air no longer there.

We brought Rex into the house, letting him run free to get to know his new home.

When I married Tanner, I promised him that I would do everything I could to make him happy. He promised me the same and ever since, we had done that. Even if it was just something small.

Being with Tanner made me realize that there was no before him.

It was just us. Always us.

Tanner and Busy.

With our kids and Rex, nothing else mattered.

THE END

Add Finally Us (Next Generation Novel, #5) to your TBR list!

https://www.goodreads.com/book/show/54102534-finally-us

ACKNOWLEDGEMENTS

Angie: Thank you as always for helping me with each and every book. Can you believe how many we've been through together already?? And there's SO many more to come! I love you, lady!

Jen and Christina: Thank you both for going through my books and helping me make them so much better. I couldn't do this without you girls.

Joanne: Thank you for not just editing for me but for also teaching me. Although, it does take me several books to remember the correct way to do some things. You have the patience of a Saint and I couldn't ask for a better editor at my side.

J.M.'s Jems: Because of you I continue to write. Your encouragement, your support and more, is constantly noticed. Thank you for being my rock when I need it most. You're not only my reader group but my family as well. Each of you hold a special spot in my heart, even if we've never talked.

Authors and bloggers: Thank you for helping me spread the word on my books. Thank you for reading and thank you for just being one of the best parts of this amazing community!

All the readers: YOU ARE WHY WE WRITE! Thank you for taking a chance on each of us. I know there are so many authors out there and I also know that 2020 has been quite the ride! Thank you for reading and I hope that our books can help you escape even if it's just for an hour or two.

JM
XX

ABOUT

J.M. Walker is an Amazon bestselling author who also hit USA Today with Wanted: An Outlaw Anthology. She loves all things books, pigs and lip gloss. She is happily married to the man who inspires all of her Heroes and continues to make her weak in the knees every single day.

"Above all, be the HEROINE of your own life..." ~ Nora Ephron

Website: http://www.aboutjmwalker.com/
Facebook: https://www.facebook.com/jm.walker.author
Reader Group: https://www.facebook.com/groups/JMsJems/
Twitter: https://twitter.com/jmwlkr
Instagram: https://www.instagram.com/jmwlkr/
Goodreads: https://www.goodreads.com/author/show/5132169.J_M_Walker
BookBub: https://www.bookbub.com/authors/j-m-walker
Amazon: https://tinyurl.com/y7dpjkud
Newsletter: https://tinyurl.com/ya9hycak

Want more? Head on over to my website for my complete backlist!
https://www.aboutjmwalker.com/books